GW01091230

CARROLL & GRAF

Also from Carroll & Graf:

Oyster
Oyster II

THE OYSTER III

ANONYMOUS

Carroll & Graf Publishers, Inc.
New York

Copyright © 1988 by Glenthorpe Historical Research Associates

All rights reserved

First Carroll & Graf edition 1989

Carroll & Graf Publishers, Inc.
260 Fifth Avenue
New York, NY 10001

ISBN: 0-88184-558-2

Manufactured in the United States of America

Preface

Since the rediscovery of *The Oyster* in the mid 1980s, there has been much speculation as to just who were the authors of this infamous Victorian underground magazine.

In her preface to *Oyster 1*, Professor Antoinette Hillman-Strauss suggested that the unknown 'Sir Andrew Scott', whose autobiographical novel *A Fond Recollection Of Youthful Days* – concluded here – made up the contents of *Oyster 1* and *Oyster 2*, was probably a journalist on one of the fledgling popular publications being produced for the more literate public of the 1880s.

And indeed sexologist Oliver Panther, in his introduction to *Oyster 2*, names the late Victorian pulp-fiction writer Gerald Burdett (who was known to have written for *The Ram*, a similar illicit journal in the same vein as *The Pearl* and *The Oyster*) as our possible scribe, though Dr Terence Cooney speculates that the work may be that of more than one scribbler.

However, there is no problem in identifying one writer in this third book of material culled from the pages of *The Oyster*, a journal that flourished throughout the 1880s, only to disappear without trace during the next decade.

Doctor Edward Parsifal (1840–1928) enjoyed a controversial medical career. During his heyday in the 1880s, he headed a most profitable practice in the West End of London which was patronised by many members of London Society. One of his patients was Lord Arthur Somerset, an equerry of The Prince of Wales, who was forced to flee to France during the Cleveland Street scandal in 1888 when Scotland Yard finally acted against the owner of a brothel for upper class homosexuals. In all probability, the Lord S----- mentioned in the latter half of the script is indeed the disgraced Lord Arthur who lived a lonely life in Northern France until his death some thirty years later.

By the end of the 1880s, Doctor Parsifal had amassed a considerable fortune. He lived in style in a fine country mansion in rural North Finchley (as it was then), though as we note from his book, he kept a London apartment for his many assignations.

In the end, his voracious sexual appetites led to his downfall when, at the ripe age of forty-six, he was named co-respondent in a divorce petition involving the pretty Mrs Denise Wright, the twenty-three-year-old wife of a wealthy businessman who had consulted our hero about some 'nervous complaint'. As we can see from his memoir, this lady was just one of many to fall for the charms of the handsome doctor who was indeed fortunate to escape the strictures of the General Medical Council.

In fact, Teddy Parsifal gave up medicine after the case and he then became an extremely wealthy gentleman of leisure. Already possessing a healthy bank account, he dabbled successfully in the Stock Exchange under the guidance of his old friends Rufus Isaacs and Sir Ronnie Dunn and, indeed, his estate was worth more than £750,000 when he died just sixty years ago in December, 1928.

What possessed Teddy Parsifal to reveal his intimate secrets to the readers of *The Oyster*? The script was written immediately after the well-publicised divorce case which he knew would effectively end his medical career, so perhaps he wrote his apologia in a simple spirit of careless bravado.

It must have distressed his wife, the Society belle Lady Sarah Andrews, though their union survived all his amorous encounters. Indeed, to Lady Sarah, her handsome rogue was a model husband and father to the family. And indeed, according to his eldest son, Adrian, the blissfully happy Lady Sarah never suspected Teddy of the slightest infidelity and knew nothing of the robust secret life enjoyed by the naughty doctor until his eightieth year.

This third selection of material from *The Oyster* is concluded with an episode of Sir Andrew Scott's autobiography *A Memoir of Youthful Days* which was first published in *The Pearl* (*The Pearl III*, New English Library, 1984) and continued in *The Oyster* (*The Oyster 1* and *The Oyster 2*, New English

Library, 1987). The unknown author (for 'Andrew Scott' is a pseudonym) writes with gusto and occasionally with a stylish wit which has led some authorities to wonder whether the young Oscar Wilde might have contributed to the manuscript. Both he and Lord Alfred Douglas were known to be aficionados of underground magazines such as *The Pearl* and *The Oyster* that surfaced during the 1880s but which sank without trace after Wilde's trial in the early 1890s.

Happily, a set of *The Oyster* dating from 1887 was recently discovered in the locked drawing cabinet inside a large Derbyshire country house. This has afforded us the opportunity to relive the exciting, amorous lives of Doctor Teddy Parsifal and 'Sir Andrew Scott' – tales that show a completely different side to Victorian manners and mores, so very different from the starched picture usually used to portray these fascinating years.

Graham Grafton
Manchester
November, 1988

The sublime and the ridiculous are often so nearly related that it is difficult to class them separately. One step above the sublime makes the ridiculous; and one step above the ridiculous makes the sublime again.

Thomas Paine
(1737–1809)

The Private and Unexpurgated Memoirs of a Medical Gentleman in Great Britain and the New World

Author's Introduction

Dear reader, I earnestly hope you derive pleasure from this set of memoirs culled from my memories of many glorious years spent in perfecting *l'art de faire l'amour*.

Many readers of this distinguished journal are members of Society, so my name will not be unknown to them. After all, Doctor Edward Marmaduke DuCane Parsifal, Member of the Royal College of Physicians, Fellow of the Royal College of Surgeons and Sometime Visiting Professor at the Universities of Washington and Bombay, is a name with whom the very highest in the land have been well acquainted. Not that I am one to stand upon ceremony, you understand. I far prefer the simple soubriquet of Doctor Teddy than any other mode of address.

I hope to entertain you with the recall of some of the bizarre, intimate incidents of my younger days, already recorded in a secret journal, but which the editor of *The Oyster*, whose name must never be mentioned for fear of police informants, and my dear old friends Doctor Jonathan Arkley and Sir Clive Freedman, have persuaded me are worthy of a wider readership amongst the cognoscenti.

So the time has come to share my most exciting experiences of a personal nature, and I must warn readers of a delicate disposition that, unfashionable though it be in this age of euphemism, I insist on calling a spade a spade and refuse to mince words for the benefit of mealy-mouthed hypocrites who wish to bowdlerise our good old-fashioned Anglo-Saxon vulgarities. I doubt, however, that there are many such personages amongst the readership of this robust journal!

So settle down and enjoy my jottings, and may I take this opportunity of wishing you all, ladies and gentlemen, a Happy New Year of licking and lapping, sucking and fucking in 1887.

Doctor Teddy Parsifal
Ford Manor
Sussex, December 1886

My Early Days

As my old friend Lady Pokingham has written, the natural instinct of the ancients was that copulation was the direct and most acceptable form of worship they could offer to their deities.

I am convinced that there cannot be any great sin in giving way to natural desires and enjoying to the utmost those delicious sensations with which the Creator has endowed us.

So no apology will be forthcoming for the unashamed voluptuousness of this memoir and without further ado, let me begin my narrative.

My earliest years were spent in Canada and India as my Papa was attached to the Diplomatic Service. I shall not bore you with the details but until the age of ten I had hardly lived in this sceptred isle of Albion more than six months or so. But on my eleventh birthday I was sent to school in England where my elder brother, Cecil (more of him will appear later in this tale), was already a student, though we returned home to Mama and Papa in the holidays wherever they happened to be living at the time.

Even at this tender age I evinced a taste for the fair sex and I will never forget our governess, Mrs Radlett, who proudly displayed what appeared to my young eyes an enormous pair of breasts in the tightest of bodices, creating a cleavage that caused many a visitor to make excuses to visit the nursery, the avowed purpose being to see the youngsters, but in reality to see Mrs Radlett bending forward. I recall that in Toronto (Mrs Radlett travelled with us wherever Papa was sent on command of the government) one visitor, Doctor Dunn, always managed to drop his handkerchief or some other trifle so that Mrs Radlett bent down to retrieve it. I realise now that the good doctor was not as clumsy as he seemed!

I recall that often at night, Mrs Radlett would undress in front of Cecil and myself and as those magnificent breasts cascaded from their cramped confines, she would sigh with relief and gently massage them to restore lost circulation. If we had been good boys that day, our kind governess would allow us each to massage a breast for her. We enjoyed this small chore as did Mrs Radlett, who whimpered with pleasure as we performed the task with vigour. She asked us to roll her stalky red titties on the palms of our hands and after a minute or so she would breathe more rapidly, squeeze her thighs together and emit a strange grunt and shudder all over in what to us was a rather alarming fashion. She would then thank Cecil and I for our labours, asking us to promise not to tell anyone of our little game.

On one occasion I recall passing by Mrs Radlett's bedroom and the door was slightly ajar. I peeped round and saw our governess naked on the bed, completely oblivious to the world, making those strange noises of pleasure she emitted whilst Cecil and I were rubbing her teats. But this time, she was engaged in self-gratification of her own. So massive were her titties that she had been able to place one erect nipple in her mouth and she was busy sucking it to great effect. This breast was supported by one hand whilst the other was plunged inside the hairy black bush of hair between her legs, and I looked on with interest as she plunged her fingers in and out of this mound. I watched, mesmerised by this act as again she squeezed her thighs and with a little scream, shuddered violently and then lay back exhausted, withdrawing her hand from her mossy growth, a hand that I noticed was strangely moist (had she wet herself, I wondered in my innocence) which she wiped across her great breasts, smearing them with what, of course, was her cunney juice.

This strange experience led to my first footsteps across the Rubicon to complete sexual happiness. For whilst I had been gawping at this handsome naked woman, my little cock had begun to swell inside my trousers. I unbuttoned my trousers and felt for the stiff little shaft inside my underpants, enjoying a sensation of a somewhat uncomfortable pleasure.

This feeling was further heightened when Mrs Radlett heaved herself off the bed and I saw the massively hairy black bush of hair between her legs. She picked up a small towel and rubbed it between her legs, threw it down onto the bed and then sauntered into her bathroom to soak in her tub. When she closed the door behind her I sneaked into the room, my cock still as hard as a rock, picked up the towel and instantly caught the aroma of her most intimate parts. This aroma was to haunt me for the rest of my life and prove to be an instant stimulant for sexual arousal.

I pulled the towel down to my cock which was pulsating with excitement. I rubbed the shaft furiously whereupon a glistening of white fluid appeared on the tip, and as the surge of pleasure coursed through my body, I felt a jet of liquid squirt out – fortunately it soaked into the towel or I would have been forced to make a confession as to how Mrs Radlett's carpet came to be stained! I was both alarmed and excited at this happening. Luckily my dear Papa had decided that it was time for my sexual education to begin, so (as he had done with my brothers) he had left by my bedside only weeks before a copy of *Human Procreation Explained For Boys and Girls* by the celebrated Doctor Roy Stevenson, the well known authority on sexuality.

So fortunately, unlike so many of my unhappy contemporaries, I had no great fear of guilt about tossing off. As Sir Andrew Scott has rightly pointed out in previous editions of *The Oyster*, several misguided physicians hold that wanking can produce the most dreadful physical and mental ailments. But I hold to the view of Doctor Stevenson who ridicules this view. After all, he argues, all boys play with themselves and this practice has no bearing upon the ability to reach a ripe old age. What harm can there be in self-stimulation of the prick – or, come to that, the cunney? Certainly, no-one ever caught an unwanted infection through tossing off, and no lady ever suffered an unwanted swollen belly through finger fucking.

But to return to my narrative – I sneaked back into my own room still clutching the towel, locked the door and threw off all my clothes. I wrapped the still-damp towel around my semi-erect cock and within seconds it stood upright again amidst the tiny first sprouts of pubic hair. Carefully, I rolled back the foreskin from the swollen red dome and manipulated the shaft up and down in my cupped hand, unwittingly mimicking the sliding of the prick through the cunney lips into the juicy love-channel of the cunt. I closed my eyes and in my imagination saw again Mrs Radlett's enormous naked titties and I thought how wonderful it would be to place my prick between them. At that age of course, it takes only the merest stimulation to spend, and all too soon I felt the boiling of the spunk in my tight little balls and the frothy jet of white spunk fairly flew out the top of my cock in a miniature white fountain. I gasped with delight as my first real spend cascaded out of my pulsating prick.

I mopped up as best I could the spunk from the eiderdown and placed the damp towel in the dirty linen basket.

After that first encounter with some of the more intimate parts of the female body, life became somewhat more mundane. The next interesting extract from my private diary comes when I was at a more advanced age of sexual awareness – fourteen. By now I was fully aware of the pubertal happenings that my body had undergone. I had grown quite tall for a chap of my age. In fact, I was the tallest in my class and also the most well developed. I had a facial growth that necessitated regular shaving as well as the beginnings of some bodily hair growth. Pubic hair grew in a tight knot above my male member. This was also seemingly well grown for, after games, my friends would all look on in amazement at not only the length but the thickness of it. Modestly comparing it with my closer friends (as one does at that age), I would judge it to be at least twice as thick as theirs and nearly half as long again.

I was educated up to the age of seventeen at Cockshall Manor in Arundel, under the excellent tutorship of Professor James Bagshott-Coleman. At the end of one particular term of schooling, I returned home after the final, rousing game of footer between the two top houses. Being a big chap, I was the captain of my house and led the team to victory. I thus returned home rather dirty, streaked with the mud and sweat of a good, hard-fought game. I came back with my school report sealed in the ominous brown envelope, conveying either a good summer, being treated well by Papa, or a miserable one spent swatting at the subjects in which I was least good. Thank goodness my report was a good one. Papa was pleased that I had done well in the classics and in sport, winning the junior Victor Ludorum that year as best all round sports chap. Thus praised, I went off to have a soak in a well-deserved bath that

Alice the upstairs maid had drawn for me. Papa told me to join the rest of the family on the lawn for tea when I had bathed and changed.

After my luxurious soak in a steaming bath, I dried myself off in front of the mirror, feeling very pleased with myself and really looking forward to a super fun summer break. As I dried myself, I lightly stroked my member, which instantly caused it to spring to life, it almost having a will of its own. I found that it would grow and swell very rapidly to its stiff proud self at the slightest stimulation. As I have intimated before, it had developed into a weapon of inordinate size and when proudly erect was measured by my closest friend, Terence, to be nearly one foot in length. Its thickness was at least twice that of my nearest rival.

As I was standing there admiring myself, I saw in the mirror that the young maid Alice was standing to one side of me at the doorway, staring at my body. I hurriedly grabbed a towel to cover myself, when she came into the room and quickly locked the door. I was so shocked at her doing this that I dropped my towel, exposing my slowly shrinking member.

'Oh, young master Teddy, you *are* well developed are you not? A good boy like you with your school report and such an enormous cock deserves a treat.' So saying, she came over to where I was standing next to the mirror, knelt down in front of me and proceeded to take my penis in her warm, soft hands. It immediately began to swell to its fullest extent, needing little or no encouragement to do so. Alice cupped my ball-sack with one hand and gently squeezed them, whilst running her other hand up and down the shaft of my tool. The feeling I experienced was one of the utmost delight, far better than the feeling I got when playing with myself. I uttered a little groan as the feeling built up in my balls. 'Do you like that, Master Teddy?' whispered Alice. All I could do was to nod my head as I was far too excited to reply coherently.

'Well, if you like that, young master, see what you think of this.' With that she leant right forward and to my amazement took my now throbbing prick and proceeded to put it into her hot wet mouth. The feeling was unbelievable. Her darting tongue moved to and fro along the shaft of my by now aching cock. As she licked the tip of it, I felt my balls begin to swell and fill with come. I thrust frenziedly into her hot mouth, almost choking her. I knew I was close to shooting my cum in her mouth even though she had been sucking me for barely thirty seconds. Alice also felt my urgency, for she sucked good and hard, at the same time squeezing my balls hard. The exquisite pain of her hard squeezing, together with her darting tongue, caused a rush of spunk up the channel of my pulsating shaft which exploded into her mouth as it jerked and emptied my balls of steaming hot spunk. I could not believe the sensation as she drank my cum. My balls contracted as she squeezed the last drop out. I must have really shot a great load of cum, for even though Alice greedily swallowed my juice she could not contend with the gush I produced. My spunk seemed to fill her mouth and gushed out the sides, down her chin and onto her cleavage. After finally sucking every drop of juice, she gently kissed my still rock hard member, wiped the cum off her chest and sucked her fingers clean.

'My, you have got the biggest tool I have ever seen for a lad of your age,' said Alice. 'And I have never known anyone to spunk like that. I can normally swallow it all, but you were drowning me with it.'

I stood there, dazed, as she tidied herself and lifted up her skirt. 'Goodness. I'm soaking wet here,' she said as she pulled her knickers down to reveal a wet patch on them. At the sight of the dark patch of pubic hair adorning her private parts, my semi-limp rod instantly hardened again, bringing back distant memories of my governess. As it leapt back to hardness, Alice looked up in amazement.

'Are you ready again?' she asked. 'You have only just shot your load! Well, if that's the case, young master, we can't go wasting such a lovely erection, can we? I was going to save the pleasure of you fucking my cunt 'til another day. But seeing as my cunt is so wet and ready, we will introduce you to the delights of a soaking wet fanny. This is your first time with a woman, isn't it?'

I replied that that was indeed the case. She quickly slipped off her now considerably wet drawers and tucked them in her pocket. As she bent down I noticed her pert young breasts spill over the top of her maid's blouse. I reached forward and cupped one in my hand. It felt so soft and tender. I brushed the pinky-brown nipple and felt it harden beneath by fingers. Alice gasped a little, stood up and took both ripe pears out. She took my hand and guided it to her now sopping wet juice-box. At the same time, she forced my head to her breasts and with no encouragement I greedily sucked her now erect nipples.

This was my first experience of actually touching the previously hidden areas of a woman's body. The feeling of a pert nipple in my mouth, together with the wetness of Alice's quim made me groan with delight and I realised that I would soon spunk again. Alice, being the experienced girl she was, aware of the build-up of spunk in my balls and the imminent explosion, quickly extricated herself from me and lay on the bed with her legs wide open, allowing me to see for the first time in my life the pink portal to heaven. Alice noted my interest in her cut so obligingly spread her cunt lips widely with her finger, revealing the very depth of the hole from which I could see her love-juice slowly dribble. As soon as I saw this my knob began to throb. Alice, seeing the closeness of my state of coming, beckoned me over. With expert hands she guided my rod to the entrance of her cunney. Thus placed, I needed no other encouragement than Alice whispering, 'Go on, big boy, fuck my juice-box like you have always dreamed of.' With that I plunged my now dribbling great cock deep into her beckoning cunt. It felt like nothing I had ever experienced before. I instinctively rammed my cock hard into her, whilst she wrapped her legs around me holding me firmly inside her. I shafted in and out, in rhythm with the ever quickening thrusts of her hips. Suddenly, I could feel her love-box begin to tighten. 'Oh fuck me hard Teddy,' she gasped, 'I'm coming.' As she said that, I could feel a surge build up inside her. The contraction of her wet pussey was enough to cause my balls to explode and, as she shuddered in ecstasy, my hot sticky cream poured into her, mingling with the soaking wetness of her juices. I pumped and pumped until my balls were totally voided. The feeling of my first sexual dalliance was a rare one. I lay back bewildered and spent. Alice looked over to me and said: 'Master Teddy, there you are, a treat for doing so well at school. But my, aren't you well endowed. You're as big as ever I've had and without doubt the thickest. I could feel you fill up my cunny and I can normally take them with room to spare! With a cock like that, young master, you will keep many a young girl happy and sore.'

With that, she quickly tidied herself up, but did not put back on her wet knickers. She checked herself in the mirror, tidied her dark locks, ran to the door, looked back and threw her panties to me.

'There,' she said, 'a prize for your first time. Your father did not get a pair the first time he fucked me, so you really are going to be good.' With that amazing remark, she left me holding her sopping panties and looking at my father in a new light.

So, dear reader, you are now privy to my first encounter with the fair sex. I was but a young stripling of just fourteen years of age at the time, and since then I must have fucked at least four hundred women, but the memory of that glorious initiation into the delights of sexual intercourse remains as bright as if it happened but yesterday.

However, let us return to my story. That last remark uttered by Alice, casual though it may have been for her, came as a total shock to me. Could she be telling the truth about Papa? I had always looked up to my father with total respect and awe as befitted a young man of my upbringing. I asked Alice repeatedly to enlarge upon her words, but the little minx refused to say anything further on this subject which, for the time, had to remain a closed book.

I still found it difficult to conceive that my Pater, a regular churchgoer and pillar of the local community, could have succombed to Alice's ministrations. And yet, I decided finally to take Alice's word that Papa had been dipping his wick, and I was forced to look upon Papa in a new and somewhat more critical light!

I saw Alice daily as she continued to perform the services of an upstairs maid, but regretfully I must admit that nothing of a titivating nature occurred until the end of the summer vacation. Unless, of course, one took into account the provocative looks she would often give me, gazing directly between my legs and licking her lips in a most lascivious way. This led to almost instant erections and often I would leave my room, meet Alice on the landing and then dash back inside my room, lock the door, hastily unbutton my trousers and take solace in a frenzied tossing-off. Just the merest thought of her pert titties and juicy cunt sent my right hand shooting down to my throbbing shaft, but this regular masturbatory activity was but a poor substitute for the richness of a real fuck.

Nevertheless, those summer months were quite the most eventful I had ever experienced and I recall those days with gladness. I was most fortunate to have a close friend, Terence Browner, living close by (many of you will remember his later exploits with the 69th Lancers on the North West Frontier) and we remained close friends for many years. General Browner (as of course he is now entitled to be addressed) still lives in Delhi and we correspond on a regular basis. He was a great cocksman and I am sure he will relish the retelling of some of our joint escapades together when we were but lads.

Our summer hideaway was a disused farmhouse and assorted outbuildings. Well, disused is perhaps too strong an adjective. The land had been farmed by a tenant of Lord Friary who had decamped suddenly to the New World in search of wealth during the California gold rush of '49. No-one had taken up the tenancy and the place had remained vacant. Terry and I had played many a childish game there but at the end of this fateful summer, we played games of a more adult kind!

One of the most memorable and highly enjoyable days occurred when Terence and I believed ourselves to be alone in the house. We were sitting in the lounge discussing, as I recollect, the chances of my ever being able to fuck Alice again and also – a very important matter to Terence – whether she might accommodate my best friend who was extremely anxious to lose his unwanted virginity.

'Are you certain that you are ready for such an experience?' I said earnestly. 'After all, you are three months younger than me and anyhow, very few boys of our age can have had the opportunity to enjoy a good fuck.'

'I'm as ready as I ever will be,' said Terence indignantly. 'Why, my cock is almost as big as yours, Teddy, even though you probably have the thickest prick of all the third formers.'

'That's awfully kind of you,' I replied modestly. 'However, you and young Bob Cripps must come joint second behind me.'

'Do you really think so? It's surprising that Bob has a sizeable cock as he is the shortest chap in the whole year.'

'Oh, yes, without a doubt. Indeed, I have often thought that it is highly inappropriate for that new prefect Davis to call Bob a little prick.'

'Ha! Ha! Ha! That's a good one. Anyhow, Teddy, where is that curious book you promised me?'

'It's a book of photographs by Harold Sailor. I heard Pater talk about this man to his friend Colonel Golthorpe. It seems that he has a special shop in Piccadilly where people can buy something Pater called "gallant literature". Anyhow, I heard the Colonel ask Pater to keep this book for him until he returned from India.'

'Gosh, let's have a look at it,' said Terence eagerly, his eyes sparkling with animation. 'I should wonderfully like to look at it.'

'Here it is, Terence, only I hope it won't excite you too much. You can look it over by yourself as I read the newspaper,' I said, placing it in his eager grasp.

He sat close to me in an easy lounging chair, and I watched him carefully over the top of the newspaper as he turned over the pages and gloated over the beautiful plates. There was a superb collection in there, which I had already seen, of coloured plates of boys and girls in the nude, both singly and together, and towards the end of the book, some of the photographs showed a fine young couple enjoying a good bout of fucking.

I could see Terence's cock harden in his trousers until it was quite stiff and rampant.

'Well, well,' I said, laying my hand on his bursting prick. 'What a tosser yours has grown up to since I gave you that book. We must compare our cocks as I think that yours must be almost as big as mine.'

'I told you I am ready for my first fuck,' he said with a laugh. 'Yes, do let's see which prick is the biggest,' and opening his trousers, he pulled out his fine red-headed cock, which stood in all its manly glory, stiff and hard as marble, with the hot blood making it warm to my touch. He then helped me pull out my own thick stiff truncheon, frigging it up to its fullest measure.

We proceeded to handle each other in an ecstacy of delight which ended with us tossing each other off and aiming each other's jets of frothy white spunk into the fireplace.

'Ah well,' sighed Terence. 'I enjoyed that but I am sure it it not as satisfying as the real thing.'

I was about to make a soothing reply when we were both startled by what sounded like an ornament crashing to the ground just outside in the hall.

'What was that?' asked Terence.

'I don't know but let's find out!' I replied grimly, and arming myself with a poker from the fireplace, I rushed to the door.

I had no need of the poker, dear reader, for the noise in the hall had been made by Charlotte, the seventeen-year-old parlourmaid who had been doing some menial task in the scullery and had crept upstairs when she heard our voices as she too thought that the house was unoccupied except for her. But when she had heard us talk and saw us play with ourselves, she stayed to view more closely as she had never seen a naked stiff cock before and the sight of not just one but two had fascinated her!

Unfortunately, in her attempt to steal away unnoticed, she had bumped into a small vase on a mantelshelf which had fallen down and shattered on the parquet floor.

'You won't tell on me, Master Teddy, will you? Please don't tell or I'll lose my job', she begged me.

'I don't know about that', I said severely. 'It's a pretty serious matter.'

'I'll do anything you want', she said with imploring eyes.

'Anything at all?' said Terence quickly. 'How about letting us fuck you?'

'Now, now,' I said reprovingly, 'that's not fair. As it says in Doctor Stevenson's book, a man must never blackmail or cheat his way into a girl's bed.'

'Oh, you are kind, Master Teddy. I am a virgin and I've never even let a boy slip his fingers in my cunney,' cried the pretty girl.

'Goodness, you must have had a boy friend', said Terence.

'Not really, Master Terry. I have never had the pleasure of having male arms around me except Mister Baigue the butler who always pinches my bum when I walk past him.'

'Don't you ever feel you want to be fucked, Charlotte?' I asked.

'Of course I do, Master Teddy. We girls like to imagine lustful matters just the same as you boys', she said. 'Why, don't you think we can enjoy ourselves in sole fashion just like you do?'

'Girls can spend by themselves?' said Terence in amazement.

'Of course they can', laughed Charlotte who was now quite at ease. 'Shall I tell you how I do it?'

'Yes, please', we chorused and I added that this recounting of her secret pleasures would constitute a sufficient punishment for breaking the vase and that I would not peach on her to my parents.

'Well,' Charlotte began, 'I like to start after I have had a bath. I then stand in front of the bathroom mirror, slowly drying myself with a towel. On a summer morning, if the sun is shining like today, a gleam of light beams in making my body shine with a golden glow. Still looking in the mirror I let my gaze run down to my dark, thick pussey hair that curls round my crack. I then slowly rub my clitty and that makes me feel good all over.

'Then I scuttle into my bedroom and pick up a hand mirror and the dildo that I have taken from Alice's room. She is unaware that I know of its existence. I then place the mirror on the floor between my legs and, by crouching down, I have a lovely view of my cunt lips. I then separate my pussey lips and I can see to the very depths of my now damp, tight cunt. Then I push two or three fingers up to get my juices flowing and as soon as my cunney is dripping wet, I pick up the dildo and slowly rub it up and down my slit, rubbing my little clitty until it throbs and tingles.

'After a few moments, I push the dildo between my pussey lips and then gently take it out – at first slowly and then faster and faster and deeper and deeper until wooosh! My body is enveloped in a beautiful, most wonderful ecstasy as my cunney explodes and my love juices flow unabated. Afterwards, I lick my creamy cum from the dildo which also sends shudders of pleasure throughout my entire frame. This all takes about ten minutes and leaves me feeling drained but I feel sprightly and rejuvenated quite soon afterwards.'

This racy narrative excited both Terence and myself so much that our cocks were fairly bursting out of our breeches and we were forced to unbutton ourselves to be comfortable.

Charlotte blushed when she saw our two stiff cocks standing

stiffly to attention, but she said shyly: 'Would you like me to rub these for you? I've never done this before, but I've seen Alice and her friend Pelham, the Vicar's coachman, together and Alice rubs and even sucks his prick. I'll have a go, if you like.'

We readily gave our assent and her delicate little hands were soon grasping two eager thick pricks. Terence was so excited that he spent almost immediately Charlotte squeezed his shaft, but I lasted a little longer before I too jetted gushes of hot spunk onto the rug.

'Damn, how are we going to get the sperm stains out of the rug?' wailed Terence and I must confess that the problem had me most concerned.

Fortunately, Charlotte had the answer. 'Don't worry, boys, I know how to clean the rug so well that no-one will ever know that you spunked onto it. I'll rub in some of Doctor Watkins' cough medicine!'

'A cough medicine, that's odd,' I said.

'Yes, but it works wonders. Alice showed me how to take the sperm and cunney juice stains out of her sheets after a good bout of fucking with young Pelham,' said Charlotte with an infectious little giggle.

'Mama gave me some of that stuff when I had a cough last year,' said Terence. 'I'll never ever swallow another mouthful!'

'Oh, I wouldn't worry, Master Terence. Old Giddens the gardener puts some on his roses – and they won a prize at the village fête last week.'

We collapsed with laughter. Charlotte unbuttoned her blouse and showed us her curvey breasts. Plump and white they were, tipped by rose-red little stalks that I tweaked and rubbed against my palms. Alas, we were interrupted by the noise of a carriage drawing up outside for otherwise I am sure that Charlotte and Terence would both have crossed the Rubicon that morning, but as matters stood, both had to wait a little longer before ridding themselves of their virginity.

I was to see both Charlotte and Alice regularly over the next few days. I was certain that they had confessed of their sexual exploits with Terence and myself though nothing took place of a sensuous nature until the beginning of the following week, despite some provocative lip-smacking by Alice when she passed by me in the house. This often caused my cock to swell straight up and made my cheeks crimson with embarrassment. After all, at fourteen years of age, how was I to know the delights that a young stiff prick could afford a lustful young lass like Alice?

So, for a week, I sat in my bedroom, tossing myself off as I daydreamed of Charlotte's pert breasts and Alice's juicy cunney. But after the riches of genuine fucking, self-stimulation was but a poor substitute.

Matters came to a head after I decided to send Alice a love-letter. I first thought of writing some verses myself but truth to tell, I am no poet. Terence offered some verses which I copied down:

How oft I've sworn to Alice dear,
The world no sight can show,
To match her locks, her lips divine,
Her bosom's hills of snow.
But oh! I find myself forsworn,
Two lips I have beheld;
Still lovelier, on this happy morn,
A mount that those excell'd!
Her bosom boasts no swell so fair
No tints that these eclipse;
Her head has no such suburn hair,
Nor such enchanting lips!
Yes, I've beheld the mossy mount,
Where all the graces centre;
I've seen the rosy nectar'd cunt,
Where he she fucks will enter!

'Terence, you are a genius!' I said warmly. 'If this works, I shall entreat Alice to let you fuck her as well.'

'That's kind of you, old boy,' said Terence. 'Let's see if it works. Gad, though, what about fucking both Alice and Charlotte together in a whoresome foursome!'

What a splendid idea. I thought as I sat down and composed a covering letter to go with the poem. I wrote:

Dear Alice,

I dedicate this piece of verse to you. It is sent with my

heartfelt thanks to you for initiating me into the mysteries and joys of coition. I think long and hard about that glorious romp and since then my desire for you has been ever heightened. Do let us enjoy ourselves again before I go back to school.

With gratitude and affection,

Teddy Parsifal

After checking that the coast was clear, I placed the note and verse in an envelope which I slid under the door of her room later that day. My parents and I dined at our friends, Lord Gordon and Lady McChesney, so I had no opportunity to see Alice until after breakfast the next day.

I was sitting in the study reading what appeared to be a geography textbook (but I had pages from *The Pearl* pasted inside the volume!) when Alice suddenly breezed in, ostensibly to dust the room. As she dusted she came close to me and whispered that she loved my letter but that she could not read very well and so Charlotte had read my poem to her! I must have looked somewhat shocked for she added that Charlotte could be trusted implicitly and indeed would not be averse to taking part in a little romp that afternoon – especially if 'that handsome young Master Terence would come along'.

We arranged to meet at two o'clock, in the old barn that stood, disused for some years, in Farmer Phillips' field, adjacent to our own grounds. I knew that Terence was more than keen to take part in a most wondrous and joyful new experience. How time stood still as we impatiently counted the very minutes until two thirty!

At two thirty four Terence said gloomily: 'I bet they won't come. She was having you on, Teddy. They have made monkeys of us both.'

'What sort of monkeys, Master Terry?' broke in a female voice from the entrance. It was Charlotte who asked the question, and to our delight we saw that she was not alone. Alice was with her, carrying a couple of blankets across her arms.

'You *are* monkeys,' chided Alice. 'Did you really think that I would tease you about such a serious matter as fucking? Shame on you both.'

We apologised profusely and we helped Alice spread the two blankets on the ground.

'Oh damnation, I've forgotten the pillows,' said Alice. 'I'll have to go back to the house and get them.'

'Don't worry on our account,' said Terence, but Alice insisted that we needed pillows 'for our heads and our bums' and that it was foolish to spoil the ship for a ha'porth of tar.

'Charlotte can begin the game,' she said, as she turned to trudge back to the house. 'I just hope you two young sparks won't spunk off too much whilst I'm gone. I'm looking to a good fuck just as much as you are!'

To put Charlotte at ease, I decided to take no part in the introductory fondling and petting. After all, I knew that the sweet girl's desire was to make love to Terence, so I resolved to be the gentleman, though my own prick began to swell in my breeches as the young pair moved towards each other as if drawn by a giant, invisible magnet.

Terence clasped the trembling young girl in his arms and they exchanged a most passionate kiss as they sank down upon the blanket. Terence's nervous fingers fumbled with Charlotte's blouse so the clever girl quickly stripped off all her clothes and she lay back so that both Terence and myself could have full view of her naked charms.

Gad, Charlotte was a beauty! Her bare breasts rose and fell and the firm swell of those succulent young globes was such that my hand automatically went to my prick which I hastily let out of my trousers before any damage was done to myself or the trouser material! What lovely titties they were, well separated, each looking a little away from each other and tapering in well proportioned curves until they came to two crimson points. Those taut nipples acted as magical magnets to Terence's hands which squeezed and moulded those succulent spheres, the very first time that those deliciously hard and pouting stalks had ever been felt by his eager fingers.

She then slid her hands to the front of his trousers and deftly unbuttoned him as my best friend wrenched off his belt. As he pulled off his shirt, she pulled down his drawers and her hands grasped his swollen shaft, jerking up and down, faster and faster until seconds later the white love juice gushed out of his purple helmet like a miniature fountain.

This exciting sight was too much for me to view and I pulled off my clothes and knelt in front of Charlotte, pushing my rampant, hard cock in front of her face. Her blood was up and she licked her lips before flicking out her pink little tongue to tease the uncovered mushroom head of my prick. Emboldened, she now opened her lips wide and encircled my cock as I instinctively moved forward to push my yearning prick even further into her mouth. Her magic tongue circled my knob end, savouring the juices, and her teeth scraped the tender flesh as she drew me in between those luscious lips, sucking slowly from base to top again and again, delighting me to experience new heights of unbelievable pleasure.

She stroked her tongue up and down along the underside of my bursting cock, making it ache with excitement as it throbbed with ever increasing urgency. Then she cupped my balls in her hand, gently stroking them as she slowly sucked my prick even deeper inside her mouth. She squeezed her free hand under the base of my shaft, sucking me harder and harder until I felt my balls hardening and I shouted that my climax was imminent.

'I'm going to spend, Charlotte!' I cried out, trying to take out my cock from the sweet prison of her warm, wet mouth.

But she was enjoying the taste of my prick in her mouth so much that she grasped the cheeks of my bottom, moving me backwards and forwards until with a final throb, I spunked a hot stream of sperm into Charlotte's willing mouth. She swallowed my copious emission and licked all round the head of my cock to take up the last drains of love juice.

'M'mmmm, that was delicious, Master Teddy. I've often thought about what it must be like to suck a cock and Alice has told me how delightful it can be – especially as there is no chance of a swollen belly afterwards.'

She lay back and her soft, white belly was bared to our eyes and exposed to our lascivious gaze, hidden in a luxuriant growth of curly black hair, was her superbly chiselled crack with its large pouting lips which she parted with her fingers to reveal a gleaming little clitty.

'Come on now, Master Teddy,' she said. 'I've sucked you off

so how about repaying the compliment? Or perhaps Master Terence would like to have a try.'

I looked up to see if Terry would take up the invitation but my priapic partner shook his head. He was, as he later confessed, frightened to accept Charlotte's kind offer, as he was unsure as to exactly what was required of him.

I must swiftly digress here to note how poorly Englishmen perform in this particular amatory art. All the Continentals, especially the French and Italians, suck a lady's pussey with far more aplomb than the sons of Albion. Whilst this is a technique that could hardly ever find its way onto a syllabus of a learned institution – except perhaps at Nottsgrove Academy, where my old friend Doctor Simon White now presides [see *The Oyster 1*, Editor] – it is an art that needs to be practised far more widely and with far greater skill than at present.

'Show me how to eat pussey,' whispered Terence. And to his immense delight, I instructed him although my experience was to say the least limited to reading Doctor Roy Stevenson's fascinating manual on *les affaires d'amour*.

I let my tongue travel down the length of her velvety body, lingering briefly at her belly button before sliding down to her thighs.

I was still in a kneeling position when I parted the curly thatch of dark hair to reveal her damp, inviting slit. As I worked my face down into the cleft between her thighs, I could not help but notice how appealing her pussey looked and how delicate was the faint aroma that drifted towards my nose.

By this time, I was now down on my stomach, between her legs, with one hand under her gorgeous bottom to provide a little elevation and the other reaching around her thigh so that I was able to spread her pussey lips with my thumb and middle finger. I placed my lips over her swollen clitty and sucked it into my mouth, where the tip of my tongue began to explore it from all directions. I could feel it grow larger as her legs wiggled and twitched up and down along the side of my body. More by luck than judgement, if truth be told, I found the base of her clitty, and began to twirl my tongue around it. As I flicked it up and down rapidly, she became very excited and I discovered that the faster I vibrated my tongue, the more of a reaction I wrenched out of her, a valuable lesson to both Terence and myself and one that we never forgot in our many muff-diving expeditions in later life.

Meanwhile we had not noticed that Alice had returned with the pillows and, in a mock serious voice, she said: 'I see that you have begun the game without waiting for me! Well, boys, I think I'd like to wait a while as far as you two are concerned because I want your cocks to be as big as possible when I give you both something to think about!

'Meanwhile, Charlotte and I will give you a little exhibition that will show you that despite what you may have been told, we girls can enjoy ourselves even when there are no pricks around. Shall we do that, Charlotte?'

The younger girl nodded her assent and Alice began to undress. First she unbuttoned the little mother of pearl buttons on her tightly stretched blouse revealing her large breasts with their quivering hard nipples that were soon exposed in their glorious nakedness. Then she slipped off her shoes and stockings and as she rolled down her skirt, we saw that she was wearing no underwear. I saw Terence's cock rise as she bared her delicious bum cheeks in front of him. I was equally excited by her titties and the thatch of blonde hair that barely covered her prominent pussey lips, which she stroked lasciviously, saying to Charlotte: 'You've been a naughty girl, Charlotte. You know what happens to naughty girls, don't you?'

'Yes, Alice,' said Charlotte meekly, rolling her lovely naked body over towards Alice and finishing on her belly, exposing her luscious bum-cheeks to us all. To my surprise, Alice began to smack Charlotte's beautiful bottom, lightly but quickly as Charlotte cried out: 'Oooh! Ooooh! Alice! Mercy, mercy! No more, I beg of you, please, enough now, finish me off, please finish me off!' as she winced and wriggled as her skin turned from milk white to a rosy pink.

'All in good time,' said Alice, continuing her chastisement of Charlotte's bum. 'You deserve this and besides, I love to see your lovely arse change colour. It should always be this fine shade of pink and I just adore the way your cheeks jiggle as I slap them!'

But in the end she relented and I passed Alice a pillow so that Charlotte could lie back with her tingling bum resting on something softer than the mossy ground. Alice knelt between

Charlotte's legs and my cock stiffened perceptively as she began to slowly lick the inside of the young girl's thighs with sensuous, unhurried movements. Charlotte was now totally aroused as she pulled Alice's face downwards, ramming it between her long legs. Charlotte lay back with her legs high in the air as Alice muzzled and slurped the love-juice that was now pouring from Charlotte's cunney.

'Oh, Alice, you are the best clitty sucker in the world!' cried Charlotte. 'You make me wild with desire. Can you feel my love juice squirting all over your face. AAAH!'

The lovely girl screamed out with delight as Alice slipped a hand behind her and began to frig her arse as she continued to lick and lap at her dripping cunt. I sat back looking on with rapturous attention as the two tribades moved into a *soixante neuf* position, each tonguing the other's cunt, licking, lapping each other's quims. I could see Alice's juices dribbling like honey from her parted pussey lips as Charlotte flicked gently with her wet darting tongue at Alice's erect little pink clitty. Clutching my now rock-hard prick, I moved round to see Alice give Charlotte's furry bush a thorough tonguing, soaking her curly hairs with sweet saliva and working her tongue deeper and deeper into her soaking snatch.

Alice saw me and grabbed my cock and before going down again on Charlotte cried out: 'Oh, Charlotte, look, I'm tossing off Master Teddy's thick prick. He's going to empty his balls any second now, I can feel it! I can feel his juices beginning to flow. Finish yourself off, Master Teddy, I must see to Charlotte!'

She let go of my cock but I needed no urging to take over where she had left off. I rubbed my shaft up and down, covering and uncovering my glistening red knob and as the girls jerked in a mad frenzy against each other, panting and biting, then screaming with excitement as their orgasms came jointly as they shuddered to their mutual climax. At the same time I thrust my hips together and spurted my jets of frothy white spunk over Alice's face as she shrieked in delight, rubbing it all over her face and breasts. When the juices finally stopped cascading out, she milked my still throbbing cock of all its jism by sucking the very last few drops from the knob. And not to be outdone, Charlotte was sucking hard on Terence's cock as he stood over her until with a squeal of joy she took his prick out of her mouth and let her titties be drenched with the jets of spunk that squirted out of his mushroom-domed knob.

'There you are,' said Alice. 'That's a lesson they don't teach you at school, and I hope you enjoyed it.'

'What's that, Alice?' I panted.

'Well, you saw Charlotte and I lick each other's cunneys and frig each other's arses. And the lesson is that only women really know where those special areas of pussey exist, those that drive us wild with excitement. We know just where to lick and suck and probe. Mind, I still enjoy a good thick cock up my cunt more than anything else, truth be told.

'You do seem to be able to spunk deliciously, Master Teddy. I wonder if after a little rest we can all fuck together to finish off the afternoon's entertainment?'

As far as Terence and I were concerned the question was unnecessary! We were ready in almost a trice. Gad! In those days I could fuck all day and night and be ready with a stiff cock the next morning. And if I only knew as much about fucking then as I do today. Good Heavens, I can hardly bear to think about it. Still, as my old friend Oscar Wilde said to me quite recently: 'Youth is wasted on the young!'

It took little time before we were ready and waiting for a whoresome foursome. Terence started the ball rolling by covering Charlotte's mouth with a burning kiss and the lovely girl responded by reaching out for his stiffening prick, holding it firmly yet gently between her long, tapering fingers.

'Go on, Master Terence, giver her a good fucking!' cried out Alice as Charlotte moaned with pleasure as my friend slid a hand between her legs, feeling her hairy crack, rousing her to new bouts of passion. As they rolled together on the blanket Terence tenderly opened her tender pussey lips, sliding his fingers into that dainty slit that was already moistening to a delicious wetness. He continued to frig her with one, two and then three fingers as she took hold of his cock with both hands and wriggling across him bent forward to receive the uncapped red knob between her eager lips. She sucked at the mushroomed head, her soft tongue rolling over and over, slipping her hands now underneath to cup his tight little ballsack.

She rolled on to her back, eyes closed, mouth open. She was ready to be fucked – and Terence too was ready, as he positioned himself on top of her – while Alice took hold of his bursting cock and placed it between lips that opened wide to receive it. Terence thrust forward, sending his shaft deep inside her willing cunt. Charlotte cried out as she felt his prick fully inside her. She wrapped her legs around his waist as she bucked to and fro with her buttocks coming off the blanket as she gyrated faster and faster. Charlotte began to grunt, her breathing heavy and strained as her movements quickened and suddenly she was like a wild animal as he pounded to and fro and the surging cries of fulfilment echoed throughout the old barn as Charlotte began to milk the thick cock thrusting in and out of her soft, wet cunt.

'Ah, Terreeeee!, push harder, again, and again, there!' she screamed in ecstacy as they came together. She arched her hips, forcing Terence to withdraw. Alice grabbed his swollen red prick to squirt his hot jets of spunk across Charlotte's belly as the young couple sank down into the reverie that follows the opening of the gates of the reservoir of love.

My own cock was again as stiff as a poker as Alice whispered: 'Just lie back, Master Teddy, just lie back and leave the rest to me.'

I did as I was told and Alice gently stroked the underside of my cock, allowing her fingers to trace a path around and underneath my balls which made my whole body tingle with gratification. After a while she closed her hand round the throbbing shaft and suddenly her tousled mane of blonde hair was between my legs as she sucked lustily upon my rampant cock.

'Oooh! Oooh! I'm going to spend, Alice, I'm going to spend!' I cried out desperately.

Immediately she ceased her sucking and struggled up standing over me, legs apart like some divine female Colossus. Her teeth flashed in a lustful smile, her eyes twinkled as she slowly lowered herself upon me. She rubbed her cunney over the tip of my red-headed shaft and then expertly slid herself right down on me, my prick sliding straight between her pussey lips and into her moist cunney at the first attempt. I felt her muscles contract and relax as she rocked up and down my shaft. I flexed myself to thrust into that exquisite silky wetness as she pumped her tight little bum cheeks furiously up and down, digging her fingernails into my flesh as she held on to my body. Each voluptuous shove was accompanied by a wail of ecstacy as I grabbed her large breasts and brought my head up to suck and lap on those rosy nipples.

We both began the final ride to our climax and I felt her cunney grip my cock even harder as we entered the last moments. She shivered and trembled as she reached the haven first, pulling me in as tightly as possible until, with a final push upwards, I too began to spend, spurting my hot love juice into her willing cunt. Alice gurgled with joy as the frothy white cream flooded into her and I felt her shudder as she drained me of every last drop of jism.

The four of us lay panting with exhaustion for a while and then we developed a superb fucking chain with Charlotte on her knees, leaning forward to gobble my cock and Terence pushing his cock into her from behind whilst he frigged Alice's cunt as the dear girl exchanged passionate kisses with me while I fondled her crimson nipples that were as hard as two miniature little pricks to my touch.

To end with, the girls lay down and played with each other's pussies, each rubbing and fingering the other while Terence and I knelt down to have our cocks sucked, mine by Charlotte and Terence's by Alice.

As my old friend Sir Andrew Scott has written, first love can be idyllic – or disastrous. Which it will be depends much on the partners concerned and to a very great extent upon our own selves. Terence and I were naive and perhaps bewildered by our experiences but there can be no doubt how fortunate we were to make our first journeys down the highways of love with such willing, loving girls who were willing to cater to our every desires. The old country law says that one's first experience should be in an open field, at night, under the stars. Maybe so, but our romp in the old barn, which was also Terence's introduction to fucking, certainly did us a power of good. We learned much from our joust, not least the need to experiment until one finds the best way to please both oneself and one's partner. This was a maxim I have never forgotten and have always urged the lucky young men just about to begin their first rides on the roundabouts of love-joys.

Later that evening I found myself alone with Alice, as Charlotte had been given the evening off – and as you can guess, dear reader, she and Terence spent the evening down nearby Lovers' Lane sucking and fucking until his cock and her cunney were just too sore to continue!

Not that Alice and I were doing anything very different up in my bedroom! We had enjoyed a grand session of fucking and we were lying sated on my bed, with Alice toying with my cock in her hand.

'Have you taken part in a great deal of fucking?' I asked Alice somewhat artlessly.

'Not as much as I would like, Master Teddy, but that's because I'm careful in choosing the days. I'd rather go without or use a dildo than rely on you boys to take your cocks out just before you're about to spend.

'I was always careful about letting a cock up my pussey – even the very first time, when I wanted it so badly,' she added.

'Oh, you must tell me all about that,' I said eagerly.

'Well, if you really want to know, Master Teddy, I lost my virginity working in my last situation.'

'Do tell me about it, Alice,' I begged. 'I'm sure that will make my cock swell up again. After all, I've only come twice and Mama said they would be returning late tonight. I want to fuck you at least twice more before they come back.'

'My, could you really? I've been looking at that book by Doctor Roy Stevenson that your Papa gave you and he says that too much fucking is as bad as too little.'

'Oh, never mind all that!' I exclaimed. 'Tell me about the first time you fucked.'

She smiled and said: 'Well, all right, I will tell you all about it. I was working as a kitchen maid in a big house in North London. My employer was a publisher and he often brought home books for the servants to read. Well, one afternoon, I was walking down Holywell Street and I thought I would look into one of the bookshops there. I noticed there were several shops selling prints but I did not know that this was a notorious centre for smutty books. After all, I was just a simple country girl of sixteen years of age. I couldn't help noticing that some of the prints displayed outside Toby Watson's bookshop looked rather rude. Of course, I did not know that the prints that had caught my eye were classic sketches by the great caricaturist Thomas Rowlandson.

'Suddenly a man's voice behind me said: "Do you like the work of Rowlandson? There are prudes who would wish to ban his drawings but I think the man was a great artist, don't you?"

'I blushed and turned round to see who was speaking to me. He turned out to be a good-looking man in his late twenties or early thirties, smartly but not richly dressed. We struck up a conversation but I could tell that from the way he was staring at my white frilly blouse that he was attracted to me – as I was, it must be confessed, to him.

'We engaged in conversation for about five minutes and then he offered to take me to a public house for a drink. I liked him even more when he did not demur after I said that I would prefer a nice cup of tea. So he took me to Bourne's Coffee House in Gray's Inn Road and we chatted away animatedly over tea and cakes. He told me that his name was Kenneth Kenhall-Watkins and that he worked as a salesman for a big London publisher. And what a coincidence! He worked for Goulthorpes, the company for whom my employer, Professor Pelham, was the chief editor.

'He lodged nearby in John Street and I needed little encouragement to agree to see the etchings he had purchased the previous week which were, of course, in his rooms.

'So very soon afterwards, I found myself sitting on a couch in Kenneth's room, looking at a book of very saucy prints. There was one particular print that I shall always remember as it sent shivers of lust throughout my body. Indeed, it makes me randy now just thinking about it.

'The scene was of a richly decorated bedroom and upon the bed lay a ravishingly beautiful young girl in a state of deshabille. She lay with her eyes closed, her petticoat and shift thrown up, her thighs wide apart, revealing to my burning gaze a rounded white belly the bottom part of which was covered by a generous growth of jet black hair; and from between the locks that grew over the mount above a delicious-looking little crack, I could perceive two rosy lips slightly gaping open, from which oozed traces of whitish-looking foam. Next to the girl was standing a handsome young man, totally naked, whose huge erect prick was being lovingly grasped by the reclining girl whose mouth was open, teasingly near the uncapped knob and ready to perform sweet suction upon this lucky youth's stiff cock.

'You may well guess what happened very after that, Master Teddy! I hardly noticed the dashing rogue raise my petticoats and inserting his hand between my legs, letting it rest on the golden covering of blonde hair that covered my delicate little crack.

'With the other he dexterously undid the top two buttons of my blouse to view better the firm swell of my breasts. I was unsure as to how best to react – but for better or worse I was given little time to think about it as he suddenly pressed his face close to mine and kissed me passionately upon the lips.

'In spite of my surprise, I felt a rush of excitement surge through my veins. There was something about Kenneth's kiss that made it impossible not to respond. His hand slipped down to close gently over my breast as his other began to stroke my dampening pussey thorugh the thin cotton material of my drawers.

'Everything was now happening so fast that my memory is but a fond blur. I do remember though that I didn't try to resist him although being a gentleman, Kenneth later assured me, he would have acceeded to my wishes if I had wished to break away from his embrace.

'Be that as it may, his hand reached the top of my legs as I pressed my lips more firmly against his, he now stroking my pussey harder with his thumb, his fingers probing and caressing the lips of my cunney. Then I felt my whole body vibrate with excitement as his thumb found my clitty! He began rubbing it with a steadily increasing pace that had me swooning with delight. Ah, at that moment, I must confess, I knew for certain that I would be glad and willing to let him do anything he wished with me.

'Kenneth now let go of my breast and began to undo the buttons at the back of my blouse. Then he slipped it off me completely and ran his hands over my naked breasts, tracing circles around the stiffening nipples with the tips of his fingers. Then he bent his head down and took one of my erect teats in his mouth, and the wet friction of his tongue made me gasp with bliss as he sucked firm and deep.

'Now I culd feel him tugging at my drawers and I lifted my bum off the seat automatically to assist him as he pulled them down. I was feeling incredibly aroused and when Kenneth took hold of my hand and planted it firmly between his legs, I knew I just had to be fucked by this sweet man. My whole body panted for him! My breasts seemed to be swelling as if they would burst and the little red cherry-tipped nipples were as hard as peas and tickling me! And as for my cunt, oh, such a throbbing as went on in it as I had never felt before.

'"Now, Alice,' he said tenderly. "I do so want to fuck you. Would you like that, my darling?"

'"Very much so!" I replied quietly and with that Kenneth swiftly undressed and I gazed with longing at his thick, stiff cock which stood up so proudly, attended above by a fine swatch of thick black hair and underneath by the velvety wrinkled ballsbag. I might never have been fucked before but I had seen a few cocks before then, from the time I played "Doctors and Nurses" with Dudley Lovell, my cousin, at his fourteenth birthday party, to the extraordinarily thick but battered-looking prick belonging to Taylor, the Scottish butler at the house where I worked, whom I saw fucking the cook and the youngest pantrymaid one after the other on the kitchen table just a few weeks before. Fortunately I had been warned to keep away from this man who was well-known for his propensity to stick his enormous truncheon up any skirt given half a chance.

'But Kenneth looked so handsome without a stitch of clothing on him. He looked so powerful, so lithe! His shoulders were as broad as mine were narrow and his deep and manly chest, coverd lightly with dark hair contrasted so well with my graceful, swelling bosoms. He stretched me out on the big couch and knelt alongside me, kissing my titties and belly and running his hand up and down my thighs.

'My excitement grew even more stronger as I lovingly clutched his head, moaning my approval as he pressed his lips down onto my bushy mound. He worked his tongue up and around my clitty, sucking and lapping my soaking pussey as I ground my slit against his mouth. He was an excellent pussey-eater, one moment gently nibbling my cunney lips and the next sucking on clitty until I just could not wait any longer for his cock to nestle down between my legs.

'"Please, please fuck me, Kenneth!" I implored.

'"But I want to make sure you wish to lose your hymen," he muttered, not leaving his stimulation of my pussey for more than a moment.

'"I lost that by fingerfucking years ago," I said. "I want your cock, though, to be the first to enter my slit especially as it's a good time of the month to let you come inside me."

'"I don't want to play Vatican roulette," said Kenneth. "But 'pon my soul, you are such a beautiful girl, I don't think my cock would ever forgive me if I did not place him in your dear little pussey."

'Kenneth needed no further urging as he climbed over me and I eagerly lifted my hips to welcome his thrusting prick that slid easily between the lips of my pussey. His cock was thick and long, as I said, and I squirmed in sheer ecstasy as for the first time I experienced the joy of a throbbing, hot cock pump in and out of my love-channel. I was in heaven having waited so long for this moment to arrive. Kenneth was an expert at fucking, or *l'art de faire l'amour*, in a salute to the French whom he insisted made their love-making far more fun than in our stuffy old country.

'Still, his prick was a perfect fit for my nest. I remember the way he played with my breasts as my titties bounced back and forth in rhythm to his thrusts. My pussey was soaking with love juices but it was still tight and I loved the way – how shall I put it – well, how my pussey lips and clitty appeared to move to and fro, sending me into a delicious spend as Kenneth thrust and thrust again as he clasped me to him and in a convulsive thrill he pumped a luscious flood of creamy spunk into my womb!

'There, Master Teddy! That's how I lost my virginity. Did you find that an exciting story?'

'Your tale certainly has made me feel randy again, Alice,' I replied. 'Why, look at my cock! It's swelling up again beautifully.'

'So it is, Master Teddy! My, you are lucky to have such a big cock. It's even fatter than my last friend's tool and his was quite enormous. His name was Trevor Williams, an assistant in John Hotten's special bookshop in Piccadilly and I think he must have enlarged his tool by playing with it all day while reading all those naughty books!'*

[EDITOR'S NOTE: The bookshop to which Alice refers was well known to the cognoscenti of erotic literature one hundred years ago. The owner, John Camden Hotten, enjoyed a tremendous reputation as a publisher and distributor of banned books, magazines and photographs. Among those known to have frequented the shop which was situated near the junction of Piccadilly and Albemarle Street were the Prince of Wales's equerry, Lord Arthur Somerset, H. Spencer Ashbee, Sir Lionel Trapes, the noted war correspondent George Augustus Sala, and the Cambridge Univeristy don, Professor Norman Blakeley.]

As we lay back on the bed, I felt her warm hand encircle my throbbing cock. She turned onto her back and whispered to me to stroke her. My hand glided smoothly over her white skin, brushing lightly over her breasts, her hard, erect nipples and then down over her stomach. When I reached her pussey, she opened her legs for me. My fingers slipped over the moist lips of her cunt and when I found her clitty, her hand tightened around my shaft.

She said: 'Oh, Teddy, lie down beside me with your head towards my feet. Do you know how to taste a girl?'

'Not really, Alice.'

'Just lick me,' she instructed. 'Slide your tongue slowly over my cunney lips. Once you do it you will see how naturally it comes to you.'

And she was right! Once I had got a taste of her creamy cunt, my tongue seemed to develop a life of its own, whipping back and forth, up and down, boring deep inside her tender love channel. I felt her tongue flick over my knob, down the shaft and over my balls and then reversing the route back to the top. Dear Alice, few girls know how to suck cock better than she!

With one gulp, she slipped the remainder of my shaft in the wet warmth of her mouth and lying on our sides, we sucked away at each other until she spent, grinding her soppy pussey against my face. Suddenly, she backed away from me and my cock slipped out of her mouth. She raised her knees up, legs wide apart and told me to put my trusty tool inside her.

Nothing loath, I leaned forward, pressing into her until my entire shaft was buried in her snatch. She cried with delight as I pumped away, pressing to meet my thrusts to make certain that every inch of cock was inside her juicy pussey. Naturally, it took only a short time before I felt myself ready to climax and I shot great globs of white frothy sperm inside the lovely girl's cunt.

We lay panting after this lustful emission but later that afternoon she showed me the joys of tit-fucking and how to squirt my spunk over her breasts. Alice taught me many of the secrets of sexual pleasures that summer. She was patient and loving and every woman I've made love to since has benefitted from her kind tutelage. I am glad to say that Alice married a young teacher and emigrated to Australia where they now live, happily in considerable prosperity near the town of Melbourne.

This summer of my fifteenth year was truly a memorable time. For I must now pass on quickly to an event that occured just two or three days after my glorious joust with Alice.

We were enjoying a quiet breakfast when my father suddenly broke off from reading *The Times* to say: 'Ada, boys, listen to me. There is a most interesting item in the newspaper this morning.'

'What is it, Father?' enquired Cecil, who I should mention was now seventeen and a lordly sixth former at Cockshall Manor Academy.

'Do you remember that Swedish gentleman, Mr Karl Andersson* [*Editor's note: Mr Parsifal must have been referring to the distinguished Scandinavian explorer Karl Johann Andersson, who was rated as only second to Livingstone. He died while trying to reach the source of the Cunene river*]? You will doubtless have recalled that we met him at Sir Douglas Walker's reception in aid of the West London Home for Unmarried Fathers. Well, he has written a letter to *The Times* from East Africa about his experiences with elephants. You will be fascinated by what he has to say.'

'Who cares a shit about that boring old fart?' muttered Cecil under his breath. Fortunately Father did not quite catch what was said and registered his disapproval only by a glare.

'Oh, do read the letter to us,' said Mother placatingly, though I am sure that she had no real desire to listen to my Father. Actually, I was rather interested, not having met the gentleman concerned and I had just finished reading an exciting adventure about explorers in the Dark Continent.

'Very well, my dear,' said Father. 'Pay attention, boys. The letter begins: "I address you now from the wilds of unexplored country about a hundred and fifty miles from Nairobi. During my travels I encountered a very considerable number of elephants but unfortunately chiefly cows with their young which are both dangerous and unprofitable. I have had some perilous adventures with these animals and have been taught some severe lessons which I am not likely ever to forget. If I have not obtained a great deal of ivory I have gained a great deal of experience and some interesting insights into the natural history of the African elephant.

'"Nothing gives a person a better idea of the elephants' stupendous powers than a day's walk through one of their favourite haunts. There may be seen whole tracts of forest laid prostrate and such trees sometimes! The trees, which for the main part are of a brittle nature, are usually broken off short by the beasts; but when they meet with a tree that seems to them too tough to snap at once, up it goes, root and all.

'"The other day, after many hours of fatiguing tracking, I was closing with a very large troop of elephants, consisting chiefly of females, when to my left I suddenly espied another troop of what I took to be males. I at once left the first troop to attack the second. I stalked unperceived to within twenty-five paces of the herd when to my annoyance, I discovered that they were also mostly cows and calves. There were however, a couple of fine bulls among them, one evidently acting as paterfamilias to the herd. This beast's position was unfavourable and I was waiting for him to present a better mark when to my astonishment they all made off.

'"As they were disappearing into the brushwood I fired at one of the hindermost – a male, as I imagined. In an instant the herd wheeled about, and with a terrific rush came crashing through the bushes nearly in a direct line towards me. But after running for about sixty or seventy paces they stopped short, evidently annoyed at not finding the enemy.

'"I felt very much inclined to take to my heels, but a moment's reflection convinced me that safety lay only in keeping close; and it was as well I did so for in a few moments the paterfamilias made an oblique rush through the jungle with such force as to actually send a whole tree that he had uprooted in his headlong course spinning in the air. A huge branch remained fixed to one of his tusks. His head he carried aloft, his huge ears were spread to the full, while with his trunk he sniffed the air impatiently. In this position, and when within less than a dozen paces of me he remained, I should say, for about half a minute. I think it was the most striking and thrilling sporting scene that I ever saw . . .

'"I have shot many giraffes, gnus, hartebeests besides elephants but I make a point of not destroying unless absolutely in want of meat to feed either my party or the hundreds of poor devils constantly following my track."'

'Well, that sounds very exciting, doesn't it, lads?' said Father, folding the newspaper and putting it down on the table.

'I don't like the idea of killing for sport,' I said.

'Neither do I,' said Cecil. 'I am glad that Mr Andersson only shot those poor animals for food and not simply wantonly as do so many hunters.'

'I am in agreement with you, boys,' said Mother. 'Your sentiments certainly do you proud.'

'Yes, I would not disagree with that,' said Father. 'Anyhow, the reason that I read that passage to you is that Jumbo the elephant is at the London Zoological Gardens in Regent's Park just now and I thought that we would take a train up to town and see him. Would you like to go?'

What a splendid treat lay in store, I thought, as Cecil and I chorused our assent. But Mother declined the invitation as she was due to take tea that afternoon with the squire's wife, Lady Le Baique, and felt it would be impolite to cancel the arrangement at such short notice.

'But you three men must go!' said Mother kindly. 'I will go another time and anyhow, your Papa and I saw Jumbo last year when we went up to town for Lord Bourne's Autumn Ball.'

'Very well, my dear, I will call young Owen to take us to the railway station so as we can catch the noon train. It so happens that I want to see my old friend Sir Lionel Trapes who lives nearby in St John's Wood so I shall be able, if you will forgive the perhaps inappropriate colloquialism, to kill two birds with one stone.'

We travelled up to town on the good old London, Brighton and South Coast Railway and the train pulled into Victoria Station within a minute of its scheduled time of arrival. We disembarked and strode up the station platform to the cab rank. We were waiting in a fairly long queue when Father suddenly snapped his fingers and grimaced.

'Boys, I have just remembered that I promised to undertake a chore for Sir Lionel which will necessitate my leaving you to visit the Zoo by yourselves,' said Father.

'I promised to pick up a book for him, some learned text or other that has been ordered especially for him from the Continent. The bookseller promised it would be ready for collection today so I wrote to my friend and said that I would collect it and save him a journey or the cost of postage.

'So here are two sovereigns, Cecil. You and Teddy can take a cab directly to the Zoo. I think it best if you meet me at Sir Lionel's this afternoon. In case you have forgotten his address, here is his card. Be there by five o'clock. I will have to see Jumbo another time. And perhaps I will be able to take your mother with me,' he concluded.

The day was turning into a great adventure indeed. We waited with Father for our separate cabs and he warned us of the dangers of pickpockets who lurk round railway stations and any large gathering of people.

'You can sometimes tell the thieves by an unrest about them, for they seldom journey on a train,' explained Father. 'They hang around the ticket offices or queues like this. When they see people engaged in conversation they go up to them and plant themselves by their side while the others cover their movements. Then one might pretend to bump into the victim and extract his wallet, for these thieves have very quick fingers. So be warned, and keep an eye out for your money and your pocket-watch.'

With those words, Father climbed into a cab and fortunately a second cab soon appeared and Cecil and I were off to the Zoo.

'I say, Cecil, what sort of book is Father getting for Sir Lionel?'

'Something he'd never let us see, like French postcards or a copy of the *Cremorne*!' said Cecil. 'Did you know that Sir Lionel's nephew is in my form at school? And from what young Daley tells me, old Sir Lionel's a bit of a sportsman. He belongs to the Jim-Jam Club in Great Windmill Street. Now that's run by Major Ferguson, whose nephew is also in the Lower Sixth at Cockshall Manor. And Scott Ferguson told the prefects that all the London swells go there to fuck, if you know what that means.'

'Of course I know what that means!' I cried indignantly. 'Why, I've already fucked two girls myself this summer.'

'Gosh, have you really? One of them must be Alice. No, no, no, you must not tell me, Teddy, for a gentleman never ever reveals the names of girls he has fucked unless he has caught a dose of clap from them. And then, in that case, it is his bounden duty to inform his friends. Still, good luck to you, little brother. I didn't think you could even manage a cockstand yet,' smiled Cecil. 'However, I don't suppose you would be interested in having a fuck at a rather special private club I know. After all, I'm sure you would much prefer to see the animals at the Zoo.'

'Don't tease me, Cecil,' I said. 'You know bloody well that I would give up my house cricket colours for the chance of another fuck. But Father has always warned us against loose women. Won't we be risking catching some awful pox?'

'Father is quite right. You must never pick up a woman in the street. But the girls at the private clubs cater exclusively for gentlemen and they are checked every so often for any problems. Don't worry, Teddy, your cock and balls are quite safe at Maison Alfred's.'

'Well, I'm game if you really mean it. But how about lucre? We've only got Father's two sovereigns between us and we'll want some tea and then we'll need another cab to be at Sir Lionel's by five o'clock, won't we?'

'No problem, young brother. I've five pounds here that Father's cousin, Doctor Arkley, gave me for coming first in the Public Schools' cross-country race last April. I can't think of a better use for the cash than to spend it on two lovely girls, a slap up spread and a magnum of bubbly, can you?'

Cecil instructed the driver to change his route though, as it happens, Maison Alfred's was not all that far away from the Zoological Gardens, being situated at the north end of

Marylebone High Street.

The club was in a private house and Cecil gave five sharp raps on the door with the heavy brass lion's head knocker.

'That's a signal known only to club members,' he told me.

The door was opened by a rather stout maitre d'hotel, who asked Cecil for his membership card which he fished out of his waistcoat pocket.

'I'll sign in my brother,' said Cecil breezily.

'I regret that the minimum age for entry is sixteen, Mr Parsifal,' intoned the attendant.

'Well, young Teddy's sixteen, Soames.'

'He looks far younger, sir. We would require proof of his age. Have either of you any such proof?'

'How about this?' said Cecil, slipping a sovereign into the man's hand.

'That will do nicely,' said Soames happily. 'May I recommend the Chelsea Room on the first floor. Polly and Sophie are awaiting custom.'

'Excellent, excellent. Send up a cold collation with a magnum of fizz in as soon as possible. Look, Soames, I'll leave five pounds here, that should cover it and leave a fair old tip for you, right?'

'You're very generous, Mister Parsifal,' murmured the servant as Cecil led the way up to our salon. He tapped on the door and opened it. I peered from behind him and saw an exquisitely furnished room that had a small table near the windows which overlooked Marylebone High Street and two couches drawn up near the fireplace though naturally at the height of a warm summer's day, the fires had not yet been lit.

And sitting on one of the couches were two of the prettiest girls I have ever seen in my life. One was slender and of medium height of no more than at most eighteen years of age with a merry little face which was sheer perfection. Her chin was charmingly dimpled, her lips, full and pouting, slightly open, gave just a glimpse of two rows of ivory that appeared set in the deep rosy flesh of her small and elegant mouth. Her nose was of the Roman cast, her eyes a sparkling lustrous dark brown and her forehead was middling high, setting off a mop of brown, shiny hair.

She wore an emerald green dress, low-cut with a long wide

skirt, nipped in at the waist and her nipples were only barely concealed by the fabric for her corset thrust forward her pert young breasts and my eyes were immediately riveted upon those white alabaster beauties.

The other exquisite creature was red-headed, her hair drawn back in a bun which she was in the act of loosening when Cecil opened the door. Her skin was white and of a clarity that it seemed illumined from within. She was wearing a cream coloured outfit, the jacket of which, being fashioned tightly to her torso and waist, allowed me to see the perfect development of her fully-rounded breasts while her lower limbs were clad in a long, pleated skirt. Her features were finely shaped, the best features being a *retroussé* nose and sparkling light blue eyes.

'Well, do you like what you see or do you want to send us back to the shop?' said the divine-looking redhead.

'No, no, not at all. It's just that my young brother and I have been struck dumb by this exciting sight of two luscious lovelies such as yourselves,' stammered out Cecil.

'How kind of you to say so,' chipped in the brunette. 'In that case we had better introduce ourselves. I am Sophie and this is my sister Polly.'

'Heavens, two brothers and two sisters together, how exciting!' said Cecil.

'Ha, ha, ha! Yes, well actually Sophie is only my half sister but I love her very much!' cried Polly.

'I'm sure you do,' rejoined my brother. 'Anyhow, I am Cecil Parsifal and this is Teddy, my young rogue of a full brother. At least, to the best of my knowledge he is my full brother although I must confess that Nature has been kinder to him than me as I hear from a variety of sources that he possesses the biggest prick in Cockshall Manor!'

'My, he's rather young, isn't he? How old are you, Teddy?' asked Polly.

'Old enough!' I replied. 'I'm sixteen years old next week.'

I believe that the girls saw through my unblushing lie but they smiled and said nothing more about my age. I think they both fancied a fuck with a young teenaged boy after having to deal with older men who frankly often had trouble keeping it up.

'I've made all the arrangements with Soames,' said Cecil,

who was obviously eager to get on with the action. 'He'll have a cold collation and some bubbly up here soon.'

'Oh, he won't be here for at least an hour,' said Sophie. 'It's very hot in here, boys, why don't we take off some clothes and let the pleasant warm air get to our bodies.'

We needed no further bidding but perhaps it was the first time Cecil and I had undressed together for many years, we were both somewhat inhibited and I found to my surprise that unusually, my cock stayed flapping down between my legs. I stole a glance at Cecil and saw that he too was at half-mast, his knob being only partially uncovered by his foreskin.

'Those look like sizeable weapons once they are primed,' laughed Polly.

'Yes, you're right. What can we do to stiffen their cocks?' Sophie pondered. 'I know, let's tan their hides!'

'What a good idea, Sophie,' chirped Polly. 'Now, who is going to be first. You are the older, Cecil so let us begin. Bend down, sir and touch your toes.'

Quite nude, my brother did as he was told, opening his legs slightly so we had fair view of his hanging balls. Sophie passed a hand lightly across his bare bum cheeks and then she nodded and they immediately began to smack Cecil's arse with their palms. As one girl smacked his bum, the other began to undress so by the time Cecil's bum was rosy coloured from their sweet slapping, both the girls were stark naked.

'There, you naughty boy. How dare you come to us with a limp prick?'

'Such an impudent boy! There, take that, and that, and that!'

I craned my head forward and observed a very perceptible rising in his cock which had swelled up and soon stood out up against his belly in a rampant state of erection. I had not even noticed that my own prick had also stiffened up to its fullest height and was also standing high majestically against my flat belly.

'They're both ready now,' cried Polly. 'Now, Cecil, your poor bum took a beating so you can fuck first!'

And with that she grabbed hold of Cecil and after a cheerful preliminary embrace the lovely girl stretched herself out on the luxuriously thick carpet. She was absolutely beautiful with extremely large breasts topped by equally well proportioned aureoles and nipples. Her mound was covered with a profusion of rich reddish hair and the glowing chink between the slips of her cunney looked highly inviting.

Cecil took a deep breath, blew out his cheeks as he expelled the air from his lungs and took his rock-hard cock in his hand. As he knelt down he drew back the foreskin, making his purple knob bound and swell.

Polly heaved herself up and she too knelt forward, pushing out the chubby cheeks of her bum to afford me a truly excellent view of both her cunt and her arsehole. This excited me no end and it was all I could do to restrain myself from frigging off there and then.

She grasped Cecil's cock with both hands and slowly began first to lick my lucky brother's knob and then, after giving the shaft a good rub, taking almost the whole length in her mouth until it must have surely been touching the back of her throat. Then she began to suck noisily on Cecil's bursting prick, moving her head to and fro so that his shaft moved smoothly back and forth though always a part was engulfed between Polly's pouting lips. Meanwhile, she played with his balls, gently squeezing them until she felt that Cecil was near the peak of pleasure.

Now she took his throbbing member out of her mouth and, still keeping tight hold of his shaft, gently whispered to him to lie down on his back. Cecil obeyed without demur and lay flat on the carpet, his rampant cock sticking up as firmly as a flagpole under the gorgeous Polly's expert handling.

The delicious girl rose up, and still keeping my brother's prick in her hand, turned her peachy bum cheeks to his belly and calmly proceeded to sit firmly on his cock, straddled over his lap in a position that I was later to learn enabled her to enjoy the very last fraction of a cock length in her heated cunney. They stayed almost motionless for a few moments as in a tableau vivant, enjoying the mutual sensations of repletion and possession so delightful to each of the players of the glorious game.

Then they commenced those soul-stirring movements that led inexorably to a grande finale of frenzy. One could almost feel their muscles contract and relax as she rocked up and down on Cecil's cock.

As their orgasm approached, Polly drove down hard with a delighted squeal, spearing herself on Cecil's bursting prick which was glistening wet from her cunt juice. The pair then melted into a torrent of mutual spendings as they came together with great cries and Cecil shot a great gushing stream of spunk into her womb.

Now it was my turn to join in this erotic frolic. Sophie and I were now both stark naked and the gorgeous girl embraced me passionately as we stood belly to belly, with only my thick, hard cock being squeezed delightfully between our tummies.

'What a monster,' laughed Sophie lasciviously. 'My goodness, Teddy, you have a gigantic prick for such a young fellow. I do believe it is even bigger than that of Peter Stockman, that young theology student who fucked me so divinely last Thursday.'

'Do you think so?' said Polly with interest. 'Well, let us see if he can use it as well as Peter who you said was the best fuck you have enjoyed since you had the Bishop of Finchley.'

I inclined the willing wench backwards upon the soft carpet and we lay at full length, side by side, both of us eager as possible for the game; my head was buried between Sophie's loving thighs, with which she pressed me most amorously, as I inserted my tongue into her inviting little crack, making her gasp with passion. She sucked my stiff prick, handling and kissing my balls till I spent in her mouth as her tongue washed my knob. She sucked down my copious emission whilst I repaid her loving attentions to the best of my ability with my own active tongue.

I rolled over this delicious minx, spreading her legs wide as she grasped my cock to feed it to her juicy pussey. She rolled back my foreskin and kissed the shiny dome as she guided my knob to the lips of her hot pussey and slowly, thrillingly, I inched my shaft inside her willing cunney as it sucked in my throbbing prick. I fucked her with long, smooth strokes and we laughed merrily as I hovered above her, supporting myself on my arms. My balls slapped in slow cadence on her buttocks and thighs as I moved down, up and down again, increasing the pace as I thrust with a new intensity, cheered on by Cecil and Polly who were greatly impressed, and I apologise if I do sound boastful of my prowess in *l'art de faire l'amour*.

As I approached the heights, I changed the tempo to one of swift, short jabs as she rotated her bum cheeks as I pulsed in and out of her squelchy pussey. We climaxed together as my cock squirted out jets of spunk that mingled exquisitely with her own stream of cunney juice. Now she had tasted me Sophie wanted more, so she rubbed up my cock to a second fine erection and I took her doggy fashion, gripping her hips as I thrust my rampant tool deep into her cunt from behind, my balls jiggling against her firm and nicely rounded bum cheeks. I fucked away energetically just as if I had never spent just minutes before, as the throbbing and contracting of her inner cunney muscles on my enraptured prick spurred me to further efforts until with a hoarse cry I pumped a second stream of sperm into her willing womb. I fell on top of the sweet girl and we sank down exhausted entwined in each other's arms to enjoy the lovely lethargy that comes after a fine bout of fucking.

None of us had noticed that whilst we had been fucking, Soames had entered the room and set up a table upon which he had placed a selection of cold meats, fruits, and a magnum of champagne in an ice-bucket.

(I understand that the contract for the club's ice was so valuable that the tradesman concerned, a Mr Tong, slipped Soames a five pound note the first Friday of every month but that is neither here nor there).

We were so warm from our games that we stayed quite naked as we ate and drank our way through the informal little luncheon. It transpired that both the girls were well educated young ladies and had entered their work not so much from want as from sheer enjoyment of the business involved and Cecil and I enjoyed a very interesting conversation with them as we sipped our nice champagne.

We sat idly around talking of this and that when Sophie said: 'I must say that I really enjoyed my lunchtime fuck. You boys are in the first flush of youth and eager to please your girls.

'But you would really be amazed at the ignorance and sheer, utter selfishness which Polly, myself and all the working girls at Maison Alfred and other private clubs encounter daily.

'Now I know you gentlemen are paying for your pleasures but if, for example, some customer actually took the trouble to ask if there was a particular mode of fucking I preferred, I would be so grateful that I would be able to give him that little bit extra – that certain *je ne sais quoi* that stands between a good fuck and a great one,' she added warmly.

'I must agree with every word you say,' said Polly. 'I know that different men have different preferences and indeed their performances are governed by both physical and mental factors.

'And yes, many only want to fuck in one specific fashion. But I must add that I have no objection, and nor I am sure have you to giving relief to those men whose own upbringing (let alone that of their wives) mean that they cannot enjoy the full flavour of the fruits of the marital bed. I mean, incredible though it may seem to liberated girls like us, many women recoil with distaste at the very notion of sucking a prick! Is that not quite astonishing?'

'They just cannot know what they are missing?' chimed in Sophie.

'Perhaps it is as well, my dear, or you would both be out of business,' said Cecil and we all laughed heartily at his quick-minded wit.

'Ah, I would wager a day's pay that your Papa has a copy of Doctor Roy Stevenson's manual in his library,' said Polly, her eyes twinkling with merriment. 'I recall the passage where the good doctor lays down the rule that between lovers there should be no rules.'

'You would win your wager, Polly,' said Cecil. 'However, I was actually thinking of what Doctor Stevenson says about rear entry.'

'Oh, about how some folk believe it is not quite genteel to poke in your prick from behind?' smiled Sophie. 'Why, I enjoy that position immensely. How some people can believe that the manner in which most mammals copulate is somehow unnatural is almost past my comprehension. I also enjoy the sensation of a lovely smooth cock entering my pussey from behind. I believe this position allows an extra inch or two of the shaft to enter the cunney and that it always a bonus.'

'Indeed it is,' mused Polly. 'And I do believe that it allows the knob of the cock to touch the clitty which is even nicer! Why, just feeling a knob against my clitty and cunney lips brings me off in a trice.'

'Let us put into practice what we have been talking about,' said Cecil, massaging his cock up to a fine state of stiffness.

'Very well, Cecil dear. But do have patience as I would like to have young Teddy fuck me from the rear,' said Polly, looking with interest at my youthful prick which was rising majestically upwards as she was speaking until it stood upright in all its glory, the rich red ruby dome uncapped as it throbbed out its need for a juicy quim in which to bury itself.

Sophie took hold of my cock as Polly leaned over the arm of the couch, spreading her legs a little and raising her bum so that both her arsehole and cunt were waiting for my arrival.

'Would you like this colossal cock up your bum, darling?' enquired Sophie, with characteristic eloquence.

'No, not now, but thank you so much for asking, my sweet. But please put Teddy's prick in my cunney, there's a dear, as I have a great fancy for it just now. I want to feel his hot cock nudge between my bum-cheeks until his knob touches my cunt lips.'

The lovely girl grasped my cock firmly and soon the red head of Cupid's battering ram was brought to the charge. Sophie opened the lips of Polly's cunt and placed my cock just on the edges, whispering to me: 'Push on, push on, Polly has a marvellously tight little pussey! And she really wants to feel every inch of your big cock inside her!'

I moved my hips in rhythm so that with each plunge forward, an extra inch of my shaft was embedded in Polly's sopping cunney. We enjoyed a most pleasurable fuck, moving slowly at first till her rapid motions spurred me to faster plunges, her deliciously tight pussey holding me like a warm, silken hand. Her juices lubricated her cunney walls so that soon my shaft was sliding in and out with ease though I was able to feel my foreskin drawn backwards and forwards with every shove.

'Ah! You dear boy, push on! Come now, Teddy, empty your balls!' she screamed in ecstasy as we came together though I was too tongue-tied to be profuse in my terms of endearment. As we lay still after it was over, her tight little pussey seemed to hold and continually squeeze my delighted cock by its contractions and throbbings and it was only a few minutes before we ran another thrilling course in this most voluptuous way imaginable.

By this time Sophie was down on her knees lustily sucking on Cecil's stiff prick. He had his hands on her head as she sucked greedily on his shaft, caressing his large balls with one hand and frigging herself with the other, the fingers vigorously sliding in and out of her hairy cunt.

She changed course after a minute or two and clasped my brother's buttocks and squeezed him close up to her mouth till his balls slapped against her chin.

Cecil shouted: 'My God! I'm going to spend! Suck me harder! Oh yes, that's it! I can feel my cream coming! I'm going to shoot my spunk!'

And with short convulsive jerks of his dimpled bum, he shot wads of spunk into Sophie's willing mouth. She swallowed his copious emission joyfully, smacking her lips as she milked Cecil's prick of the last frothy drops of spunk as he quivered with convulsions of delight, sinking to his knees to join her as they wrapped their arms around each other and sealed their joy with a passionate kiss.

We stayed a while longer to enjoy the pleasure of the company of these two delightful girls. We had strength for a final round of fucking before we pulled on our clothes and made ready to go.

For time was now pressing as we had to meet Father at Sir Lionel Trapes' imposing town-house off Avenue Road in St John's Wood and we had promised to be there by five o'clock. So we made our farewells and Sophie slipped me a piece of paper with her home address written on it saying that she had enjoyed our fucking so much that I would be a most welcome guest in her West Hampstead apartment at any time and that the fucking would be free of charge.

'Quite a compliment,' said Cecil with a wry chuckle as we climbed into the cab that the thoughtful Soames had called for us.

'Do you think she means it?' I said.

'Perhaps yes, perhaps no. After all, she has to earn her daily bread so she cannot be expected to let you fuck her for nothing. If she were a milliner, for example, she would hardly be expected to give away her hats!'

'Well, I am sure that she would be generous to her friends.'

'And in no time she would be out of business, for once you

start giving something away nobody else will pay for it,' said my cynical brother.

I shrugged my shoulders and smiled as Cecil took out an afternoon newspaper he had picked up from the hallway table at Maison Alfred.

'This is very interesting, Teddy,' he said. 'Look, you are thinking of taking up medicine, aren't you? Now here is a most interesting news item about a Mancunian consultant, a Professor McChesney, who says that smiling is good for you.'

'Well, it doesn't need a consultant to state the obvious, Cecil, does it?'

'No, no, there's more to it than that. Professor McChesney maintains that when we smile we push our facial muscles against bones, we temporarily divert the blood flow from the brain to the face. This may influence brain temperature and stimulate the production of endorphins, the body's own natural pain killers.'

'So smilng is good for you not just because it makes you feel better but it is actually beneficial regarding body chemistry?'

'Precisely, Teddy. I think I will ask Father if we can come up to town next week to hear Professor McChesney lecture at the Aeolian Hall.'

'Is he speaking about smiling?'

'Indirectly perhaps,' said Cecil. 'The lecture is entitled "On Natural Relief of Piles". No doubt anyone who is relieved will smile quite broadly afterwards!'

The roads were quite busy as many people had decided to spend the very pleasant afternoon taking the air in Regents Park. Inside the park, the air was strangely still and I was reminded of the lovely words of Goethe we had been diligently studying at Cockshall Manor under the stern guidance of Herr Grossputz. I can still recite much of Goethe's verse from memory. Despite the prejudice against a sometimes gutteral tongue, I believe that German can sometimes sound as melodic as the Latin languages.

Anyway, the words that came into my mind are from Wanderers Nachtlied:

> Uber allen Gipfein
> Ist Ruh,

In allen Wipfeln
Spurest du
Kaum einen Hauch;
Die Vogelein schweigen im Walde.
Warte nur, balde
Ruhest du auch.

I will translate for those of my readers unfamiliar with German:

O'er all the hill-tops
Is quiet now,
In all the tree-tops
Hearest thou
Hardly a breath;
The birds are asleep in the trees:
Wait; soon like these
Thou too shall rest.

But I was rudely awakened from my reveries by my brother who suddenly grabbed hold of my right knee and hissed: 'Hell's bells, Teddy! See what I've found!'

'What is it?' I asked a little irritably. 'Have you left something behind at the Club?'

'No, no, no. It's what I've picked up there, young fellow-me-lad.'

'Not a sore prick or worse,' I suggested facetiously.

'Not that either,' rejoined Cecil. 'But I did pick up something at Maison Alfred all right. Look, Teddy, you see this newspaper that I took from the hall table. Well, I didn't actually ask Soames if I could take it as he was busy hailing a cab for us. Anyhow, I decided that the gentleman who had purchased the paper would hardly miss it and in any case he would in all probability want to buy a later edition.

'But the chap who left it out in the hall has left a letter inside the paper and it's pretty hot stuff, I can tell you. Would you like to read it? It's addressed to a Miss Kitty Easthouse from – My God, Teddy! It's from our Uncle Arthur!!!'

Our Uncle Arthur was a respected lawyer who had only recently been appointed one of Her Majesty's judges in the

High Court. What was Uncle Arthur doing at Maison Alfred – as if we didn't know!

'Be sure your sin will find you out, Reverend Shackleton would say,' said Cecil. 'Funny though, I thought that Uncle Arthur was only keen on polo especially as Aunt Philothea has a figure roughly approximate to a pony's backside.'

'Well, he wasn't about to play a chukka at Maison Alfred.' I commented. 'The old devil! Mind, it might be useful to tackle him about it if we ever find ourselves in trouble with the law! Anyway, let me read it.'

With a guffaw Cecil passed over the closely written sheets. 'What a twerp to keep such an intimate letter inside your newspaper.'

'He has simply put it there prior to posting it,' I said.

'I know,' said Cecil. 'Let's post it for him!'

'That is very kind of you.'

'Not really, Teddy, as I aim to compose a rather interesting post-script.'

'What on earth do you mean?'

'Wait, we're almost at Sir Lionel's. I'll tell you about my plan as soon as possible.'

Cecil paid off the cab and we knocked on the door of Sir Lionel's rather grand house which was situated off Avenue Road at the North end of Regent's Park. His butler, Denis, answered the door and informed us that we were expected. He showed us into a beautifully decorated drawing room. We did not have to wait long before Sir Lionel and Father came in from the library. After exchanging greetings, Father told us that we were to be given an extra treat.

'I am going home now and must leave shortly to catch the six o'clock train. But Sir Lionel has generously suggested that you two boys might like to stay over in London tonight. He has tickets for the theatre which he cannot use and rather than let his box be empty, he is offering it to you.'

'How kind of you, Sir Lionel. Teddy and I would like to thank you for your hospitality.'

'Not at all, not at all,' said the genial baronet. 'It so happens that some of your clothes are still here from your previous visit last Spring, when your dear Mama took you both to the Italian Opera. The only slight inconvenience will be that you will have to share a bedroom as my two spare rooms are being redecorated and the smell of the paint which was applied today is really quite overpowering. You'll both be far better off sharing a room – so long as neither of you snores!'

'It is good of you, Lionel,' said my Father. 'You are so fond of the theatre that I am surprised that you would miss seeing the great Charles Irving play Macbeth.'

A great pity, I thought, that Sir Lionel did not patronise the music halls which at this time were just beginning in their present form, but as we were studying this play at school I knew that seeing it acted would help me pass my summer examinations *cum laude*.

'Well, yes, ordinarily I would most certainly attend the performance,' said Sir Lionel. 'But I have been asked to go to a lecture by Jonathan Arkley. It seems that the whole of Society is under the spell of one Professor McChesney from Manchester who is supposed to be an expert on self-healing.

'Arkley is sure that the fellow is a charlatan and plans to stand up during question time and expose him. That should be quite fun so I don't expect the evening to be all as dull as it sounds and I can see Irving tomorrow night with Lord Bracknell who is always glad to escape one of his wife's ghastly dinner parties. Lord Bracknell is a good example to show you boys why I never married.'

'McChesney will be piles of laughs!' muttered Cecil and I only just managed to keep a straight face.

After Father left, Denis showed us to our room. Fortunately, we both had full evening dress hanging in the wardrobe so we could go to the Lyceum properly turned out. At our request Denis prepared a hot bath and Sir Lionel popped his head round the door to tell us that he had written a note to the Secretary of his Club to enable us to eat there afterwards, for his cook was unwell and that we would do far better at the Savile. His carriage too was at our disposal as he would be travelling to the Aeolian Hall with Doctor Arkley.

'Here's a five-pound note for use in an emergency, plus your return railway tickets for tomorrow. I'm dining at the Travellers with Doctor Arkley who will be here any minute as we have some previous business to finish before leaving for Professor McChesney's lecture.'

We wished each other a pleasant evening and after luxuriating in a hot tub and dressing myself up to the nines I felt like a real man about town.

Cecil and I were sipping whisky and sodas in Sir Lionel's drawing room when Cecil produced Uncle Arthur's letter.

'You'll have a good laugh reading this, Teddy,' he said, passing the letter to me.

I have kept the letter (throughout my life I have been an inveterate collector of ephemera) and so I can reproduce it in its entirety. Here it is:

> My Darling Kitty,
>
> How my mouth yearns for another kiss of your succulent cunney lips! The last time I buried my face in your hairy bush was so delightful that I can hardly wait for the next time! I dream of you constantly and sometimes fancy that I am back on your bed with your lovely naked bottom sitting on my face so that I can kiss and suck your pussey!
>
> At other times in my dreams you catch hold of my cock and rub it up to a fine erection, saying sweetly: 'I refuse to let you go, Mr Pego, unless you promise to fuck me!'
>
> You cannot wonder at these dreams, sweetheart, for they are only repetitions of the facts of the day!
>
> Give my love to your beautiful cunt which I hope will be conjoined with my prick very, very soon.
>
> From your own ever devoted admirer,
>
> Arthur

'Good grief, what on earth shall we do about Uncle Arthur?' I exclaimed.

'Well, I don't suggest we should peach on him to Aunt Philothea,' said Cecil warmly. 'After all, I would imagine that she only opens her legs once a month if he's lucky. Although with her looks he probably doesn't want any more fucking than that – at least, with her.

'However, the silly clot deserves to be taught a lesson for his carelessness. After all, he has not only compromised himself but also Kitty Easthouse. Now where do I know that name? I am sure it rings a bell somewhere in my memory. Anyhow, I have an idea for a jolly jape. I'm going to write another letter to Miss Easthouse and I'll get old Pemberfield, Sir Lionel's coachman, to deliver them both in the same envelope – look, Uncle has written her address down on his letter. My, what a coincidence, she lives only three minutes walk away in St John's Wood High Street.'

'What are you going to write?' I asked, my curiosity being aroused to the highest pitch.

'Come over to the desk and simply watch me write the letter,' rejoined my brother, who was to show me, not for the first time, that he possessed a most creative imagination, for this is what he wrote:

Dearest Kitty,

I quite forgot to mention that my two young nephews, Cecil and Teddy Parsifal will be in London today (Wednesday, June 17th). Teddy had just celebrated his fifteenth birthday and I cannot think of a finer present for the young scamp than to become acquainted with your lovely pussey! His brother Cecil, although only seventeen, is, I am reliably informed by our mutual friend the Rev. Robert Bacon, extraordinarily fond of fucking and indeed is quite expert in *l'art de faire l'amour*. I believe his special delight is having his tool sucked and I know how much he will enjoy thrusting his young cock between your lips to be milked by your ever eager tongue and mouth. My own prick is rising just by thinking about such a naughty scenario!

As you well know, jealousy is not among my mortal sins, so you have my full permission to fuck both the boys. I would suggest that to begin with you should let Cecil fuck you from behind whilst Teddy eats your juicy pussey. But I am quite happy to leave the details to you.

I would always expect to spend at least fifty guineas on young Teddy's birthday present so if you are agreeable I will send you a cheque for that amount. They are staying the night in town with that old reprobate Sir Lionel Trapes whose penis must one day fall off if there is any justice in the world – the rogue rogered my dear lady wife only last

Thursday – but I must admit that Lionel would never peach to the boys' Papa so my birthday present would remain a secret.

The lads are going to the theatre tonight. They could be with you at around eleven o'clock. Send a note back to them via Pemberfield, Sir Lionel's coachman and they will attend you at that time.

My love as always,

Arthur

P.S. I have dictated this letter to Miss Formby of the Jim Jam Club who is kindly acting as my personal secretary whilst my own factotum Mr Nettleton is away in India supervising my business interests in the Punjab.

'You are not really going to send that letter, Cecil?' I gasped.

'Just watch me!' said Cecil merrily, ringing the bell for the butler.

'Ah, Denis,' said Cecil as the old butler came in. 'I want this letter to be sent round as soon as possible. And would you please ask Pemberfield to wait as there will be an immediate reply.'

'Very good, sir,' said Denis. 'I will see to the matter straight away.'

'Good fellow that,' said Cecil as Denis left the room. 'He knows the secrets of at least half of London Society. But he will never reveal what he knows. Last month I heard Sir Lionel tell Father that some brash young journalist tried to bribe Denis to spill the beans about Lord Alfred Douglas and his telegraph boys.

'And even though Denis even knows the vintage of the bottle of port Lady Pence attempted to stick up Lord Euston's bottom, not a word passed his lips. Oh, he is the very soul of discretion and we can roll in at two in the morning without any trouble. Mind, I'll slip him a sov. for having to stay up so late.'

'You are pretty certain that Kitty Easthouse will agree to the terms?' I asked.

'I would swear a thousand pounds on it,' said Cecil with

great confidence. 'Why the very thought of it makes my prick really swell up!'

I looked across and saw the bulge in my brother's breeches and he undid his buttons to let out his rampant red-headed cock, caressing it in his hand until it stood in all its manly glory, stiff and hard as marble with the hot blood looking ready to burst from his distended veins.

'Put it away, Cecil,' I hissed. 'Suppose one of the servants came in.'

'I wouldn't mind,' said Cecil, happily stroking his shaft. 'Indeed young Millie the parlourmaid could do a far better job than I on my cock! Whoops, I'm going to come, Teddy!'

Always a considerate fellow, Cecil moved to the fireplace in order to steer the jets of spunk that shot out from his cock into the empty grate.

'I wonder if sperm is inflammable,' he said thoughtfully, buttoning up his flies.

'It may surprise you but I've never attempted to set light to mine,' I said with heavy sarcasm.

'All right, all right,' said Cecil with his usual good humour. 'Look, I'm quite respectable now. Let's have a whisky and soda whilst we wait for Pemberfield to return.'

Neither of us have ever been great imbibers of spirits although Dr Arkley has always assured me that an occasional nip of Scotch is truly beneficial to one's continuing good health. However, we enjoyed our little drink and read the newspapers until in just only an hour or even a little less, old Pemberfield returned.

Fortunately, I had not taken up my elder brother's wager for indeed, Miss Easthouse had readily consented to meet us at her house after the theatre. What a night beckoned us onwards! Truly, this would be an evening to remember!

Indeed, after Cecil had torn open the pink envelope in which Kitty Easthouse had couched her reply, I could scarcely contain my excitement. And this was further heightened when Cecil passed over to me Kitty's response to 'Uncle Arthur's' invitation.

It read as follows:

'Dear Cecil and Teddy,

I have received a lovely letter from your dear Uncle Arthur asking me to provide a very special birthday treat for young Teddy – and I agree absolutely with your thoughtful uncle that it would be wrong for Cecil to miss out on some saucy sport as from what he tells me, Cecil has a taste for the delights of love.

I look forward to meeting you both then, at eleven o'clock at my house. To get you both in the mood, perhaps you would like to know how I first met your sweet Uncle. It so happened that I was caught in a sudden shower of rain some six weeks ago whilst taking a stroll through Regent's Park. Your uncle was also passing the afternoon listening to the military band but he had wisely brought an umbrella along with him. He walked briskly over to the tree under which I was attempting to take shelter and said: 'Madam, please allow me to offer you the protection of my umbrella as the branches of this beech are proving inadequate to the task of protecting your beautiful dress.'

Well, such gallantry deserved a reward for I have always believed that manners maketh the man and no man however wealthy or good-looking could hope to win my heart (or my cunt) if he behaved in a boorish fashion.

Anyhow, he asked me to dine with him at Fine's Chop House that evening and I accepted his invitation. We drank champagne throughout the evening and this is a drink that always puts me in the mood. Our conversation over dinner was animated and I must confess that a large part of my attention was concentrated on my new beau and what I'd like to do with him.

You will soon know how it is when you are sexually attracted to someone – there is a real energy that magnetically connects you both and the plain truth of the matter was that all I wanted to do was to lunge across the table, kiss him long and wet and get my hands down around his thick, delicious cock and ravish him completely.

We exchanged heated glances across the table and I knew that Arthur was just as randy as I was! I was wearing a black evening dress with a low neckline and I calculated that if leaned forward in a certain way he would be given a clear view of my ripe breasts. Just the thought of this had my titties standing erect and longing to be loved and sucked.

It was all too much to bear so I slipped off my shoes and moved a silk-clad foot up between his legs. Under the cover of the linen tablecloth I was able to feel the meaty bulge between his legs and soon I was stroking the stiff length of his shaft with my foot. He began grinding his groin against me in desire but above the table was all calm as I softly declined the waiter's offer to refill my glass with some more bubbly. Arthur too looked stoical and except for the odd steamy glance when he thought no-one was looking, he never let on that his prick was threatening to burst out of the confines of his trousers.

As perhaps you know, Arthur has a great sense of humour and before I knew it, he too had slipped off a shoe and I felt his foot insinuate itself between my legs. I was so aroused as his toes rubbed around my crotch that my silky knickers were soon wet with my juices.

We could hardly wait to finish our meal and it was even more difficult to contain ourselves in the cab. But we managed to restrain ourselves until we were back in Arthur's London *pied a terre* in Welbeck Mews. No sooner had we walked into his front room than we began to tear off our clothes. Arthur has a fine physique and I admired his thick prick which was swelling by the second. I stood there trembling with excitement in the middle of his living room in just my silken knickers and stockings held up by my frilly garters.

He took me in his arms and we kissed passionately. His cologne smelled beautifully and I adored the sensation of his abundant chest hair tickling my nipples. He put his hands around my bottom and presented his cock into my belly. I didn't touch it at first as I had no desire to appear a wanton but as he took my hand and wrapped my fingers around the throbbing shaft, I gently peeled back his foreskin whilst his fingertips slid their way into my now juicy pussey.

"Egad! What a lovely little filly you are, Kitty! I must have you here and now," said Arthur softly. "Come into the bedroom and I am going to take you from behind. You will enjoy it, I promise you."

Somewhat nervously I followed him into the bedroom and watched with interest as he smeared pomade on his burgeoning cock. Dear Arthur motioned me to stand by the side of the bed and then placed my left knee on the quilt. I leaned forward looking a little apprehensively over my shoulder as Arthur smoothed his hands over my buttocks and then pulled them apart as I felt his gorgeous knob jiggling between my now dripping cunney lips.

He slowly slid his rampant pole into my juicy cunt and then withdrew all but an inch before slowly sliding it in again. He increased the tempo as he felt my excitement rising until with a grunt he slammed the entire length of his thick shaft inside me so that his black mossy grove of pubic hair brushed sensuously against my bum. Oh, how exciting it all was! In no time at all I was bucking and writhing like a crazed beast and I shouted out "Fuck me! Fuck me, darling Arthur!" in sheer unadulterated lust!

Arthur too was now past the point of any return – "I am going to spunk into you, Kitty!" he shouted. "Here it comes!" – and with a delighted yell he pumped his jets of love juice just as I too reached the dazzling heights of a magnificent spend. What a fantastic fuck this was – and it was the first time I had been fucked "doggie style" (if you will pardon the popular description of the act). But as Arthur explained to me later, despite the mendacious warnings from the pulpits and elsewhere, a fuck from behind is often extremely pleasing for the woman as it enables her clitty to be more stimulated than when a shaft enters the cunt from the front.

Enough now, for all these lewd memories are making me eager for immediate relief and I must wait until eleven o'clock when I hope that both of you will be able to satisfy my voracious sensual desires. If either of you can perform even half as well as your Uncle, I shall not have waited in vain!

Kitty Easthouse

Cecil breathed heavily as I passed the letter back to him.

'Well, young Teddy, no tossing off for you tonight!' he exclaimed. 'You will enjoy a grand fuck with Kitty and I. Let's first have a bite of supper and then on to the theatre.

'But do not drink too much for you remember what the Porter in Macbeth says of the effects of drink to Macduff: "Lechery, sir, it provokes and unprovokes; it provokes the desire, but it takes away the performance: therefore much drink may be said to be an equivocator with lechery: it makes him and it mars him; it sets him on and it takes him off; it persuades him and disheartens him; makes him stand to, and not stand to; in conclusion, equivocates him in a sleep, and giving him the life, leaves him."'

Although I well realise that those reading my memoirs in *The Oyster* (long may it flourish!) are perhaps more interested in my exploits *in flagrante delicto,* I am sure there are many, in a minority, perhaps, who will readily forgive my noting down in some detail now my remembrances of that magnificent production of the Scottish play staged at the Lyceum by the company lead by Mr Irving.

Cecil and I sat transfixed by the power of his performance and the quality of the entertainment. In the foyer beforehand we listened to the rumours on the cost of the production – on the costumes and on the scenery. Sir Arthur Sullivan's music was known only to a select few; people whispered of a golden dinner service for the banqueting scene; the three witches were to be such as never been before beheld.

We were not to be disappointed; Mr Irving is a tragedian of the finest rank. In the latter part of the play especially, he rose in awesome power as the toils gather round Macbeth. All through the scenes up to the final struggle nothing could well be better than Mr Irving's picture of the man. His courage is undaunted and he will fight against any odds until he finds on Macduff's avowal that he was from his mother's womb 'untimely torn' that the weird sisters have paltered him in a double sense. Then his arm falls powerless, he reels like one smitten with disease, he seeks to avoid the encounter until, stung by Macduff's taunts, the old courage flashes up – 'before my body I throw my warlike shield' – and the noblest part of him is his death.

Miss Ellen Terry's presence as Lady Macbeth added an extra lustre to this admirable *coup de theatre*. Our senses were spellbound as that enchanting being in gorgeous robes reads her husband's letter and determines that nothing can come between the new Thane of Cawdor and the throne of Scotland. Yet soon afterwards we suspend our disbelief that this glorious looking woman is capable of calling upon the spirits to unsex her and fill her with the direst cruelties, a woman capable of urging her consort onwards to deeds of unspeakable horror.

One last word on this magnificent spectacle. The scene in which the weird sisters appear for the final time is admirably managed. The cauldron-work and the procession of grisly kings, even the witches disappear; and Sir Arthur Sullivan's lovely music breaks upon the audience as the gloom and darkness of witchcraft melt into space whilst a glorious dawn is greeted by white-robed spirits who sing 'Come away, come away.' – a surpassingly beautiful scene as gradually the sky changes from rosy dawn to noontide light, the curtain falls on a picture which precipitates Mr Irving's appearance. And as Cecil and I heard Sir Richard Segal say afterwards, this Lyceum *Macbeth* was about the grandest revival that, in this age of theatrical art, the present generation has seen. Mr Irving, Miss Terry and the entire company well deserved all the praise and honours lavished upon them by the critics.

Now I return to my narrative proper and again crave the indulgence of those readers uninterested in the theatre (of which I myself have always been extremely fond) but they have naught to fear for there are many further stories, all true, of my own and several other people's intimate affairs.

And so, as Pepys nightly commented, to bed. But what a bedroom frolic my brother Cecil and I enjoyed with Kitty Easthouse, one of the most enthusiastic girls with whom I have ever cavorted.

Beforehand, Cecil and I had little knowledge of her expertise in *l'art de fair l'amour* although her spectacularly rude letter to us boded well for the hours ahead.

We were shown into Kitty's opulently furnished drawing room by a silver haired old butler and after just a few moments, an enchanting creature entered the room – no wonder my Uncle Arthur had offered to shield her from the rain regardless as to whether his own clothes would be left without protection from however hard a downpour!

Kitty could not have been more than twenty-eight years of age (I found out later that in fact she was only twenty-five) and she looked ravishing in an emerald green dress cut low in the front which accentuated her exquisitely large, well-proportioned breasts. Kitty was head-turningly pretty, being of dark complexion with large, languid hazel eyes. Her full lips were a succulent shade of red, earlier moistened by a sip or two of claret and when she smiled a welcome to us she showed pearl white teeth which sparkled through even the muted electric light of her tastefully fashioned home.

'Hello boys,' she said in a soft sensual voice, 'you must be Cecil being the taller and this is obviously young Teddy of whom I have heard so much from your Uncle Arthur.'

For some moments Cecil and I stood transfixed by the beauty of this delicious girl. Kitty smiled at our shyness and said: 'Come now, you two, there is no need to be bashful. Sit down on this couch and let us see if you two are really chips off the old block as Uncle Arthur has intimated to me.'

We did as we were bid and she sat between us, her hands touching each of our thighs in turn. 'You know,' she murmured, 'my breasts are so sensitive. Why, I can spend just by having my titties played with. Would you two nice boys like to see that?'

We nodded our assent and Kitty unbuttoned the French silk blouse that Uncle Arthur had purchased for her at Madame Adrienne's famous Mayfair establishment. She shrugged the garment from her shoulders and (for as we were to discover very soon she was wearing no underclothes that evening) her splendidly round succulent breasts were naked to our delighted view.

Kitty's fingers deftly unbuttoned our trousers and our two naked stiff cocks were soon in her sweet grasp. I thought that I would spunk just by drinking in the beauty of Kitty's beautiful breasts which were as big as those I had seen in the picture book of *poses plastiques* one of the boys in school had smuggled in from Paris last term. Her brown nipples were as hard as little rocks, sticking out at least a whole inch in length. Following the dear girl's directions, I held one tittie and Cecil held the other and we squeezed and rubbed them as she wriggled and squirmed with pleasure, holding on to our cocks all the while as her whole frame shook with the pleasures of her climax.

So quickly had she climaxed that neither Cecil nor myself had squirted our sperm and I watched as Kitty let go my cock and slid to the carpet, holding on to Cecil's cock which she placed between her magnificent breasts, squeezing them together so that my brother was treated to a most delicious tittie-fuck. 'Now then Teddy, kiss my pussey!' she cried out so I knelt down behind Cecil and as I put my head under her dress Kitty wrapped her legs around my neck. I buried my face in her silky thatch of black pubic hair. I kissed her salivating pussey lips and began licking her slit with long, lascivious swipes. Her vermilion pussey lips parted and between them I felt with my tongue for her stiff little clitty which I rolled around in my mouth.

'Oooh! Oooh! Ahh! Ahh! AHH!' cried Kitty. 'Suck harder Teddy, suck harder and make me come!'

I sucked and slurped with great ardour, rolling my tongue round and round, lapping up the sweet love juices which were now flowing freely from Kitty's juicy cunt. She began to spend as her hips bucked violently, her back rippled and then from her cunney spurted a fine creamy emission that flooded my mouth with a milky essence which I greedily lapped up until Kitty shuddered into limpness as the delicious crisis slowly melted away.

Cecil's cock was still being massaged between those hugh globes and Kitty pulled his bum cheeks forward so that he was sitting astride her as she slipped his throbbing shaft between her red painted lips and gave my brother a most delightful sucking off. Her mouth worked up and down, licking the length of his prick, taking playful little licks at the uncapped knob with her little tongue. When she felt Cecil was about to spend, her hands gripped the base of his cock and pumped up and down as she sucked his balls but quickly transferred her mouth back to his cock to milk his prick of every last drop of milky froth.

Somehow I had just managed to refrain from handling my own cock although the temptation to toss myself off was almost overpowering. My reward was now to come as Cecil moved off Kitty who quickly tugged her dress over her shoulders and now quite nude she turned round and climbed on top of me, straddling my cock with her still wet, juicy slit.

Treating me to a long ride, she fucked me slowly, taking in every inch I had to offer, sitting flat on my crotch, moving back and forth as my cock prepared to pump spouts of spunk inside her eager cunney.

I grabbed her hips and began to fuck her from underneath, working my cock into a frenzy. I could no longer wait to spend and that is exactly what I did after a few deep thrusts. Kitty moaned with pleasure as the sperm boiled up in my balls and shot out of my shaft into her warm, inviting pussey. Even after my abundant drenching of her womb, Kitty continued to move up and down on my now deflating cock, hoping to milk more spunk out of my twitching tool.

Cecil stood up and padded across to the table and opened a bottle of Bollinger '72 (Kitty knew the difference between good and indifferent champagne) and after she had refreshed herself she said: 'I don't think it fair that only Teddy should have the pleasure of fucking my cunt. I'm quite ready for another joust if you two are feeling up to it. Let us go into the bedroom and continue our sport in there. Teddy, perhaps you would kindly bring another bottle of champagne and our glasses – there is a tray just behind you. Cecil, you come with me.' She grasped my brother by his cock and led him not unwillingly to the bedroom as I did as I was told and followed them into the room.

We now removed our remaining clothes and I sat on a chair as Kitty pulled Cecil close to her and said: 'My darling boy! Tell me how you are going to fuck me!'

From an early age Cecil was always the most articulate member of the family and with only a momentary pause as he slipped his hands around her back to caress the plump cheeks of her warm bottom, he murmured: 'You wish to know how I am going to fuck you, Kitty? Well, I shall first mount you and then I shall decide which way we shall take our pleasure. But first I shall lie upon your belly and insert my thick, long cock slowly in your deliciously inviting little snatch. Then, by moving my rod in and out of your juicy cranny we shall be jointly intoxicated with delight and each shall expel our liquid pleasures – you upon my cock and balls and I by the velvety clinging of your slit.'

'Oh, that's well said, Cecil my dear boy,' she breathed, 'so please let me feel the actions to follow those lovely words and fuck the arse off me!'

How splendid the two lovers looked as Kitty slowly ran her tongue down my brother's slim body. Cecil's prick began to rise again almost with the tenderness of a butterfly's flight as Kitty's mouth reached his naval. He writhed in delicious agony as her silky dark hair brushed against his now throbbing member which ached for further attention. She brushed his cock with her cheek and caressed his heavy, hanging balls with her warm, wet lips.

It appeared to me that Cecil's testicles were appreciably larger than mine, but then I recalled the good Doctor Stevenson's book which assured its readers that there was not the slightest medical connection between the size of the testes and their spunk-producing function.

But I digress – Kitty's smooth hands smoothed over Cecil's slender frame, sending him into fresh raptures of delight. Then, moving quickly, sliding herself on top of him, hungrily searching for his lips, they kissed passionately, moving their thighs together until their pubic muffs rubbed roughly against each other. Cecil's stiff cock probed the entrance to the exquisite little crack, throbbing with a powerful intensity until Kitty eased her hips, grunting with delight as the swollen knob forced its way between her pussey lips, massaging her clitty until Cecil arched his own frame upwards, plunging his trusty tool inside her wetness.

I could not bear to stand motionless any longer as Kitty shouted: 'Oh, Cecil, keep sliding that lovely cock in and out! What a marvellous young lover you are! More, more, more!'

My own right hand simply flew to my own proudly erect prick and I quickly frigged myself off. Wave after wave of pleasure engulfed me as I pumped spurt after spurt of my hot, sticky cream over the entwined lovers, who oblivious to my coating of the pair with jism, were still jerking in new paroxyms, panting and biting,then screaming, with excitement as the summit of the mountain of love was finally scaled and they sank back, sated, on the soft sheets.

I joined the happy couple and Kitty laughed, saying: 'Let us see if Teddy's young cock and balls are in top working order!' And without giving me further time to recover my senses, the lewd girl commenced immediately to play with my prick which she hugged, pressing it to her large breasts, squeezing it between them, pressing it against her cheeks, gently rubbing it with her hands and taking the uncapped head between her lips, softly biting it and tickling it with the end of her tongue. Then she suddenly thrust the whole shaft into her mouth and by her exquisite palating and sucking, proudly erected the monster till her little lips could hardly clasp it.

Cecil was lying on his back, his cock again now stiff as a flagpole and Kitty gently eased herself upon it and began to pump herself forwards and backwards.

'Ah, Teddy,' she gasped, easing my cock from her mouth, 'will you give me the double pleasure of fucking my bottom whilst I ride Cecil? Go behind me and wet your cock with some pomade, which you will find in that little pink jar on the side table. Then come back and slowly shove your gorgeous cock up my bum.

Ever obedient, I did what was gently requested and knelt behind Kitty who thrust herself forwards as far as possible and raised her beautiful bum cheeks so that I was given full view of her little wrinkled arse-hole that beckoned me in so invitingly. I took hold of my cock in my hand and carefully positioned my knob between her bottom cheeks, which I grasped and opened wide the crack in between so that her bum-hole was fully opened to my impending attack. Then I pushed forward and despite my initial worry that I might injure the dear girl, I shoved slowly and steadily until it felt impossible to reach any further.

Kitty writhed and twisted so much that she could hardly keep Cecil's cock inside her but soon I could feel my prick rubbing against his with only the thin divisional membrane between them. It was all so exciting that we both spent quickly, our joint spunking deluging both cunt and arse, spurting the frothy jism over each other's balls at every thrust.

Cecil was now *hors de combat* and was forced to retire but Kitty saw that my cock still seemed to have a twitch of life about it.

'Are you still able to continue, Teddy?' Kitty asked me, with a roguish twinkle in her eye.

'I believe I can enjoy one further ride on the roundabout of love,' I proudly answered. And without further ado, I sank to my knees in front of her lusciously juicy cunney. Like nipples, like clitty, say the Hussars, and Kitty proved the truth of the adage, her stiff little clitty gleaming long and erect through the bush of her mossy black pubic grove.

I let my tongue travel the length of Kitty's velvety smooth body, lingering briefly at her belly button before sliding down to her thighs. I was still in a kneeling position when I parted her soft, lightly scented pubic hair with my fingertips to reveal her swollen clitty. As I worked my face into the cleft between her thighs, I could not help but notice how clean and appealing her pussey looked after its coating of love juices.

I placed my lips over her clitoris and sucked it into my mouth where the tip of my tongue began to explore it from all directions and I could feel it growing even larger as her legs wriggled and twitched up and down along the sides of my body.

But just as I was about to proceed further I heard a door open and a girl's voice cry out: 'Kitty! What an earth do you think you're doing?'

'I am having my cunney sucked, my dear Rosemary, what do you think I am doing, playing cricket?' said Kitty coldly, angry that her enjoyment was being interrupted.

Of course, the surprise led me to wrench my lips away from the succulent morsel upon which I was chewing so nicely and I looked up to see a pretty red-haired girl looking across the room at us with ill-concealed irritation.

'Just what are these men doing in our bedroom?' said this petite sprite with some sharpness.

'Our bedroom?' repeated Cecil, raising his eyebrows.

'Yes, our bedroom, if you must know,' she said. 'Pray leave us immediately, gentlemen, you have no further business here.'

'Oh, I think that is rather for me to decide,' drawled Kitty. 'Rosemary, may I introduce Cecil and Teddy Parsifal to you – and gentlemen, let me introduce Miss Rosemary Sharpe-Somerset who resides with me when she is staying in London.

'Rosemary, you will enjoy fucking these two boys – Cecil is an accomplished lover and young Teddy here has the most extraordinary staying power for one of such tender years.'

So here was a potentially most embarrassing situation. I had no real experience of tribades and Rosemary's preference for her own sex in matters of *l'amour* was for me a strange affair.

Meanwhile Rosemary began to berate Kitty for welcoming boys into her bed. 'Fucking remains a means of making a woman inferior!' she trumpeted. 'All that pushing and thrusting simply represents the male acting out his supposed domination of us, the inferior sex.

'Historically, women have always had their sexuality controlled. For most of us the opportunity to define our own wants and desires does not exist. We who reject men are forced to keep our secret as such thoughts are taboo and we must find our pleasures where we can. Now you are betraying the cause!'

'Oh, come now, that's going a bit far!' protested Cecil.

'Indeed it is,' cried Kitty, a flush of anger now clearly visible on her face. 'I fully believe in the freedom of adults to do anything they like to each in bed as long as both consent and, as Mrs. Campbell says, they don't do it in the street and frighten the horses. But I enjoy having a strong, thick prick up my cunney just as much as a dildoe or even your wicked little fingers, so there!'

'Oooh! You cat!' squealed Rosemary and forgetting, perhaps, that Cecil and I were there, she sat down on the bed and stripped off her clothes in amazingly quick time. She possessed a boyish figure, with small but nicely rounded breasts and both her cherry-red nipples were like erect little stalks. She may have been small but she was strong for, before you could say Jack Robinson, she had turned Kitty on to her tummy and exposed her generous bum cheeks to our delighted gaze. Rosemary then began to smack Kitty's beautiful bum, lightly at first but then harder and in rapid succession until the poor girl cried out: 'Oh! Oh! Oh, no more, Rosie, I beg of you. No, no, no, no more. Ow! Ow! OW! Ooooh!' as she wriggled and winced as her skin turned from milk white to bright pink.

'Quiet now, Kitty!' snapped Rosemary. 'You have been a very naughty girl and all naughty girls get slapped. Besides I just adore to see your bum change colour. It should always have that pinkish tinge and anyway I love the way your bottom cheeks jiggle as I slap them!'

By now, both Cecil's cock and my own were rock-hard as we watched this stimulating exhibition. In no time Cecil was on his knees next to Kitty who, despite her tingling bum, eagerly clamped her full red lips around Cecil's cock and began sucking his prick with unashamed gusto.

'Come here, you wretched boy!' Rosemary called out to me, without missing one beat of her rhythm as she continued to slap Kitty's bum. 'I suppose I must give you the same treatment for as a good Socialist I believe in fair shares for all!'

I needed no second invitation as I jumped on the bed to complete the quartet. Mercifully for Kitty's bum, Rosemary ceased her spanking and circled her hands around my pulsating prick which already had a blob of milky spunk on the knob. She jammed down my foreskin and bending low, lashed her tongue round my pole thudding away like a steamhammer. I could see that Kitty's ministrations with her mouth had already brought Cecil to the point of climax and Kitty greedily milked his cock of spunk as she sucked up noisily every drain of love-juice.

Now Kitty raised herself on her hands and knees and lowering her pretty head began to kiss Rosemary's mossy ginger bush which I could see was already damp with excitement. Her pink tongue slipped effortlessly in and out of her friend's cunt.

Now I pulled my prick out of Rosemary's mouth and positioned myself behind Kitty whose rounded bottom cheeks were moving in fine rhythm as she sucked contentedly on Rosemary's pussey. The darling girl then reached out behind her and took hold of my throbbing cock and directed its purple domed knob to the glorious cheeks of her bum and to the tight-looking wrinkled brown hole that lay between them.

Cecil thoughtfully plastered my prick with the pomade as I attacked the fortress with vigour. 'Aaah! Not so deep, my dear Teddy, not so deep! Oh, pray, enough – Oh! Oh! Ah, yes, you're there!' she shrieked.

I rested a moment or two and then began slowly to pull in and out as I fucked her arse-hole. I could tell by the wriggling of her plump bum that she was enjoying it as much as I was and she took my hands to her front so that I could frig her cunt as all the while she licked and lapped at Rosemary's pussey which was now expelling a veritable flood of love-juice.

Rosemary's wriggling about and the delicious contractions of her bum-hole brought down a copious discharge of the nectar of love.

'Oh, heavens!' she exclaimed. 'Ah! what pleasure I feel rushing into me! How hot it is and – yes, now I come too; it is running from me. My God! What delight! Ah, what lus – lus – luscious pleasure!'

She almost swooned away in delight for as I was fucking her bum and frigging her clitty at the same time, she was procured of the exquisite double pleasure.

So you see, dear reader, both Kitty and Rosemary were capable of extracting pleasure from intimate relations with both genders, an ability which I must confess I do not share, keeping my bed strictly reserved for members of the female sex.

We were now totally exhausted and so we refreshed ourselves with some more champagne. It was now so late that we sent word that we would not be returning to Sir Lionel's until after breakfast. I was concerned that Father would hear of our escapade but Cecil said: 'Don't worry, Teddy, Sir Lionel is a man of the world and won't preach – and I don't think that Uncle Arthur will say anything when he finds out because if he says anything, he'll have to do an awful lot of explaining to Aunt Ada!'

I talked at some length with Rosemary, who was studying political economy at the nearby Bedford College. Although her father was the possessor of a vast hereditary estate in Cumberland, Rosemary had become an ardent Socialist. I had no great interest in politics (our family were to a man supporters of Mr Gladstone and of course a distant cousin, Oliver Parsifal, has been for many years the Liberal MP for a Cornish constituency) but I was curious to know what had attracted this rich young girl to sit at the feet of Burns, O'Driscoll and Mann.

Rosemary explained: 'We have witnessed during this century an unparalleled sudden increase in our powers of production, resulting in huge accumulations of wealth. But only the owners of capital have benefitted, while for the great numbers there has been an increase only in misery and insecurity. Unskilled labourers are falling into destitution and even the best-paid artisans labour under the permanent menace of being thrown out of work in consequence of some of the continuous and unavoidable fluctuations of industry and caprices of capital.

'The chasm between the modern millionaire who squanders

all in a vain, gorgeous luxury and the pauper reduced to a mere existence is growing more and more. The working classes will no longer endure this unfair division of society and in proportion, as all classes take a more lively part in public affairs, their longing for equality will rightly become stronger and their demands for reform become louder and louder until they can be ignored no more.

'The worker is entitled to claim his share in the wealth that he creates – not only in management of production but the additional well-being in the higher enjoyments of science and art. These claims conform with my natural feelings of justice and they find support in a daily growing minority amongst the privileged classes themselves.

'Socialism has thus become *the* idea of the nineteenth century and neither coercion nor pseudo-reforms can stop its further growth!'

This was quite a speech and we sat silently contemplating her words, which frankly made little sense to me, until Cecil broke the serious mood that had descended upon us by saying: 'Well, if Socialism means fair shares for all, then I am all in favour! Especially if it means a fair share of pussey!' he roared, tossing back a bumper of champagne and presenting the company with a capital stiff-stander.

But Kitty, between whose bum cheeks he had placed his prick, wriggled across to Rosemary saying: 'Oh, darling, you are such an orator. Let us celebrate your discourse with some love-making.'

And the two girls dissolved into a passionate embrace kissing rapturously and thrusting their tongues into each other's mouths. Rosemary clasped Kitty firmly by the buttocks whilst with two fingers of her right hand frigged the girl's bottom and pussey at the same time. She then laid Kitty down kissing her lips gently whilst softly rubbing her huge breasts until the nipples stiffened into hard little cherry bullets. Then she stroked Kitty's pussey as the girl opened her legs wide giving a glorious view of the paraphenalia of love. She had a quite splendid mount covered with glossy black hair; the serrated lips of her cunt slightly parted from which projected quite three inches I am sure, a stiff fleshy clitoris as big as a thumb. Rosemary opened the lips with her fingers then bending her head down, passed her tongue lasciviously around the sensitive parts, taking that lovely clitty in her mouth, rolling her tongue around it and playfully biting it with her little teeth.

It was exciting to watch and all too exciting for Kitty who cried: 'Oh! Oh! You make me come, darling!' as she spent profusely all over Rosemary's mouth and chin.

'Now it is my turn to repay the delicious pleasure I owe you,' sighed Kitty as she sat up and pulled Rosemary down beside her, kissing her rapturously and with her fingers, opening the pussey lips hidden in Rosemary's ginger bush and rolling on top of her, directing her stiff clitty into Rosemary's crack, closing the lips upon it with her hand in a novel yet delightful conjunction. Without separating for a moment, the girls writhed and rubbed against each other, swimming in a veritable sea of lubricity until they both reached the acme of pleasure and sank back exhausted, their arms wrapped tightly round each other.

Cecil and I looked on in no little bewilderment. How were these girls introduced to all-girl sexual encounters? wondered my brother.

'I will tell you,' said Kitty. 'Like many women, I do not believe in picking up any strange man just for the sake of carnal desire, although just like you or any other man, I am in regular need of good satisfying orgasms.

'Then one day last summer in the *Morning Telegraph* I read a small advertisement that said: "Woman to Woman: A selective group of attractive ladies wish to meet others to join their circle. Write to Lady SL for full details."

'I wondered whether this was one of the select private clubs that I knew existed in London where ladies meet to relieve each other's sexual tension. I had heard how they fondle breasts, suck pussies and use dildoes on each other to achieve the peaks of pleasure and I found the idea somewhat fascinating. After all, it was better than sitting at home alone, playing with yourself!

'So I wrote to "Lady SL" (who turned out to be none other than Susannah Loomlane, whose sister Brenda was an old schoolfriend of mine back home in Hertfordshire and she invited me immediately to a meeting at her grand house in Lots Road, Chelsea.

'For the sake of the family fortunes, which had been badly depleted by some most unwise speculation by her Papa, Susannah had married a dour Edinburgh gentleman some years her senior, one Geoffrey Hurton, who spent more time in the Highlands tracking down antiquarian books for his library than in his own bedchamber. Considering that Susannah was a most attractive lady in her middle twenties, I think I can say without fear of contradiction that not only was Sir Geoffrey a very great bookworm but an exceedingly foolish old fart!

'You must remember that at this time I was totally unaware of the joys of tribadism. Anyhow, I went round to Lots Road and Susannah showed me round her large home. A most interesting feature was a small cabin that had been erected in the garden. She told me that this is where her circle met regularly and I thought to myself that this seemed a small edifice for a ladies' meeting.

'But after I accepted her invitation to go inside, things became clearer. The floor of the cabin had been partially scooped out and a tiled bath – or perhaps a miniature swimming pool would best describe it – had been laid. It was fully plumbed with both hot and cold water and splashing around in the pool were two beautiful naked girls of about my own age, nineteen, whom Susannah introduced to me as Nancy and Alexandra.

'Do join us, Rosie,' said Nancy, shaking long blonde tresses of her away from her pretty face. 'Take off your clothes and jump in with us. The water is deliciously warm.'

'What a splendid idea,' said Susannah.' I have to entertain the artist Mr Lawrence Judd-Hughes for a while as I have to negotiate a fee for him to paint the charming views from our country home near Tunbridge Wells. But I am sure that Nancy and Alex will deputise most effectively as hostess whilst I am away.'

'I was somewhat shy at first but eventually I was persuaded to disrobe and I stepped gingerly into the pool. Actually, Nancy had been telling nothing but the truth, for the water was indeed nicely warm and we splashed around gaily. Then, as I rested momentarily at the side of the pool, Alex began to rub my crotch with the palm of her hand. The sensation was frankly delicious and I relaxed totally. Soon, I found myself being seduced by the two harpies. On one side Nancy was caressing my breasts and tweaking my nipples to full erection whilst Alex ran her hands between my legs, playing with my clitty.

'It was very erotic, especially as Nancy began whispering what she would like to do to me. She was rubbing my breasts and kissing my titties whilst at the same time murmuring about all the sensual things she wanted to do to me – like how she wanted to stick her tongue up my cunt and rub her face all around my hot, wet crotch and suck my clitty till I spent!

'I was so fired up by her words that I took her hand and placed it next to Alex's between my legs. Her fingers became alive as she started diddling me. Then Alexandra said: 'You cannot eat pussey under water.' So we all got out of the huge tub, dried ourselves and went into an adjacent little room which was just big enough to accommodate a large double bed upon which had been laid the most luxurious silken sheets.

'I was gently laid down on the bed and Alexandra began to stroke the insides of my thighs, opening my legs to accommodate Nancy who began to lick and lap at my wet pussey, sending me into spasms of desire and wanting desperately to be fucked. The little minx was licking along the insides of my labia, not putting her tongue inside me. I told her how hot she was making me and how I could feel an orgasm coming on. I told her to finish me off by fucking me with her tongue but then I heard Alex's voice saying: 'It's all right, Rosie, dear, I'll do that for you.'

'I opened my eyes and saw that the sweet girl had strapped on a belt round her waist which at the front had attached a black wooden affair shaped exactly like a giant cock, complete with carefully fashioned balls. This was the first time I had seen a didlo although of course I had read about these affairs in Doctor Roy Stevenson's famous manual – ah, I see you are acquainted with this excellent tome of which I believe no fewer than one million copies have been subscribed all over the world – so I was unsure as to what to expect.

'Anyhow, I spread-eagled my legs as Alexandra climbed on top of me, giving me a passionate kiss on the lips as she reached down and inserted the head of this wooden cock between my pussey lips. It certainly had the desired effect! I wrapped my legs around her waist and locked my ankles together. Then she leaned forwards and the dildo began to slide into my sopping cunney and I gasped with pleasure, urging her on. It took only a little while to get the rythm right but once I did, I discovered that the dildo gave me great joy. Every time she thrust forwards it rubbed against my clitty and at the end of each thrust, when the dildo was in as far as it could go, it would rub into my deepest recesses and send sparks through my entire body.

'It only took a few minutes before I spent, my cunney disgorging a flood of love juice and Alexandra spent too, so fucking me that we both managed to finish off together. We had so much fun that afternoon, especially when Susannah returned to join in the games, that I have almost gone off fucking with men, and especially since I began to share my bed with Kitty.'

'Have you ever strapped on a dildo?' Cecil asked Kitty.

'Yes, quite often, although Rosie and I take turns to play the masculine role,' she replied. 'Something happens to me when I put one on. I feel powerful for suddenly I have a cock mounted between my legs and I can thrust it into another girl and give her an orgasm just like a man whilst I can enjoy one too!

'It's difficult to describe how this feels but the last thing I want to do is try to replace men. I still feel that there is nothing like sucking a good stiff cock and then fucking it!

'But playing around with other girls makes me randy. I remember one day last week Rosie and I were sitting on the bed, our legs spread apart and our fingers buried in each other's pussies when your Uncle Arthur walked in. I was almost ready to come and I wasn't about to let Rosemary stop what she was doing so I unbuttoned his trousers, took out his prick and sucked him off. Then when he had recovered he fucked us both.

'I enjoy threesomes of any computation of the sexes. I believe that threesomes offer the most intimacy. When there are three persons, you feel like you are sharing something very special. We don't have to worry about embarrassing ourselves and my, we can have such fun' she added.

Perhaps it was just as well that we had no further time to explore this newly proposed avenue of pleasure. For, as you may well imagine, dear reader, Cecil and I were by now completely *hors de combat*. I do not believe that either of us, after all the priapic exercises I have already described, could have managed another cockstand even at the appearance of Lily Langtry, Gwendolen Bracknell or even Jenny Everleigh who is reputed to have been fucked by both Lord Robert Cripps and Major General David Haines after a wild country house party in Cheshire.

However, we left our ladies with the fondest salutations and the sworn promise to return to see them on our next visit to London. Whether Uncle Arthur would have approved is another story but as my wise older brother Cecil succinctly commented when I ventured to bring up this point: 'Uncle Arthur can go and fuck himself.'

We were forced to catch a slow train back home as workmen were carrying out maintenance work to the railway tracks near Egham. It was a bright morning and I noticed a group of chattering magpies in a high treetop where they were fluffing up their feathers and fanning their long tails.

'Why are magpies supposedly unlucky, according to superstition?' I asked Cecil. I knew he was a one for such clever brain-teasers.

My brother smiled and replied: 'Well, Teddy, the story goes that when Noah summoned the animals to enter the Ark, the magpies stayed outside to jabber maliciously at the drowning world. Another tale goes that they were further cursed with black and white plumage for refusing to go into full mourning with other birds at the Crucifixion.

'Some twerps actually doff their hats, spit towards the birds and say: 'Devil, devil, I defy thee. Two magpies, incidentally are supposed to be lucky, but all should be saluted by bowing and spitting. Mind, if you believe such nonsense, you deserve to have your arse kicked to the middle of next week!'

I laughed but noted his explanation. Even at this early age, I was already interested in folk-lore. [*Dr Parsifal was a contributor to Lore and Language in the West Midlands 1750–1880 edited by Professor Kenneth Watkins published by Singer and Le Baigue in 1890 – Editor*].

By the time we reached our station, we were feeling somewhat randy and as Cecil had surreptitiously purchased a copy of *The Pearl* from a newsvendor at Victoria, we had divided the publication into two sections and had each taken a portion to read.

'Damn me, but it's amazing how quickly one recovers from a good spell of fucking!' commented Cecil, stroking the bulge between his legs. 'After reading this randy stuff, I could really do some girl a favour!'

'Me too, 'I said. 'Mind, we are lucky that we have such big pricks. There's that fat fellow Ivor What's-his-name in the fourth form whose cock can only measure a couple of inches on the dangle though I've never seen it ready for action.'

'Don't fall into a trap here,' advised Cecil. 'Other fellows tools will often appear to be bigger than your own. This is simply because you are looking at theirs from an angle whereas you see your own cock only by looking straight down on it which is why it always will appear to be larger when viewed in a mirror.

'And as for young Ivor, his prick will probably grow as he gets older. Our bodies all mature at different rates. Anyhow, size is unimportant except I suppose that there are quite a number of girls who get excited at the sight of a really big juicy cock. Many others, however, I am told are far more aroused by a manly chest or the slim flanks of an athlete.'

But remember that there are times when small is beautiful! For example I can quote from the poet Alexander Pope who you may know was a man of very small stature. I think I can remember the very words he wrote to a lady who had dared to mock his size:

'You know where you did despise
(T'other day) my little Eyes,
Little Legs, and little Thighs,
And some things, of little Size,
    You know where.
You, tis true, have fine black eyes,
Taper Legs and tempting Thighs,
Yet what more than we all prize
Is a Thing of little Size,
    You know where.'

So it's not the size that counts, it's what you actually do with the equipment provided,' finished my brother.

Well, as chance would have it, a message was waiting for us at home from our dear parents who had been called to the bedside of my mother's aged Uncle Frederick in Brighton. As Uncle Frederick was reckoned to be worth at least a cool quarter of a million, my parents (along with other nephews and nieces) had cancelled all arrangements to journey to Brighton post-haste. Well, the old gentleman had no children – at least, none the right side of the blanket, and there were no bastards of which we knew.

Cecil and I were commanded to change into sombre clothing and join our parents forthwith. They were staying with Colonel and Mrs Bedwell, who were old friends since before Cecil and I were born. When the Colonel retired from the Army, he bought a splendid country mansion very close to Preston Park. Cecil was extremely friendly with the Bedwell's youngest son Richard, a cheery young man who was of a similar age and, as I was about to find out, a chap with similar and quite singular tastes!

Indeed, when we arrived at Bedwell Manor, we were ushered in by the butler to the billiard room where Richard was waiting to greet us.

'Hello, chaps,' he said warmly. 'How smashing to see you again. How are you keeping Cecil, old boy? Hasn't fallen off, has it? No? Well, that's a relief I'm sure and, good heavens, is this young Teddy? Christ, I would never have recognised you. You've got hairs on your chest by now, I suppose and elsewhere if you're anything like your brother!

'Dunn will take your things upstairs. We have the house to ourselves as my folks have gone with your parents to see your Great Uncle Frederick who I am sorry to say is probably on his way out this time which is quite a sad business really.

'My parents were friendly with him, you know, and I thought he was an interesting old cove. He was quite healthy until he got sozzled at a *soirée* Lady Fransmann arranged for that young Scottish poet Douglas Walker, the *protégé* of Oscar Wilde whom London Society seems to have taken to its heart.

'So an over indulgence in wine has caused his downfall,' said Cecil.

'Well, indirectly, yes,' Robert continued, 'though he could always knock back a bottle of bubbly without any problems.

What happened was that he was walking home from Lady Fransmann whose house was only down the road when he slipped upon some very fresh evidence of horses and feeling somewhat tired, he decided to sleep under the stars. Alas, he caught a chill which has settled on his chest and the quacks hold out little hope of recovery. They've even brought down Doctor Jonathan Arkley from Harley Street but it looks all up with the old boy.'

'What a deuced shame.' I said. 'How old is Great Uncle Frederick?'

'He was ninety two last month,' answered Cecil. 'So he has had a good innings. But what a way to go – slipping in a pile of horse-shit!'

'Well, he was too pissed to have smelled it,' said Robert and I'm afraid we rather inappropriately burst into peals of laugher.

Still, as the Eastern sage Mustafa Pharte says, when old words die out on the tongue, new melodies break forth from the heart.

Needless to say, our new melodies centred around l'amour and after a light luncheon, we sat in Richard's private room where he regaled us with an account of his latest conquest. I should add that he was a good-looking young man approaching eighteen years of age and many girls of all walks of life lost their hearts (and often their cherries) to the handsome boy.

As we settled down to our post-luncheon liqueurs(both Cecil and I chose brandy whilst Richard sipped at a port), our host told us of his encounter the previous night with Augusta, the pretty young daughter of Sir Clive and Lady Bonney who lived nearby.

'We had attended Colonel Burbeck's ball,' said Richard, 'and Augusta had pencilled me in for several dances. She really is an attractive young miss and she looked quite ravishing in a low-cut dark blue ball gown that accentuated rather than hid her full, snowy white breasts. She is almost as tall as I am and as we danced we found out that we shared the same birthday. 'Maybe people who were conceived at a certain time share similar characteristics' she smiled as I held her tightly in my arms. I was trying to ease her back from my erection at the time for although we had known each other for some time we were hardly bosom friends and as a gentleman I had no desire to embarrass the girl who, for all I knew, might still be a virgin.

'But as I tried to wriggle free, to my surprise, the gorgeous girl pressed herself even harder against me and softly whispered: 'My, my, my, Richard, that's quite a bulge I can feel down below. Is that all your cock or have you pushed some padding down there to make it feel bigger?'

'Certainly not,' I replied, 'But I am astounded to hear you talk so freely of such matters, Augusta, I really am.'

'But you are not sorry, are you, Richard?' she twinkled, squeezing my cock with her hand as we waltzed our way into a secluded corner. 'If you have had enough dancing, shall we take the air outside? It is so warm this evening, is it not?'

'As you may well imagine, I hardly needed a second invitation and with alacrity piloted her through the crowds and we stepped out on the patio and then walked down the path towards the little gardener's shed where to my amazement a key was in the lock and Augusta motioned me inside. 'I borrow the key from old Newman, the head gardener, for five shillings and no questions asked,' she whispered. 'And I have spent another ten shillings getting my maid Elizabeth to clean out the shed and lay down a nice mattress on the floor. Several of the girls clubbed together to buy the mattress and we take it with us to all the dances around the country. We take it in turns to use it although if it is one's turn and there is no boy worth fucking, then a postponement is permitted. The Hon. Celia Nutworthy is secretary of our little circle and she keeps our accounts.'

'What a splendid idea,' I exclaimed. 'Yes, and as you are the boy I have chosen tonight, I am sure that you will not mind reimbursing us for the cost of bribing the servants and other incidental expenses,' said Augusta.

'I readily agreed to pay up and my offer of a guinea was deemed acceptable by Augusta who pulled me to her ample charms. We sank down onto the soft mattress and kissed and embraced with ardour. I peeled open the buttons on her dress and her large breasts poured out of their cups and I gently caressed the saucer-sized nipples which rose to rosy little bullets under my touch.

'We undressed each other without difficulty as the

moonlight flooded into the shed through the large window. I gasped with delight as I ran my hands over her white globes and flat belly. Then I let a hand run through the silky dark hair of her bush and I could feel the dampness as I rubbed my knuckles over her moistening crack.

'She reached out and stroked my throbbing cock which was now as hard as rock. She pulled down my foreskin and ran her fingers over my knob. Then bending over me, she kissed and licked my pubic hair as I lay back to enjoy what was to come. She started to move her face slowly, feeling my hard prick against her soft cheek. She took strands of her long dark hair and made a web round my shaft that was by now almost bursting as it stood stiff as a flagpole as she parted her lips and sucked up my knob into the inviting warmth of her mouth. Then, taking my shaft in her hand, she bobbed her head up and down so that I was fucking her mouth in a most delightful manner. She sucked me off so beautifully that all too soon I could feel the sperm rushing up from my balls. I could not hold back as with a cry I pumped a stream of hot spunk into her mouth. Augusta sucked up and swallowed every last drop, milking my prick until it wilted under the sweet urgency it had encountered.

'What a truly magnificent fuck!' ejaculated Cecil trying hard to keep a note of envy straying into his voice.

'It was certainly extremely pleasurable,' said Richard. 'In fact, I would go as far as to say that Augusta is amongst the best three ladies I have ever fucked. She was really quite insatiable that night and just thinking about the way that her love sheath throbbed around my tool makes me very randy!'

'What a grand night of passion,' I sighed.

'Oh, but that isn't the end of the story,' laughed Richard. 'We were lying there a little exhausted after our romp, feeling a little drowsy for the makeshift bed the girls had provided was quite marvellous, with its snow white sheets and fluffy pillows that cushioned up beautifully. Anyway, I had not thought to bolt the door and for a moment I was horrified to hear footsteps outside. I lifted my head from the pillow to see the door open and I could just make out the shape of a feminine form in the moonlit shadows.

'Augusta too had been woken from our reverie and she

called out: "Who's there?" "It's only me, Penelope Hunt," said the intruder.

'"Oh, Penny, thank goodness, I thought it might have been a stranger," said Augusta with audible relief. "Penny, I think you have met Richard Bedwell, haven't you?"

'I had indeed been introduced to Penny, a tall, most striking blonde girl earlier that evening. Her Great-Uncle was Henry Hunt, the famous Radical orator who had been present at the dreadful Peterloo massacre in Manchester when the cavalry had been ordered to disperse a crowd.

'"This looks very interesting," said Penny, pulling away the thin sheet to expose our nude bodies to her enquiring gaze. "Very interesting indeed. Is this a game that only two can play or may I join in to make a threesome?"

'"I don't mind if Augusta has no objection", I said and, to my delight, Augusta smiled and indicated with a wave of her hand that Penny should join us on the bed. "Stand up Richard, and help Penny take off her clothes," ordered Augusta.

'I stood up and Penny turned round to allow me to unhook the catch at the nape of her neck. I helped pull the dress down and to my astonishment, immediately perceived that this beautiful young girl was wearing not a stitch of underwear. I marvelled as I felt her heavy breasts which were naked to my loving touch. We kissed fervently with our tongues deep in each other's mouths but I soon wrenched my lips away, moving my head down as I dropped to my knees, kissing her extraordinarily thick blonde pussey hair whilst my hands went upwards to squeeze the rich full breasts, tweaking the pert little nipples that were standing up high to my ministrations.

'My cock was now rising up to its full majestic height and Penny sank down besides Augusta to carry out a close inspection of my prick. Augusta was now bending over in front of me, the shapely, tender cheeks of her lovely young arse slap up almost against my mouth as her hands ran up and down the length of my shaft, slipping back my foreskin to uncover the red mushroomed dome as Penny began to lick and lap the tip of my hot thrusting tool.

'I soon learned that Penny's speciality was sucking rather than fucking although I would have awarded the girl at least a beta plus for the latter exercise. But her sucking certainly deserved an alpha and I was in the very seventh heaven of delight as her moist, pink tongue travelled up and down my excited cock. Augusta however was not to be denied and she began to kiss and suck my balls as my shaft slipped in and out between Penny's generously proportioned lips.

'What more could a chap desire in this world? There I was with two delicious damsels sucking me off with my left hand cupped round one girls's breasts and the other sliding in and out of the other's juicy crack.

'"May I be the first to be fucked?" gasped Penny, taking her lips away from my cock for a brief moment. She flipped over on to her back where she lay with her legs spread open and with her fingers parting her cunney iips that stood out in the midst of that hairy blonde minge. Augusta leaned over to squeeze Penny's nipples with wild thrilling pinches that brought the little cherries up to peak hardness. And it was the unselfish Augusta who took hold of my thick cock and guided it in between Penny's inviting cunney lips. I plunged my prick into her warm cavern and soon Penny and I were locked into a superb rhythm of long, sweeping strokes as my trusty truncheon slurped its way noisily in and out of her sopping cunt.

'I spurted my spunk to delicious effect but I sank back on the pillow absolutely shattered – after all, before all this fucking we had wined and dined quite sumptuously. But the two girls were still feeling randy so they turned to each other for further stimulation.

'Augusta began the proceedings by running her fingers through Penny's thatch of silky blonde public hair. She ran her hand along the length of her slit allowing it to come to rest at the base of Penny's clitty. She then grasped the trembling girl's bum cheeks, one in each hand, and gently kissed her dampening pussey, her mouth gently pressing against the soft, yielding fleshy lips, probing her utmost parameters of desire with her clever little tongue.

'Soon they were entwined in a *soixante-neuf*, Augusta's head buried between Penny's legs whilst the blonde girl's busy fingers were nipping and pinching Augusta's own finely developed clitty that stood out like a miniature cock from between her pussey lips. Penny then pulled her pussey to her own lips and nuzzled them round the curly bush that surrounded her cunt. The two tribades wriggled and cooed with delight as Penny produced an India-rubber dildo which she had hidden underneath the mattress and with a giggle passed it to me. I took hold of the dildo which was well crafted to the dimensions and shape of a good-sized prick and pressed it between Augusta's wet cunney lips. I must confess that I found the thrusting of the dildo in and out of her sopping cunney very exciting although I was just too tired to raise a decent cockstand.

'Now Augusta began to moan wildly, twisting and turning as I plunged the dildo in and out of her insatiable cunt. Penny too was madly excited and swooped her head down to my cock to suck it up to an almost full erection, with one hand on my swelling shaft and the other between her own legs as she frigged herself to an orgasm.

'Now meanwhile dear Augusta had wriggled over on her tummy and stuck her firm bum cheeks up in the air, slightly parting her legs so I could see her juices dribbling like honey from her cunt, for her pussey was by now creaming with pleasure. I looked at the wrinkled little bum hole that winked at me from between her arse-cheeks and as my cock was now standing fully at attention, I gently eased Penny's head away and getting up on my knees I slipped the head of my cock in and out of the puckered little rosette. "No, no, don't fuck my bottom," cried Augusta, "I would far rather that you dipped your cock into my cunt, I need it there so badly."

'How could I refuse such a request? I gave my cock a few rubs until it was rock-hard and, holding my red-headed weapon in my hand, I made Augusta stoop forward, as I plunged my cock into her wet welcoming crack from behind, my balls fairly bouncing against her bum.

'"Aaah! Aaaah! What a fine fucker you are, Richard, that's right, push harder now, further in, further in! Empty your balls, sir! That's it, that's it!"

'Her arse responded to every shove as I drove home until, excited to new raging peaks of lust by my lusty cock, the poor girl fainted as the maddened thrusts and contractions of her cunt sucked the sperm from my shaft. The sweet friction of her cunney lips against the head of my prick made every nerve thrill with that exquisite, unique pleasure. Happily, she soon recovered from the temporary delirium into which her senses had been plunged and she lay with her eyes beaming, her lips apart with the tip of her rosy tongue slightly protruding between two rows of the whitest pearly teeth – the very picture of sated voluptuousness!"'

'What a fantastic experience!' I said wistfully. 'I should very much like to meet those girls!'

'Would you, young Teddy?' said Richard with a smile playing about his lips. 'Well, how do you feel about it, Cecil?'

'Not without me being there,' rejoined my brother. 'You have made me so randy by telling me of your *nuit d'amour* that I think my cock will burst if I don't let it out.' And with that, he unbuttoned his fly and took out his swollen cock and began gently frigging his shaft.

'Quite a tosser you have there,' said Richard. 'But don't spoil your appetite because the lovely Augusta will be with us in less than half an hour!'

'Is that really so?' I exclaimed, feeling my own prick rise up in excitement.

'Yes, indeed, Teddy. So put your cock away, Cecil, you'll need to be in tip-top condition to satisfy Augusta.'

With difficulty, Cecil complied, stuffing his stiff cock back inside his trousers.

Richard continued: 'Oh, yes, Augusta knows all about what to expect, although I had to tell her that you, Teddy, were a little younger and I did not know if you had even fucked your first girl yet.'

'He is very advanced for his years,' grunted Cecil, 'and his cock is almost as big as yours and mine. Well, not as huge as yours Richard, but then you were the captain of the school's Thick Prick club last year. I forget which girl told me that she thought your cock reminded her of a cricket bat but it's well known that you are magnificently endowed and your story shows that you are certainly in no need of tuition in how to use your marvellous equipment. Not even Doctor Stevenson could teach you anything about *l'art de faire l'amour*.'

'Thank you very much,' said Richard modestly. 'Anyhow, Augusta is so looking forward to meeting you both. She told me later that night that wherever possible she loves to fuck three boys at the same time. This can present some practical problems but she tells me that she feels absolutely sated with a prick in her mouth whilst cocks are entering her arse-hole and cunney. Almost immediately, she experiences a huge spend, especially if the boys squeeze and caress her body with tender, loving care.

'She also likes sharing a man as she did with Penny and myself,' he added.

'What does she prefer in that case?' asked Cecil.

'Oh, simply divide the boy into two halves, so to speak. She sits on his cock whilst the other sits on his face and has her cunney sucked and then they change places *ad infinitum*. As Augusta says, a girl is far better equipped for a *ménage à trois* than a boy. For once he has spunked, it takes a while before he recovers but a girl can go on and on for quite a while until she tires or gets sore. So, as Augusta says, who says that women are the weaker sex?'

But before my question could be answered, Dunn the butler opened the door to announce that we had a visitor.

'Oh, is it the beautiful Miss Augusta, Dunn?' enquired Richard. 'She is a trifle early but no matter at all.'

'I fear not, sir,' replied the old retainer. 'It is a strange gentleman, or rather I should say a person who insists on seeing you.'

'A strange person? Whatever do you mean – did he give you his name?'

'Yes, sir. He also gave me his card and told me that he is known to you.'

How curious, I thought to myself as Dunn passed over the card and I peered over to read the ornate inscription: 'Hymie Singh Goldberg – Artists Agent.'

'That's a curious name,' I commented.

'He's a curious fellow,' grinned Richard. 'Hymie's mother was a Sikh but his Dad was the famous Issy Goldberg who was running a clothing emporium in Delhi during the Mutiny. He saved the lives of Lt. Colonel Wilson and his family by wrapping rolls of cloth round them when the mob was howling for blood and searching the shops for Europeans.'

'But didn't they want to lynch Issy?'

'They would have done but he was giving free bagels and lox

to any customer who purchased items to the value of five annas or more even on sale goods. There was already a queue and rather than have to wait before pillaging and looting the store the mob went on to the next district. By the time they returned, the Army had moved in so Issy, his store and the Wilson family were all saved.'

'That sounds an incredible tale,' said Cecil doubtfully.

'It's true, I assure you,' said Richard. 'Issy married a beautiful Sikh girl who changed her religion to his and they decided to move back to London a few years later and I believe that Hymie was born in Whitechapel.'

'How unlike the home life of our own dear Queen,' I said.

'Hymie is an art dealer,' said Richard. 'I expect he has some amazing bargains at never to be repeated prices to show me. He's quite a character so let's see what he has to offer.

'Dunn! Show the gentleman in.'

Dunn looked a mite peeved but did as he was told and retired momentarily to announce our visitor. 'Mr Hymie Singh Goldberg to see you, Mr Richard.'

Hymie came bustling in with a clutch of unframed paintings under his arm. He was a short, quite handsome man of coffee-coloured hue and he wore a deep red turban although his clothes were of a European cut.

'Ah, Hymie, how nice to see you again. These gentlemen are my house guests and I am sure they would be delighted to see the amazing world of art you have brought to sell me at extraordinarily inflated prices,' said Richard.

'Very droll, Mr Richard, very droll. I earn so little on any painting you buy it's hardly worth while making the journey. If it weren't for the fact that my old Auntie Hetty lives in Brighton I wouldn't bother, and that's a fact.'

'But now you're here you'll let me see what you have acquired. Is there anything worthwhile?'

'Anything worthwhile, he asks! Mr Richard, have I got some paintings for you! Look, here are four superb classical studies of heroines of Greek mythology. I should warn you and the other young gentlemen that the figures are undraped so if the sight of a nude girl offends, I won't take them out of the wrappers.'

'No, no, no that's quite all right,' said Cecil.

'Very well, gentlemen – here is the little collection. Now being young men of culture, you will know that without doubt the greatest single influence on Western civilisation has been the legacy of Ancient Greece. There is no corner of Art that is not founded firmly in that period and many people are well versed in the heroes of Greek mythology.

'But what about the women? We all know of Ulysses, Zeus and Hercules but what about the female counterparts? This young artist I am representing is himself a Greek who has turned his artistic talent to painting after some years making urns which was frankly not a profitable line.'

'Why, how much does a Grecian urn cost?' I asked.

'Round about two pounds or so. But that's not the point. This artist, Nedis Mousaka, has had the benefit of having those gorgeous dark-eyed Greek maidens pose for him. They have enabled him to capture the writhing golden forms of those Titans of old. Look, I'll show you what I've got.'

He unwrapped the pictures and spread the four paintings on a wall.

'Look, gentlemen, the first is a portrayal of the beautiful Andromeda, fairest daughter of Cassiopeia, the second of scheming Aphrodite, the goddess born of the sea, the goddess of sexual love, you should pardon the expression, and who was most widely worshipped of all the immortals. Then there's Maria, the mistress of Zeus, the fairest daughter of Atlas, if I am not mistaken, whilst the last is a depiction of the magnificent Nike, the mighty goddess of victory and Zeus's personal favourite.

'Now I ask you gentlemen, aren't these paintings stunning? Look at the detail, the depiction of the nude female form drawn with such power and eloquence!'

'They *are* rather good, Hymie,' said Richard, 'and if you could only provide one or more of those delicious girls to grace my bed tonight, I'd buy the lot.'

'Oh, you will have your little joke, sir. But at the price I'm asking, they must be a marvellous investment.'

We looked more closely at the paintings which were, truth to tell, rather good with the naked girls posing most sensually with complete abandon showing their breasts, bums and cunneys quite freely.

'I must say I like the look of Andromeda,' said Cecil. This painting showed the back of a girl, her hair flowing in the wind with firm, globular buttocks that fairly ached to be grabbed!

[To be continued]

Introduction to Part Two

This witty, amusing vignette was penned by Dr Jonathan Arkley, one of the leading lights of the South Hampstead set in the last twenty years or so of the nineteenth century.

It first appeared in *The Oyster* of November, 1893 just over a year before Oscar Wilde's 'The Importance of being Ernest' was first staged. I mention this because Arkley's characters – Gwendolen, Cecily, Algernon etc – all have the same names as characters in Wilde's masterpiece and it confirms that Wilde must have discussed his play with the good doctor who was known by many members of top London Society (including Lord Arthur Somerset, Sir Andrew Stuck and other well known men about town) as a consultant who might be able to cure any sexually transmitted diseases. Syphillis was rife at this time and the need for safe sex was as urgent then as it is now for the disease was as incurable as AIDS is today.

Arkley was himself somewhat of a roué, seducing many of the ladies who visited his consulting rooms in Welbeck Street. In her secret diary, Lady Danielle Freedman wrote in 1889 of the handsome Doctor Jonathan's charm which soon led me to his bed... I just hope that his enormous prick has not been inserted into too many ladies though I know for sure that Mrs Faine and Rosanne Oaklands have both been in his bed – probably together!'

Besides his interest in erotica, Arkley possessed a fine collection of early nineteenth century art and he was the author of two papers on abdominal pain that appeared in the *New England Journal of Medicine* in 1898 (Arkley's long-suffering wife was American and the family moved to New York in 1896 although they paid several visits back to Britain before the beginning of World War One).

Godfrey Goldhill

Axminster, December 1988

Sketches from Life
In which two Young Ladies enter the World of the Artist

(from *The Oyster*, November, 1893)

'Today is a very special anniversary,' said Gwendolen. 'It is two years to the very day since my first fuck.'

'Oh, how delicious,' I murmured.

'It is also,' she went on, 'the second anniversary of my second fuck, and my third.'

'Gracious,' I said. 'That sounds very exciting but also somewhat complicated.'

'Not really, Cecily,' she said. 'One day. Three fucks. All one after the other.'

'You certainly started with a bang!' I said.

'Don't be coarse,' said Gwendolen, 'or I shan't tell you all about them.'

'Oh, that would be so cruel,' I answered, 'for you know how I have always loved to talk of such things. You simply must tell me every last detail. See, I am already quite beside myself with excitement.'

With that, I squeezed my thighs together, trapping Gwendolen's hand as it teased and petted my pussey.

I should explain that we were sitting together on the top of a London omnibus. As luck would have it, we were all alone except for the driver up at the front who was far too busy guiding the horses through the traffic that seemed to come at us from all sides to have time to pay the slightest attention to what two fashionably attired young ladies might be doing snuggled together on the back seat.

I had met Gwendolen by chance two days before at a private

dance arranged by my aunt. At once we had flown into each other's arms with great squeals of recognition and joy for whilst we had been at school together, we had not seen each other for two full years or more. I, the older by a year, remembered Gwendolen as the sweetest little minx I had ever shared a bed with. Indeed, during the last year at Miss Bradshaw's Academy for Young Ladies we had truly been the most intimate of friends. But, alas, she had been forced to stay on for one further year to complete her education whilst I, heartily glad to escape from the damp glooms of Somerset, had been living in Town with my dear aunt.

So upon that chance meeting, we had rapidly made plans to see each other again and to exchange confidences for we both had much to tell and many adventures to recount. So thus it was, on this fine day in late Spring, we were journeying along the Bayswater Road with the intention of attending a private viewing of paintings by my cousin Algernon.

As soon as we were discreetly settled and it had become apparent that we were alone, Gwendolen's roving hands made it clear that she wished to resume that same loving closeness that had marked our last year together at Miss Bradshaw's Academy. Pleased though I was to receive her attentions, truth to tell, I was also a little alarmed at her disregard for any proprieties.

'Suppose someone should see us,' I had asked anxiously as I first felt her fingers begin to unbutton and burrow their way into my clothing.

'Do not worry, Cecily,' she had answered. 'Here, I have had the foresight to bring with me a good-sized travelling rug. We can tuck this round our legs and laps and anyone who notices us will simply think that we are taking sensible precautions against the chills and breezes attendant on top-deck open-air travel.'

With that, she wrapped us up firmly with a plaid rug (featuring as I recall the pattern of the Black Watch tartan) which neatly concealed the hand that now began to slip into my underclothing, sliding through the opening of my drawers and gently stroking the curls of my pussey hair. I turned my head and kissed her warmly as she for a moment, lowered her head so that it was pressed against the swell of my right breast.

'How I wish I could set your pretty titties free here and now,' she said. 'Oh, to see them spill out of your bodice. Those lovely, big titties that have given me such pleasure in the past. Oh, I do so wish I could kiss them and squeeze them and nibble at those delightful little cherries this very moment!'

'I would indeed love to feel your mouth sucking at my nipples.' I answered as a flush of desire warmed me and I could feel my nipples swelling and standing up in response to her urgings. 'But that must wait for later. Meanwhile...'

And I eased my thighs apart and felt her fingers seeking and then finding the already damp entrance to my secret cave. Suddenly she touched upon my eager clitty. I must have jumped at the thrill that shot though my whole body as Gwendolen giggled and continued to rub it firmly.

'Now, now Cecily, try to be still for we must be discreet as you so rightly said. Besides, I have so much to tell you. Let us sit here, hand-in-glove, so to speak while I begin, for as I said before, today is a very special anniversary...'

'It all started in the washplace outside our dormitory,' she began.

Here I must explain that at Miss Bradshaw's Academy for Young Ladies (situated near Petherton in the Quantock Hills), the headmistress had been particularly concerned that her charges should not be tempted into committing what she regarded as the Sin of Vanity. Consequently, she had arranged that there should be no mirrors above the washbasins where we might have been tempted into spending valuable time in such frivolities such as arranging our hair or admiring our fresh, youthful complexions. All that was needed, Miss Bradshaw had decided, were a few pier-glasses at the doorways so that we could ensure that we were neat and tidy before going out of doors.

To this day I can remember the rows of basins with chocolate brown shiny tiles behind them and the small windows which were set so high up that we could not see out of them without climbing up on the basins. Add just three baths in cubicles and a set of lockers where we kept our washing materials and our nighties and you have some idea of the spartan, indeed almost prison-like surroundings that Miss Bradshaw considered suitable for her girls.

'Oh, Gwendolen, we did have such fun, though, didn't we, all girls together,' I said, as I recalled those times of illicit evening pleasures.

It will be readily understood, I am sure, that being all of the same sex, shut up in a large and gloomy establishment in the heart of Somerset without a single member of the male species to be found anywhere on the premises, with the exception only of the old school chaplain, we explored amongst ourselves, so to speak for our pleasures. It was hardly surprising that there were many friendships of the most emotional kind flourishing amongst the young ladies and it will be further understood that within such an establishment there were many formal school rules laid down by the Headmistress and other unofficial rules created by the pupils, not written of course, but obeyed with much more care and to the very letter, far more so in fact than the official ones. Thus, only girls who were in the upper form could walk across a particular strip of grass outside the main boarding house. Senior girls were allowed to wear a plain ribbon in their straw boaters. Junior girls had to avoid looking into the prefects' day room and disobedience meant being shut up in a dark little cupboard. Such customs seem to grow up in all schools and many of them when looked on later in life appear to be very silly indeed.

However, at least in my boarding house, we did enjoy obeying one most delightful and entertaining rule. As I have said, there were no mirrors behind the washbasins in the big room where, morning and evening, we performed our ablutions. I have already touched upon the fact that, amongst two hundred and seventy girls, deprived of any contact whatsoever with the opposite sex and subject to the most repressive regime where such matters are concerned, many very intimate friendships grew up. Such passions and crushes abounded freely and many were the sighs of unrequited love and great was the gossip and whispered rumour about so-and-so and such-and-such. Many too were the intense conversations conducted quietly in corners or on staircases and many were the sly touches, the gentle pressures of hands on hands that ached for an answering response. Many an arm was slipped casually around a slim waist in the expectation of a quick smile and an equally swift hip-to-hip rub as a signal that other and greater intimacies might be enjoyed in the near future.

Yet in all these hopeful approaches and longing caresses there was as well the fear and the pain of possible rejection. Oh, the shame and embarrassment when the pretty object of one's utmost desires brushed away the half-hearted embrace or worse still, laughed and tossed her head in a gesture of scorn. And then the mortification of knowing that soon you would be the victim of giggling tales told in the dormitory or the subject of scornful notes passed between desks during lessons. Indeed, I have always maintained that one's most private pain becoming the subject of ribald public comment is without doubt one of the most humiliating things that can happen to a human being.

So, in order to lessen the chances of such unfortunate and painful occurences, a convention – one that in my experience was always complied with – had grown up at the school. If the object of one's desire was bending down at a washbasin having her before-lights-out wash, it was accepted as permissable to approach her from behind and, without a word being said, to touch and to stroke her. A finger could be gently run down her spine or the hands were allowed to cup themselves over her hips. If these advances were not checked, one might then slowly run one's pussey against the swelling cheeks of her bum.

She in turn was honour bound neither to cry out nor turn round to see who it was who had thus approached her. She could then respond, either by silently accepting or rejecting her unknown would-be friend. She might, for instance, remain quite still and make it clear that she did not welcome a continuation of this encounter. She could, if need be, gently reach back and remove the clasping hand and relieve a too insistent pressure. There are many subtle ways by which one can quietly yet firmly refuse an unwelcome attention and women are far more expert than men in expressing this unspoken language.

However, since we were for the most part a high-spirited and healthy collection of girls, it happened more often than not that this same silent language was employed to accept and even to urge on such welcome, delicate contact. In this case, still without a word being spoken or a head being turned, a simple touch could be followed by a loving, exploratory caress. How many times, whilst busily splashing myself with water or carefully soaping my face and neck, have I sensed a warm presence behind me and felt the delicate touch of soft, unknown hands running the length of my body and massaging my flesh through the thin cotton of my nightdress. Ah, and then to press and nestle against the smoothness of the unseen adventurer, to wait in thrilling anticipation for those same hands to reach round and cup one's breasts, squeezing and rubbing the titties until one's nipples rose proudly erect with swelling excitement.

Then there might come the hoped-for pressure of one's mystery partner's hairy bush being pressed against one's bottom, of hands playing with the cheeks of one's bum. How lovely too if on the other hand one were the instigator of the approach, to feel a quiver of delight course through the welcoming body of the beautiful girl, to feel the first parting of the thighs, to see her shyly raise her bum as a sign that the road ahead was clear. Then would come the magic moment when the nightdress was raised up past the hips and the rosy delights of her arse were laid bare, first for an admiring gaze and then to be kissed, stroked and perhaps lightly slapped.

Truly, there are few more pleasurable things in life for me than to feel a hand slip between my thighs, to quiver with pleasure as the long tapering fingers begin to caress my pussey, to feel an enquiring finger seek out and rub my clitty and to be laid out on my back, with my legs apart and have a head wrapped between my legs with my partner's questing tongue probing delicately round my notch, licking and lapping at my pussey.

My first experiences than occured at Miss Bradshaw's Academy – many was the time that I cradled my head on my arms against the cold rim of the basin, shuddering with anticipation as unseen hands playfully but persuasively prised open the yielding lips of my cunney. Oh, the delight as a finger slid its way into the dampening warmth of my cunt! How often have I been driven to the full ecstacy of spending, yet never turning round as the first heaving surges of pleasure have coursed through my frame and the sticky flow of love juice has soaked my curly, thick bush.

It was not unknown, I well recall, on venturing into the washplace, to find such a loving scene as I have described being enacted before one's very eyes. Then, I must confess, I too would become greatly excited and want most urgently to join in. I remember being both the recipient and the instigator of such a multiple occasion. The first time it was I who was enjoying a most complete frigging from behind when I became aware that other hands had joined in the game, that the two fingers that were delving deep within me actually belonged to two different adventurers, and that other hands were fondling my titties.

Here I must digress and admit, nay state openly, without false modesty, that my titties are not only large and most delightfully firm, but they are most exquisitely sensitive. I can be driven almost to the delirium of my coming just by their being squeezed and nibbled upon. In turn, I have often rubbed them against another's bottom and felt them swell and throb with pleasure.

I was in fact once engaged in such a activity with the prettiest little new girl in our class when I was approached from behind by a third. Obeying the rules – for I am of course fully in favour of obeying both the laws and the customs of the land as long as they seem reasonable to me – I in turn didn't turn but continued to busy myself with the pretty little newcomer whose darling little bottom was by now opening up under the careful probing of my tongue. At the same time I also felt hands reaching out to finger my pussey hair and within minutes I was playing piggy-in-the-middle as part of a wriggling threesome.

But I digress at too great length. Suffice it to say that when Gwendolen mentioned the dormitory wash place, many, many memories came flooding back to me and I had high hopes of any story that began in such a setting.

'It was an evening towards the end of the Summer Term' continued Gwendolen. 'I was, I suppose day-dreaming – or rather night-dreaming for I was looking forward to an after-lights-out assignation with someone who had recently become a very dear friend. As I slowly attended to my toilette I became aware both of a hastily suppressed giggle and of a presence behind me. Shivering slightly with excitement I waited for that first tender touch. Unseen hands clasped me firmly around the waist and I wriggled backwards at once to give me assent for anything that might follow. Surprisingly quickly the hands were withdrawn and I felt my nightie being pushed up so that I knew that I was fully exposed to sight and touch. The same hands then urged me on to spread my legs, which I did most happily. Here was the first real surprise for the unseen hands were altogether more roughened and stronger than any I had previously encountered. As one finger at once found my little clit and rubbed it to a state of upstanding excitement, another finger had most expertly penetrated by cunt lips and was exploring me in a most forthright but delightful way.

A great warmth spread over my whole body and I sighed contentedly as I felt that familiar slow wetness begin to infuse my pussey.

Suddenly the hands were withdrawn and I felt the close heat of a body pressed up against me. Then . . . Oh, Cecily . . . Something quite amazing happened. This . . . this Thing was thrust between my legs and straightaway plunged into my quim. For a moment I was quite unable to understand what was happening. Here was something quite new in my experience. Before I had a chance to consider or to do anything to sort out this puzzle, this great Thing had burrowed its way right up to its very hilt in me. Then, as it drew back, almost to the entrance to my cunt, it was thrust in again. It seemed to harden still more inside me until I was completely filled with its swollen length. Yet such was my own ever-widening instinctive response that it caused me no pain although there was no doubt in my mind that nothing so large and so forceful had ever penetrated me before.

By now all curiosity and all thought had been driven from my mind by its insistent thrusting and I surrendered myself completely to an ever mounting ecstasy. Moaning and even biting my wrist to stop myself crying out with the sheer pleasure of what was being done to me, I felt wave after wave of excitement pass through my body. My whole being, the whole world even, seemed to be concentrated in the heat of my pussey. Without knowing what I was doing, I was gripping and releasing this great pleasure instrument with internal muscles that I had not till then known I possessed as it slid ever more rapidly up and down the length of my cunt.

Then all of a sudden there was a momentary pause before a

renewed, frantic pressure as it discharged itself right in the furthest recesses of my tunnel of love. Again and again I felt a great spurting and what felt like a very torrent of juice was flooded into me.

Rapidly this delicious spurting slowed down and before I could do anything to stop it, this great engine of delight had been withdrawn. As the lips of my cunt closed I could feel the warm flow of our mingled juices running down the inside of my thighs.'

'Oh, Gwendolen', I said. 'I am so affected by your story. Please help me a little before you go on.'

With that dear Gwendolen did indeed pause in her account and with her skilful, soft fingers, opened out my own cunt and eased and teased my own clit into a most fatly happy state. Then as I snuggled up against her, I said, 'That's lovely. Please Gwendolen, go on with your story, but please also keep your hand exactly where it is now.'

'I can feel how happy you are,' she said. 'Truly you have always been the most warmly welcoming pussey of my acquaintance.'

'Then,' she went on, 'I was so overcome and still so filled with a hunger for more that I broke the rules. Panting, my hair all damp and dishevelled with the heat of the encounter, I partly turned round, having at the same time to half support myself. There in front of me was something never previously seen in a dormitory washroom in all the history of Miss Bradshaw's Academy for Young Ladies. A man. A naked man. He had a quite sun-burned body. He had wild, curling hair, a ring in one ear and strange designs tattooed on his arms and chest. But the most remarkable feature and one to which my eye was at once drawn, was this great Thing that jutted out between his legs. That very Thing with which he had just invaded my body and caused me what I knew without thinking to have been the most exciting time of my life so far.'

'Your first cock!' I exclaimed, rather too loudly in the circumstances.

'Sssh!' said Gwendolen. 'That is not a proper word for a young lady of good breeding to cry out in such a carrying way.'

'I am sorry,' I replied, as I realised that I had been so intent on her story, accompanied as it was by the steady caressing of her fingers in my pussey, that I had quite forgotten myself. Luckily the driver did not appear to have heard anything unusual coming from the back of his omnibus (although Gwendolen afterwards announced that she had seen one of the horses prick up his ears and raise his tail in surprise. However I do not quite believe this myself as I know that dearest Gwendolen cannot always resist the temptation to embroider a story in the retelling.)

'Do go on...'

'My first cock,' said Gwendolen. 'And I know now that it was a pretty handsome specimen. Anyway, as I leaned there, wondering where this sudden forbidden visitor had come from, I became aware of two other things. The first was that four of my dearest friends were with him, their eyes shining with delight and excitement at what they had just seen.'

'Your first fuck!' I exclaimed.

'My first fuck indeed,' Gwendolen replied.

'And what was the other thing you noticed?' I asked.

'That although I had been brought to the very brink of coming, I had not yet been driven over the edge. My titties were all swollen and I could see my nipples pushing out under my nightie. My legs were trembling and I could feel blood surging through all my body whilst my private parts were throbbing with an urgency I had never felt before. But as I rested against the basin, I spread my legs as though to let some cooling air in to calm the heat and the wetness of my pussey. Without thinking I fingered myself, opening myself up to my audience. Seeing my distress, two of my friends came to my aid. One, Mary quickly knelt down and, burying her face in my bush, began to lick my swollen clit. But the other, Meg...'

'I remember her,' I said. 'A tall Scottish girl...'

'Who as you might have heard, later behaved in a most immoral fashion whilst on the passage to India where her father was stationed,' said Gwendolen. 'According to her account, no less than seven young officers from one of the Mounted Regiments passed her portals, and all accomplished whilst steaming the length of the Suez Canal.'

'However, Meg...' I prompted her.

'Meg first kissed me with open-mouthed eagerness and then brought forward the strange man. Placing one hand under his still large but now limp pleasure staff, she urged me first to lick its purple end, and then inch by inch, slowly, take it into my mouth. As my lips gently slipped further and further down its length, I felt it stir in my mouth. Understanding at once what was taking place, I sucked and pulled at it with my lips. Meg meanwhile had slipped her hands beneath his balls and was very carefully squeezing them.

Before I had time properly to realise that sucking a man's cock can be a very great pleasure in its own right, he had so stiffened and enlarged that I felt in some danger of choking. At once he withdrew and as my two friends eased me down on to the floor and as I spread my legs apart, drawing my knees up so that my entire pussey was forced into full view, he entered me once again with his now glistening and re-erected member.

Cecily, I have since then seen some of the classic Indian texts on lovemaking and have studied the positions. All I can say is that I have never needed to be taught. Fucking, I now realise, comes easily to me. As if I had been doing this all my life, I raised my legs and grasped him round the waist, drawing him fully into me. There I held him for a while, savouring the delicious feeling of my cunt absolutely filled with his prick. Then, releasing my grip somewhat, I let him recommence that to-ing and fro-ing that previously he had done from behind. This time I had the added pleasure of being able to watch that great tool thrust deep into me and then slide back in order to repeat its effort.

By now my body was responding as if by instinct and I was thrusting to meet him time and time again. This time he was much much, more controlled in his fucking and as he slid back and forth like a great piston, I began to lose control once more. Then it was that I broke the second rule. I did not mean to but I could no longer stay silent. I hardly knew what I was crying out but the others later recalled that I had been shouting out "More! More! For God's Sake! Fuck me! Fuck me!" My head was twisting from side to side and I had pulled my nightdress right up over my tits. I was rubbing them, squeezing them almost to the point of pain as I felt my legs split apart as though I was trying to suck the whole of him inside me. Then my back arched and I realised in one wonderful instant that I will never ever forget, that for the first time in my life I was coming with a man inside me.'

By now I was again so excited by Gwendolen's story that I could feel an answering wetness begin to flood down me.

'Gwendolen, quick, hold on to me tight. I think I'm coming as well. No, no! That's it. I need a second finger in me. Go on. Tell me some more.'

'Well,' said Gwendolen, only a little put off her stride by my interruption, 'Suffice it to say that I came and I came and I came. It seemed as though my coming would never end. When at last he also came for the second time I was so carried away by our fucking that I bit him quite badly and scratched him all over his back. Luckily he can't have felt a thing – although later the others said they had to dab some antiseptic lotion over him. I may say that afterwards I found that he also seemed to have bitten me, for one of my nipples was very sore.

But at the time all I can remember is that I seemed to dissolve into a some sort of sticky blancmange. I swear my eyes went out of focus and all I could see was a haze. I was so drained and so happy that I would have just stayed there on the floor for ever, feeling the last waves of my coming wash over me. Then Meg and Mary and the others took charge and they lifted me up gently and put me in a warm bath. They washed me all over with great thoroughness, paying particular attention to my much exercised private parts. They were also good enough thoroughly to sponge down the strange man, who all the time had said nothing, before they led him away.

'What happened next?' I asked. By now I also had calmed down and was happily content to leave Gwendolen's hand resting gently on my more satisfied pussey.

'They dried me off and led me back to bed. Where I slept dreamlessly and deeply until the bell rang at seven o'clock the next morning. I remember half getting up and than half wondering if it had all been a dream. I sat there on the edge of my bed feeling strange and very different somehow. I think Meg must have noticed my odd expression for she came over to me and said "You weren't dreaming. You had your first fuck last night. And your second, and your third."

"Three?" I asked. "It all seems so muddled but are you *sure* there were three?"

"Definitely," she said. "One from the back. One from the front – when we had to hold you down, you were throwing yourself about so. And one with you on top, after we'd got you all clean again and towelled you down. You stood up, your eyes all glazed, dropped the bath towel we'd wrapped round you for decency's sake, wound your arms round him and almost forced him over. You were sitting on him, riding him as though you'd been doing this sort of thing all your life and at intervals you'd lean forward so that your tits brushed against him and he was sucking them and biting them while you wriggled and yelled as he impaled you on his great tool."'

'Do you know,' said Gwendolen, 'from that day to this, I simply can't remember that third time. If it really happened I must have been quite out of my mind with fucking.'

'Well it's not a bad way to go,' I said. 'But maybe Meg was exaggerating. After all, some of her stories do sound a little suspect.'

'Like seven army officers between Port Said and Suez?'

'It certainly sounds like military service on a grand scale. Three or four? Now that I can imagine. But anyway, it's a lovely story. Did you ever find out who the man was and how he came to be there? And did you get to fuck him again?'

'It was all Melissa's idea,' said Gwendolen.

I remembered Melissa. A tall well-built girl. Full of energy and mad-cap ideas, she was definitely a character. Terribly untidy and somewhat scatter-brained, she was the despair of Mrs Bradshaw and the staff. Brought up on a farm, and with a knowing eye, she had a most unladylike knowledge and interest in the less polite activities of the animals. I remember clearly an incident when we were both only just arrived at the school. There was a rather fussy little man who in those early days used to come in twice a week in order to teach music. One day he brought in his small and rather fussy little dog. Of course we all gathered round to stroke and pet the little creature. When it suddenly started yapping and then made as if to snap at one of the girls, he snatched it up.

'Bobo's a touch on the nervous side,' he twittered agitatedly. 'A highly strung little dog.'

'She's not a dog,' said Melissa. 'She's a bitch. Look, she's got nipples.' Poor Mr Fotheringay was very shocked at her plain speaking and when Melissa made things worse by going on 'All females have nipples. They're for babies to suck milk from. Young ladies have nipples too,' he became speechless and stopped the lesson there and then.

Later Miss Bartholomew, the Deputy Headmistress, sent for her and she was told in no uncertain terms that she was never never to use such language again in the school. Her parents were to be told of her misbehaviour. She was to apologise to Mr Fotheringay, who had had a severe nervous attack after the incident and she was to lose all sorts of privileges for the rest of term.

We all thought that this was absolutely beastly of Miss Bartholomew who was such a stick-like creature that in her case it was more than possible that she in fact did not have any nipples. She certainly had no visible bosom.

Anyway, Melissa had gone from bad to worse in the eyes of the Mistresses and had got better and better in the opinions of all her friends. Of course in the midst of all our passions and night-time friendships, one subject above all was the great topic of excited conversation. Men. As I have said, apart from the school chaplain, The Rev. Mr Paddlebottom, and occasional visits from Mr Fotheringay, we never saw one at close quarters on the school premises. We were terribly ignorant about Men and in particular about what Men did to Young Ladies.

Melissa inevitably was the one who told us all, when we all were in our first term. 'They have this Thing,' she told her wide-eyed audience in the dorm. 'And they have to put it in girls' wee holes so that they can have babies.'

Naturally there was a chorus of disbelief from most of us. Apart from a vague idea that having a baby involved help from a clergyman, since babies were only born after a proper Church wedding, there was a school of thought that they came out of the belly button but mostly we were just ignorant and terribly shocked.

'Ugh!' said a squat girl called Hermione, 'That sounds horrid. I certainly wouldn't want a man's Thing pushed into *my* wee-hole. I can think of nothing worse.'

At this there was quite a babble of agreement but I noticed, here and there, a number of girls with thoughtful looks on their faces who didn't join in the general outcry. I was somewhat relieved because the idea of a man's Thing one day reaching up inside me seemed a proposition not to be dismissed out of hand and one to be considered carefully for the future.

The fact was that I had already made certain discoveries about my still dormant pussey. A little gentle exploration with my own fingers had awakened feelings of pleasure and excitement. Nor, as I realised later that evening, was I alone in my discoveries. After Melissa's lecture on the Facts of Life had ended and lights were out, I voiced my thoughts on the subject of men's Things to my friend Thomasina. She at once confided that she also had engendered feelings of a quite thrilling nature in and around her hidden parts by a process of quiet self-exploration. Emboldened by our whispered conversation, I quietly did a round of the dormitory, asking a carefully picked selection of girls whether they also had any sympathy with my ideas. Quite soon seven or eight of us were sharing confessions. We all agreed that if at any time in the future, a man's Thing were to be presented to us, we would at least greet the proposition with an open mind.

In the meantime several of us agreed that if we could get such pleasure at our own hands, maybe the touch of other hands would be as nice or even better. In no time at all, amid hastily hushed giggles, a mass exploration was going on. In the darkness, unseen hands were reaching out. Demurely pressed-together knees were being eased apart and careful journeys of adventure were being made into unseen places. Of course we were still too young to understand the peaks of ecstasy that lay ahead but we had made a start.

So Melissa had entered my life and Gwendolen's early. Her night time lectures and quite explicit explanations had been our introduction to sexual matters. Now it seemed that, like the good teacher she was later to become, she had not only awakened our juvenile interests in the subject, but had set my friend her final examination – and one that she had passed with flying colours. In short, she had arranged her first fuck. But how? Where had the man, with his splendid Thing, come from? What had happened to him?

Melissa, it seemed, had finally tired of listening to the moanings and complaints about the great lack of Men during the dormitory conversations. There was Adam the school gardener. But he was reputed to have been employed by Miss Bradshaw not for his expertise in horticultural matters but because he was safe where Young Ladies were concerned. This followed an incident in the Crimea War when he had been damaged by a Russian musket shot in those parts that are the seat of the male passions. The only other man to be found within the convent-like confines of the school, Mr Fotheringay having retired to a sanitorium, was as I have said, the chaplain, Mr Paddlebottom.

He however had always restricted his attentions to the backsides of his pupils. 'Spanker' as he was called, was in the habit of indulging in regular chastisements of those of his flock who had failed to come up to his expectations where biblical knowledge was concerned. All of us had at some time or other felt his rod upon our bottom but he had never displayed any interest in our other parts. So many a maiden's prayers had gone unanswered and no man's Thing had ever raised its head within either school or pupils.

How we had bemoaned our fate. How eagerly we had chattered and dreamed about men and their Things. We made up stories and hoped that one day we would find such a combination within the school grounds. But our citadel was well guarded and its multitude of young pussies quite unapproachable. I remembered clearly those endless after-dark speculations, those moist sighs and breathless fantasies. But I digress.

Melissa, as Gwendolen recounted, had become impatient and decided that something must be done to fill certain long felt wants.

'There is a gipsy encampment on the common,' she had announced one night. Blank stares had greeted this piece of news. 'Gipsies,' she had continued, 'are well known, in lore if not in fact, for their habit of kidnapping babies and small children. Is it not time that the tables were turned? I have a splendid scheme. We will capture a gipsy.'

'Why?' several of her audience had chorused.

'Why?' she had answered. 'So that we can make use of him.'

'How,' those same voices asked.

'We will bring him back here and use him for our pleasure.'

At this there was a great hubbub of questions and objections.

'Listen' she went on. 'I have thought this out with great care. We can smuggle him into the school and keep him in the attic where all our trunks are stored. No-one ever goes in there until the end of term. I have talked to one of the village girls who works in the kitchens. She is very taken with the idea and has promised to put on one side sufficient food for us to sneak in to him.'

'But surely he will be able to escape,' Meg asked. 'We cannot mount a guard on him.'

'But will he *want* to escape?' replied Melissa. 'School food may not be enough temptation but school pussies will surely be. I am quite convinced that he will be more than ready to endure his confinement when he realises that he is to be presented with a succulent diet of unblemished fruit, ripe for the plucking.'

'It would never work,' one or two of her enthralled audience had objected, albeit wistfully.

'It could,' she answered. 'We will have to be very careful. Above all, no-one must breath a word of what is to happen. So first we must all swear on our Honour – or rather our hoped-for Dishonour – not to say anything, not even a hint, to anyone.' By now all were becoming quite wrapped up in her plan, and quickly agreed to become sworn sisters in secrecy.

There is not time to recount every detail of the plot but suffice it to say that Melissa's already well-thought-out scheme was seized upon by two of the girls whose fathers were both in the Army. Between them they had listened far too many times over the parental dinner table to accounts of military expeditions for them not to understand the necessity of good forward planning.

The key to the scheme lay in the hands of Bess, the kitchen maid who had already promised to keep back enough food for their inviting guest. Unlike the Young Ladies, she was no stranger to men and their Things.

'I'm sure I'm not much of a one for reading,' she had confided in Melissa, 'nor for either of the other two Rs, but the Three Fs are another matter. Feeling, Frolicking and Fucking are an education in themselves.' She eagerly volunteered to be their accomplice. Melissa and four of the stronger girls had slipped out into the school grounds after dark. Waiting for them was Bess. She had led them down the lane and then to the edge of the common where there was a barn, half-filled with hay.

'I think I can get him to follow me in here with no trouble at all,' she had said. 'He' was a tall gipsy in the prime of life that she had already spotted while hanging round the camp.

'And as soon as he's in here, we grab him?' said one of Melissa's press gang.

'Not if you please, Miss,' said Bess. 'Beg pardon, but I would like to be repayed for my services.'

'Of course,' Melissa had answered. 'I am sure that I can cajole a little money out of Papa when I go home...'

'Oh No, Miss! I didn't mean anything like that,' Bess had answered. 'All I know is that if I can get him excited enough to follow me in here, then I will be excited enough to want to offer him what he's after.'

'First fuck!' exclaimed Melissa.

'First fuck,' agreed Bess. 'That is only fair is it not?'

'Indeed, yes,' said Melissa. 'It was quite thoughtless of me not to have made the offer.'

'Besides,' went on Bess. 'He will be easier to capture when he is all spent. I may not have the benefits of an expensive education but kitchen work makes a girl strong in the arm and in the thighs. I can promise to quite drain him of any fighting spirit for a while.'

'So we should hide behind these bales and watch for our opportunity,' said Melissa.

'If you would, Miss. Although it is quite dark in here, I am sure that you will be able to see enough, and hear, to know when the right moment has arrived.'

They had watched from the barn as Bess had gone down to the gipsy encampment. By the light of a fire they had seen her silhouetted by the gate. They could not hear what was going on but presently they saw a tall man leave the fire, where no doubt the gipsies were engaged in roasting a hedgehog or some game poached from the neighbouring estate, and walk over to her. They had heard an enticing laugh from Bess, a murmur of conversation and then she had turned back towards the barn and the ambush that waited within. As she approached, leading him by the hand, they had all hastily retired into the dark recesses of the barn.

With a giggle, she had thrown herself down on the straw and raised her skirts to him. They saw a quick flash of naked flesh as her legs were spread in welcome. They saw him unbuckle and unbutton himself before first sinking to his knees before her and then covering her with his body. In the half-darkness, they could make out that Bess and the gipsy were clasping each other, locked in passionate kisses. Then he raised himself up and for a moment they saw his great swollen cock. Two of the party, this being their first sight of such an instrument of delight, gasped out in amazement and excitement. The gipsy, even in the throes of his pleasure, had looked up at the sound.

'That old barn owl,' Bess had said with great presence of mind. 'There is a nest up in the roof.'

Not needing much reassurance, the gipsy had fallen to his work. Bess's thighs, the black shadow of her pussey deep between them, had seized him round the waist and she had drawn his engorged prick deep inside her. Quite beside themselves with envy, the school party had watched as the two of them coupled and wrestled on the straw.

'There was such a thrusting and a panting,' Melissa had reported, 'that it seemed some great threshing machine was at work.' Bess had been crying out and wriggling her bottom as though to clamp him forever in her. But he had continued to drive his way up and down her lover's lane as it opened up before him between the dense thickets of her pussey. Then she wrestled him, still embedded in her, over on to his back and began to ride him ever faster and faster. He responded like a thoroughbred, his prick rising to meet her downward thrusts.

'I shall never ride side-saddle again,' someone had whispered in Melissa's ear as they crouched in the darkness.

Then, as Bess and the gipsy reached their climax, straw and chaff rising in a cloud around them, he bucked and moaned and the watchers sensed the cream churning and spurting up along his great member. Bess, like any good milkmaid, accepted every drop in her waiting receptacle, clutching at him and urging him on. Clamping his head in her hands, she pressed her open mouth against his as though she was trying to eat him, while his cum flooded into her and shudders of pleasure ran through both their bodies.

Then, as their movements grew less frenzied, the watchers had to pull themselves together and remember there was work to be done. The gipsy gave one last pumping heave. Bess collapsed down on him and they lay locked together for a moment or two. The ambushers crept forward, not quite certain whether now was the time to pounce. As they hesitated, Bess raised herself up, paused, and then sat back on her heels, letting his still fat but limp prick slip out of her. Bending forward, she cupped his balls between her hands, sucked hungrily at the tip of his juice-wet cock and sat back again. She raised her arms and beckoned them forward.

In a nervous scurry, Melissa and her friends scrambled across the straw and gripped and pinioned their quarry's arms and legs. Exhausted though he was, he began to struggle, looking round wildly at his attackers. Bess at once threw herself back on top of him, kissed him and whispered urgently in his ear.

'Lie still now, dear,' she had said. 'No harm is going to come to you. But there is something these friends of mine want you to do for them.'

Quickly she explained what the plan was, how he was to be secreted in the school attic for no more than three days, how she personally would make sure he had three square meals a day. 'Food prepared with my own hands,' she said, giving his cock a friendly but firm squeeze. 'Better food than you'll get round that old camp fire of yours.'

After having had to live on the school food for a number of years, there was not one of the girls who considered this possible, but a small lie was needed in the circumstances. Then, as the nature of the duties he would be called upon to perform became clear to him, at the thought of all the virgin pussey, the unawakened clits and the hitherto unpenetrated passages waiting for him, he stopped any pretence of struggle and surrendered to his fate.

So he was brought back to the school, smuggled in through a back door and led up stairs. Bess tiptoed up from the servants quarters with a big bowl of soup and several thick slices of bread. These he wolfed down like a man who hadn't eaten for days on end.

'Fucking makes you hungry,' explained Bess. 'And you've got to feed him up and keep him in condition. Anyway, I like him.' She turned to him. 'That was a fine country fuck, she said. Now you must trust these young ladies. There is a lot you can do for them. Besides, some of them are very well connected in these parts. I've no doubt that if you or your family are ever caught with the odd pheasant that you have poached, one or other of them will be able to have a quiet word with her father, invent some story of a small favour owed, a lost brooch returned, and nothing more will be said. The gipsy, who was not stupid, realised that he was being offered a free harvest of fucking followed by the free run of the game coverts of the area. He accepted this unusual turn of affairs with a good grace. Because we were all well brought up young ladies, it was arranged that he should be bathed and made quite clean before we would receive him. Bess meanwhile promised him that a message would be taken by her down to the camp to say that they were not to worry at his absence and that he would be returning to them in a day or so.

'But were you not a party to this plot?' I asked Gwendolen.

'Alas no,' she replied. 'I had had the misfortune to be confined to the school sanitorium with a slight chill for a couple of days, so knew nothing of it.'

'But they let you into the secret,' I said.

'They let the secret into me,' corrected Gwendolen. 'Both Melissa and Thomasina had absolutely insisted that, since had I been well, I would without doubt have played a leading role in our adventure, I should be given the opportunity to enjoy a Romany Ride.'

'That was very good of them' I said. 'But how long did you keep him for in the end?'

'Three nights in all,' said Gwendolen. 'On the third night, about dawn, we released him back into the wild.'

'And nothing was ever discovered?'

'Not really.'

'What do you mean, "Not really"?' I asked.

'Well, there was one tiny incident . . .' said Gwendolen. 'Do you remember Miss Brightwell?'

'The young temporary art teacher,' I said.

'Yes,' said Gwendolen. 'Well, she happened upon Bess

creeping up the back staircase that led from the kitchens to the attics. Bess had a bowl of nourishing stew under a cloth. Thinking that some sort of forbidden night-time feast was taking place in the dormitory, she had followed silently behind her. She found the gipsy, John Smith was his name, in the lumber room, giving some private tuition to two of the girls. A lesson had just finished. Meg was lying back, recovering from a most searching examination of her inner parts, while Deirdre . . .'

'That thin girl with a most active tongue,' I said.

'The same,' said Gwendolen. 'She was using the same active tongue in order to lick our tutor back into sufficient life for him to perform his duties all over again. She was most assiduously sucking and teasing his cock back to its standing position when Miss Brightwell appeared at thc door.'

'How terrible,' I said. 'What did she do?'

'She was a jolly good sport,' replied Gwendolen. 'Everyone of course had stopped what they were doing except Meg who was too far gone in her post-fuck daze to notice anything. She just lay there, stroking her exhausted quim while Mis Brightwell looked about her and the said "John Smith, believe." The gipsy turned and said "Rachel!"'

'Goodness me,' I said.

'It turned out that they had met some months previousl when she was engaged in a series of circus sketches on Blackheath in south London. That of course was immediatel prior to her having taken up a temporary position at Mis Bradshaw's. I later saw some of her drawings. They are mos exotic. Trapeze artists and acrobats are flexible beyond the imaginings of us ordinary mortals. Such contortions and such fucking and all in positions that I swear would be quit impossible without grave risk of permanent injury to someone untrained. One of the artists, wearing only a little spangle costume, had her legs locked round the back of her own nec and had then craned forward so that her face was but a few inches from this immense cock that was plunging deep into he gaping quim.'

'Gracious!' I said, 'What a coincidence.'

'Furthermore,' Gwendolen went on, 'it appeared that sh

had not restricted her activities to just recording such details. She had several times enjoyed a thorough fucking at the hands, or rather the prick, of John the Gipsy. Although these instances she had not of course been able to record in pencil or watercolour.'

'What happened then?' I asked.

'She very sportingly said that she would not report anything that she had seen just so long as she took the next turn. Miss Minge – for that was John the Gipsy's nickname for her – quickly slipped off her rather artistic and loose fitting dress and stood before us in a delightfully unashamed nakedness. She was so slim and pretty that my heart went out to her. Her breasts were quite small but she had the longest, most provoking nipples that I have ever seen.'

'Like nipples, like clitty,' I murmured.

'Indeed, yes,' said Gwendolen. 'John's gipsy tongue almost at once had all three protuberances flushed and charged. The contrast between them and her slim, white body was tantalising in the extreme. When she drew in her breath, all her ribs stood out and her hipbones framed the plumpness of her curly haired mound. They fucked standing up, very quietly and very deliberately. We were all spell-bound and I realised that the human body can indeed be a work of art in itself. Bess was standing there open-mouthed, quite forgetting the bowl of stew which was growing cold in her hands. Only when Miss Brightwell came with a little choking cry, did she remember where she was. I think we were all in something of a trance. John the Gipsy, who had been very controlled in his fucking, held on to her as she quivered and shook with her coming. He stayed in her until she had ground to a halt, supporting her until she had regained her composure.'

'One of nature's Gentlemen,' I said.

'Far more of a gentleman than some others much better born that I have entertained,' agreed Gwendolen. 'He was Consideration personified.'

'I have been secretly reading the works of Mr Engels and Mr Marx,' I said. 'And I have developed a great sympathy for the lot of the working classes.'

'And there was a lot to this member of the working classes,'

Gwendolen responded quickly. 'I may not understand the economic sciences, but I am full of admiration for the hard Labour he performed that night and the next. Of course we looked after him with care for none of us knew when we would be able to lay hands on another such rod, pole or perch.'

I smiled at her reference to our mathematics lessons.

'Or Rod, Staff and Comforter,' I riposted in what I thought a clever little allusion to Mr Paddlebottom's scripture classes.

Gwendolen looked puzzled for a moment and furrowed her dainty brow. I squeezed her hand affectionately with my thighs.

'But do go on,' I said.

'There is not much more to tell,' she said. 'Miss Brightwell returned to her room with a warning not to make any noise. "Since," as she said, "I know that your evening is not yet ended. You have my assurance both that John will be able to stand up to further exertions in a short while and that I will report nothing of what I have seen, and felt, this evening."'

She then made a firm agreement with John the Gipsy for her to come down to his encampment one night after he had been returned and commence to put together a portfolio of drawings of Romany life.

After she had withdrawn the fucking recommenced. Thomasina, who had been waiting patiently for her turn, was next. Then Meg. Melissa and I had to console ourselves, each with the other, while the rest moaned and gasped in sequence upon the floor. We had to place a firm hand over Deirdre's mouth at one juncture for it was clear that she was about to scream out in her delight. But the danger was averted and we composed ourselves, knowing that we were the first to be served the next night when our efforts were resumed.'

'So he lasted the course?' I asked.

'Towards the end of the third night he became a bit weak at the knees,' said Gwendolen. 'But as I now realise, he held out most manfully to the very end.'

So if today is the anniversary of your first three fucks, tomorrow...'

'Is the anniversary of my fourth and fifth,' Gwendolen agreed. 'And the very last, just before we had to take him back to his caravan, was most extraordinary. I actually slid down the bannisters on to his eager prick.'

'No splinters in the bum?' I asked.

'We had smeared the surface carefully with a soothing cream. It was the smoothest of descents and the easiest of entrances. I realised then that fucking would be my chief delight for the future.'

At that moment we heard the sound of another passenger clambering up to the top deck of the omnibus. Of course, being two well brought-up young ladies, we did not do anything so immodest as to turn to look at the new arrival. Indeed we both hoped that he – for it was a he as I could see from the corner of my eye – would move up to the front so that our happy intimacy, and our conversation, could not be intruded upon and we could continue to exchange information. However it was not be to be.

'Gwendolen!' exclaimed the newcomer. 'What a splendid surprise.'

Gwendolen looked round.

'George!' she answered. I too looked round at this juncture. Standing before us was a young man who I had never seen before in my life. I barely had time to register that he was dressed as though for a funeral, when he half raised his hat in greeting and extended a hand.

Here a problem arose. Gwendolin instinctively sought to half rise in response and to hold out *her* hand. Unfortunately her right hand was still beneath the travelling rug, burrowed into my underclothing and caressing my nicely damp pussey. Gwendolin though barely hesitated. Deftly she withdrew her hand from my private pleasure place and held it out to the stranger who claimed acquaintance. He took it between his own and bent to kiss it, whilst steadying himself against the end of the seat in front in order to preserve his balance since the omnibus was once more swaying and jolting through the ever heavier traffic, the driver flicking his whip and muttering uncomplimentary things about the competing drivers and cabbies. (Indeed I distinctly heard him call in question the parentage of one tradesman's van driver.)

The young gentleman warmly placed his lips upon the backs

of her fingers, lingered for a moment and then looked her steadily in the eyes, at the same time allowing himself a small smile.

'No gloves,' he said. 'And on such a cool afternoon.' Gwendolen looked a little embarrassed at his remark, particularly when he lowered his lips to her hand once more and rather boldly licked her fingertips.

'But one hardly needs gloves when one has a warm muff to hand,' he continued with a wicked little chuckle.

Then, before I had had the time to consider how I should react to his sudden turn of affairs, Gwendolen hurried to make an introduction that set my mind quite at rest concerning the propriety of the conversation.

'Cecily, this is my dear friend Mr George Russell-Lupin. Not only is he a very close friend whom I have known now for many, many months, but he has a truly gallant prick which is most prompt to stand up for any lady, no matter what the situation.

'One likes to be of service . . . ,' he responded.

'George, this is my dear, dear former schoolfriend Cecily, with whom I am resuming acquaintance after a most painful separation of two whole years. We were indeed bosom companions and I very much hope that we shall shortly be able to resume that relationship. However this is not of course a sufficiently private place for that purpose.'

Mr Russell-Lupin, or George as I had already determined to call him for I have long been opposed to over-formality in social intercourse, looked at me with a wicked gleam in his eye, then darted out his tongue to lightly touch Gwendolen's fingers again.

'Cecily,' he said, 'I look forward to holding your hand in greeting. But in the meantime, here is an unusual and enticing state of affairs. Although I have not yet touched you, I have had the priviledge of tasting you. The sensation is wholly delightful.'

'This, Sir, is a situation that I have never seen dealt with in the books of etiquette and I am somewhat covered with embarrassment.'

'Just as dear Gwendolen's hand is somewhat covered with your cum,' he answered. 'You must have both been deep in conversation when I intruded upon your privacy. Should I now withdraw and seat myself towards the front of the bus so that you can resume your intercourse.'

'No,' said Gwendolen. 'Don't be silly. We had just come to a natural pause in our conversation. Cecily also had just come, but that's by-the-by. It was all my doing for I had been recounting the events of a most important day in my life.'

'Of course,' he responded. 'It is your anniversary. Your first fuck!'

'Cecily', said Gwendolen, 'I must explain that George has already heard the story of my first fuck.'

'And her second? And her third . . ?' I murmured.

'Cecily,' said Gwendolen, 'you will gather that George is already *au fait* with every last detail of that memorable day. Indeed he was present on the first anniversary.

Not to put too fine a point on it, George was thoroughly embedded in me when I first told him the story. In spite of showing great self restraint during the account, his final reaction was the same as yours.'

'I came,' said George, 'But only after one of the longest and finest fucks of my life.'

'When George was young,' said Gwendolen, 'he was well tutored in certain Eastern arts of Love by his Nanny.'

'His Nanny!' I exclaimed.

'The family were out East. The Nanny was passed on to them by a family who were returning to England. She had the highest references. She also turned out to have spent the formative years of her life in a harem and had there learnt many of the exotic practices that are such an exciting part of Eastern tradition and culture.'

'By the time I was fourteen,' George explained, 'I could, with the aid of some strenuous mental exercises, remain erect and fully inserted for ten or more minutes. By the time I was sixteen, I had got it up to twenty minutes.'

'Got it up *for* twenty minutes, surely?' I responded. 'Is it not unusual to still have a nanny when one is sixteen, even in India.'

'Indeed, yes,' he asnwered. 'But my parents were more than happy that their, may I say it, occasionally unruly son, had been so well taken in hand. When not engaged in his Regimental duties, my father was altogether taken up in his polo and my mother was quite taken up in an illicit liason with the Adjutant.'

'Which came to an abrupt end,' interjected Gwendolen, 'when she was accidently revealed astride the Adjutant, stark naked except that she was wearing his boots, his Sam Brown belt and flourishing his riding crop.'

'As you can see,' went on George, 'my parents led a full life and were more than satisfied when it became clear that I was growing up to healthy manhood with little effort on their part.'

'So the nanny stayed,' I said.

'Indeed, yes,' he answered. 'And I quickly realised that the reason her previous employers had retained her services long past the time when most nannies have to pass on to another charge, must be connected with her very special abilities in the training of British manhood in the arts of the Orient.'

'And British womanhood, I gather,' said Gwendolen.

'I have to explain,' said George, 'that after the unfortunate public exposure of her affair with the adjutant, my mother took to her bedroom in shame for several days. Nanny, being of a kind and thoughtful disposition, spent many hours comforting her as she lay in her darkened room. She personally made sure that light meals were delivered to her. She shoo'd all the other servants away – and also my father who had been so upset when word reached him of the scandal that he fell off his polo pony and was accidentally struck on the head by the mallet of an over-enthusiastic brother officer. Mother, in the meantime, aided by the skilled ministrations of Nanny, quickly discovered a new interest in life. So enthusiastic did she become in the erotic arts of the East that she quite soon set off in disguise, with only Nanny to accompany her, on a tour of some of the more explicit Indian temple sculptures.

'You may have seen,' said Gwendolen, 'a privately printed monograph of restricted circulation entitled *An Introduction to the Eastern Art of Fucking*, by a Lady Much Experienced in Those Parts. There was a somewhat dog-eared copy in circulation in the Senior Dorm in your last year.'

'That was George's mother!' I exclaimed. 'I have long wished to meet the author, if only to encourage her to publish a sequel.'

'So there are two members of George's family who have much to thank his nanny for,' said Gwendolen.

'And may I enquire if her services extended as far as your father?' I asked.

'Alas, No,' said George. 'Remaining true to what he considered the finest traditions of the British Empire, he continued to be what is vulgarly called a 'two-minute man' and was quite soon afterwards invalided out of the army with a nasty dose of something he picked up in an Officers Only establishment in Calcutta. He retired to Ireland to breed horses and was sadly trampled to death by a mount of a nervous disposition while thrashing about in the straw of a horse box with a young girl from the village.'

'How terrible,' I said. 'Was the girl all right?'

'Bruised only,' said George. 'The family of course took pity on her – she could hardly remain in the village – and brought her over to London where she is still in service in my aunt's establishment. She recovered fully from her injuries and quickly resumed a most energetic life of fucking. I have in fact been honoured in turn to introduce her to those Eastern practices that I had learned at the hands of my nanny.'

'What a complicated family history you have,' I said. 'I am sure I should never be able to remember quite who did what and with whom.'

'Do not worry,' said Gwendolen. 'You are not about to be examined on the subject.' She must have seen the quick look of disappointment that passed across my face. 'At least not in the schoolroom sense of the word,' she went on hurriedly. 'I am sure a physical examination in the subject could be arranged.'

'An oral one too?' I asked, with a little shiver of daring.

'It would be my pleasure,' said George.

'It would be *all* our pleasures,' said Gwendolen firmly. 'George,' she went on, 'One thing I must tell you – I hope I do not embarrass you, Cecily dear – is that Cecily has a pair of the biggest, most delicious titties of anyone I know. I am almost beside myself in my desire to see them once more, and to feel them responding to my touch.'

'Oh, and your tongue too, Gwendolen dear,' I burst out. 'To feel myself being stroked and sucked into ecstasy. And then to rub them all over your own lovely titties while our fingers begin to explore each other's most secret parts. But I must not continue with these imaginings. I am becoming all wet with the thought of such an encounter.'

'We must indeed all sit quietly,' said George. 'Already I feel a bulging reminder that this is a public place and proper public behaviour is called for.' With this he sat down in the seat in front of us and began to adjust his tie and cuffs.

'But later we will all fuck,' said Gwendolen, quietly.

We began to make small talk as the top deck filled up. George asked where we were going. I explained about the Private Viewing of my cousin Algernon's paintings. George, who had been going to visit his tailor somewhere off St James', decided that instead he would accompany us if that was acceptable to the two of us. We of course quickly agreed and apart from the promising warmth of Gwendolen's body as we sat squeezed together in our seat, the rest of the journey passed without incident.

The gallery was but a short walk from the omnibus route, in one of that maze of little streets behind Bond Street. *En route* I referred glancingly to the fact that George was dressed as though on the way to a funeral. In fact it turned out that he was on the way back from a short memorial service.

'Someone close to you?' I asked.

'A family friend,' he answered. 'She had been my great aunt's companion for some years. A paragon of Good Works, always prattling on about the Deserving Poor and Visiting the Sick. Most days she went out with a servant and a bowl of nourishing soup – a rather thin and watery brew. Personally I can think of nothing worse when ill than being forcibly visited by Miss Windermere and having a quantity of undrinkable soup thrust upon me. I believe that many in the parish felt that way. But whenever anyone who came within her definition of Deserving took to their bed, you can be sure that within hours there would be a loud knock on the door and in would traipse Miss Windermere, a bunch of religious tracts in her hand and the servant struggling behind with the gruel.

There was no avoiding your fate. Miss Windermere had the most remarkable Intelligence system. The first whisper of sickness and she would swing into action. She was without doubt the most feared woman for miles around.'

'How did she die?' I asked.

'Blown up,' George answered.

'Blown up?' I exclaimed. 'Surely an unusual fate for a spinster of advanced years.'

'The outrage was quite accidental. It seems that the latest of her bed-bound victims was an elderly lady who had worked as a governess in St Petersburg many years ago and still had friends in Russia. It was the nephew of one of these friends who was inadvertently responsible for Miss Windermere's demise. An anarchist student from Minsk, he had entered this country in order to effect the assassination of some visiting Russian General who was also a relative of the Tsar.

Whilst staying with the former governess, he had been engaged in the construction of two bombs which he intended to lob at the General while he was riding in the Park. The explosives were cunningly hidden in the chamber pot that was under the governess's bed. When Miss Windermere was standing over her, asking after her spiritual welfare, she knocked over a candle that was beside the bed – the room being darkened in order to sooth the governess's headache.

The candle, in falling, set fire to a rug by the bed. In a trice this had in turn ignited the fuse and the chamber pot exploded. Miss Windermere was cut down by a hail of china splinters.

The governess however was luckier. Her bed took the main force of the explosion and collapsed on the burning remnants, largely extinguishing them. The governess, a woman of initiative and good in an emergency, quickly put out the still smoldering rug by peeing on it. She was unscathed and the servant only slightly hurt, chiefly by the scalding hot soup which was flung all over her, but Miss Windermere was already beyond the help of all but the clergy.'

'What happened to the anarchist?' I asked.

'He fled to London and I understand that Scotland Yard are searching for him all over the East End.'

'Why the East End?' I queried.

'That is where all good anarchists gather. They sit in cafés and discuss politics in loud and quarrelsome voices. The police know that, so that is where they will be looking for him.'

'So if he is a wise anarchist, he will be staying in a completely different part of London?'

'If he has any sense, yes,' he answered.

'And the memorial service?'

'A very tedious affair. After a lifetime of Good Works it was inevitable that her passing would be attended by representatives of every Charity, Mission to the Heathen and Society for Promoting This and That in the country. Pew upon pew of worthy citizens, pious expressions and a long sermon in which the Canon expressed his belief that Miss Windermere is already busy in Heaven, no doubt pursuing off-colour Angels, Saints and Martyrs with bowls of soup. I think we can expect a mass emigration from Heaven in the near future.'

'Goodness,' I said. 'What a sad tale. I do hope the anarchist is not lurking somewhere in the vicinity.'

'I did see a most furtive little man, wearing a long black cloak on the omnibus,' interposed Gwendolen at this juncture. 'He was carrying a large Gladstone bag.'

'Did you see where he alighted?' asked George.

'Oh dear! I do believe that it was at the same place that we disembarked,' said Gwendolen. 'He must be following us.'

'Unless any of us has connections with the Russian Royal Family we are unlikely to be the target of his dark plot,' said George.

'I did once have a night of passion with a Hungarian Count,' volunteered Gwendolen. 'Well, two.'

'Two nights or two Hungarian Counts,' I asked.

'Two Hungarians,' said Gwendolen. 'The Count and his Countess.'

'How advanced of you,' I said. 'And how exciting.'

'It was more strange than exciting,' replied Gwendolen. 'The Count occupied his time almost entirely by sniffing my more intimate garments and wrapping them round his body. While he then spent himself rolling around on the floor, the Countess – who had commenced by disrobing me with great care – then proceeded to chastise me with her stick, before engaging me in a positive orgy of Sapphic delights.'

'Gracious me,' I responded.

'Cecily, I learned that night that there is much that an older woman can teach a young and innocent girl.'

'Innocent. Oh Gwendolen! that is not an epithet with which I would reproach you. I, of all people know the very day on which you lost your Innocence.'

'You debauched me,' said Gwendolen.

'That is not a pretty word,' I replied crossly.

'Yours were the first hands that were ever laid on my virginal body. But, dear Cecily, I am only teasing. It was the most delicious initiation into the mysteries of love. To this day I can remember the delicate play of your fingers on my pussey. You were most gentle – and most thorough.'

At this turn of the conversation, I once more felt a familiar warmth spreading through my body. I snuggled up against Gwendolen as we walked and then reached out to draw George into our comfortable companionship.

'Is it true what Gwendolen says about your titties?' he asked, his arm linked in mine.

'Modesty forbids me to sing my own praises,' I replied. 'But they are I consider two of my finest features.'

'I look forward to feasting my eyes on them,' he continued.

'Cecily will be better pleased if you feast more than your eyes on them,' said Gwendolen. 'I have always found that Cecily most appreciates some nibbling. Not to mention a sharp nip or two when she is well advanced in her enjoyment.'

'Please stop it,' I implored them. 'Such talk is causing me positively to swell with anticipation. My nipples are rubbing most painfully against my bodice.'

'I also am swelling with anticipation,' answered George. 'We must put off all such thoughts and deeds for the near future. Where is the gallery?'

'Just around the next corner,' I said. 'I hope this will not be too stuffy an occasion. But you should enjoy my cousin's paintings. They are held in some quarters to be rather advanced.'

With that, we arrived and when he had handed over our coats and Gwendolen's tartan travelling rug, we passed into an already crowded salon. But here I must explain a little about my Cousin Algernon.

Cousin Algernon had the unusual claim to fame of having been found as a baby in a handbag in the Left Luggage Office on Brighton Station. After such a Bohemian start to life, it was suppose inevitable that he became an artist when he grew up.

Of course like all proper artists, he led a properly scandalous life, chiefly with his model Babette, a voluptuous creature who came originally from Northamptonshire and who cooked well.

Actually the fact that she came from Northamptonshire – Kettering to be precise – was not generally known. Nor was the fact that her real name was Edith. Instead like all proper artists models, it was understood that she was a *Parisienne* and had been either a seamstress or a *midinette* before a struggling and penniless artist had discovered her and transferred her to his *atelier* to grace both canvas and bed. Babette was, as I have suggested, a big woman. In fact she was huge. Cousin Algernon, himself a big man and an altogether larger-than-life character with a commendable appetite for all the good things in life, delighted in painting Babette.

Most frequently he depicted her in Classic guise. Babette, wearing little except some carefully placed, vaguely Grecian draperies or wisps of white muslin, displayed herself in a variety of mythic poses. Here she was taking part in the *Bath of Psyche*. Here she was *Diana Surprised by Actaeon*. Most frequently she was a nymph or some such, being ravished by Zeus, or on occasion by what seemed like the entire Pantheon of Greek Gods, in any number of disguises: a Swan, a Bull, a Stallion – and in one memorable instance what appeared to be a Parrot, although Cousin Algernon insisted that it was an Eagle. He did later also admit that it was one of his less successful works.

Babette was also the central figure in a completely different series of paintings. Working in what he described as his French Interior Realist mode, Cousin Algernon showed her, this time without any trace of clothing whatsoever, as a washerwoman or scrubbing floors, laying a fire or at some other domestic task.

Whether it is the habit of French servants to perform their duties stark naked I do not know, but the paintings clearly made a considerable impression in London. In truth these vigorous oils of big Babette, for instance, leaning over a tub ful of suds, her huge forearms and magnificent bosom highlighted by the painter's art, were not unpleasing, if occasionally verging on the laughable. The views of Babette scrubbing were for the most part seen from behind. The great spheres of her buttocks rose like a double moon to fill the scene. Every roll of fat was lovingly rendered and she seemed to glow with what I gather is called 'rude health.'

His latest masterpiece, *Babette at the Mangle* had quite a crowd of admirers around it. Cousin Algernon had managed to give the impression of a woman panting and heaving with her exertions, her breasts swaying and shaking as she turned the mangle while her skin glowed and there was the sheen of perspiration on her body.

I noticed that the preponderance of the people at the viewing were men, and men of a middle aged and generally prosperous men. I was told by an elderly man, who claimed some knowledge of things artistic, that Cousin Algernon had successfully created a small fashion among the *cognoscenti* for such scenes of domestic undress. A number of fellow artists, all living and working nearby in north London, had followed his lead. Known in the art world as the Crouch End School, they had a growing and enthusiastic band of collectors quite clamouring of their works.

Of course, my informant confided in me, many of the academic critics poured scorn on the Crouch End School. Mr Ruskin had described Cousin Algernon's work as 'A battery of buttocks, thrust into the Public's face' while the Academy steadfastly refused to hang his pictures. Nonetheless, as someone who dabbled in dealing, he could vouch for the fact that a surprising number of the more flamboyant *Views of Babette*, as he called them, could be seen discreetly displayed in many of the most reputable gentlemen's clubs.

'Indeed,' said my aesthetic informant, 'if one could but see through the grey facades of Pall Mall, I fancy we would be regaled with the mouth-watering sight of Babette's mountainous buttocks flaunted cheek to cheek, so to say, along almost the full length of the street.'

Be that as it may, many of the priviledged viewers at the gallery, as they gazed intently at every detail of Babette's anatomy, were showing those powers of concentration and stamina, that must have accounted for their undoubted success in business and public affairs. I noticed also that for many there was an improving moral lesson to be gained from a close perusal of the paintings.

'Ah! The dignity of Honest Toil' announced one gentleman

as he raised his *pince-nez* to his eyes, the better to scrutinise the spread of Honest Toil's thighs.

'Application and Dedication in all Endeavours, Domestic as well as Professional', agreed another.

'An Example to the Labouring Classes,' said a third, who later confided in me that an earlier work by Cousin Algernon hung in his study. '*Babette Preparing Vegetables*, it is called. So exemplary do I consider his work that on occasion I call in my housekeeper or cook after dinner so that they also can gaze upon it in my company and reflect on its moral worth.'

One senior clerical gentleman, suffering what I was later given to understand was hay fever, had to be led away, his eyes watering and his chest heaving after standing as if transfixed in front of *The Rape of the Sabine Women* in which Babette appeared in no less than twenty seven poses.

'Such flesh tones,' he had started muttering, 'And such flesh! And so much of it!' Then, as he began to stammer and had to reach out for some support, I, recognising him as a Man of the Cloth – he was in fact the Rural Dean of N——d assumed that he was in the throes of some transcendental experience. Gwendolen, who has a sharp eye for such things, claimed rather that he had become dangerously over-excited by the proximity of no less than twenty seven naked Babettes on one canvas and that he had in fact come in his trousers.

'Look on my Mighty Works and Despair' proclaimed a tall, cadaverous man as he traced out the outline of Babette's great pendulous breasts with his walking stick. 'How bounteous is Nature. See where the twin globes of her bosom seem to loom like planets in the celestial firmament of her flesh. Truly a sight to make one humble before one's Creator. All things' he went on, 'Wide and Wonderful, all Creatures great and tall . . .'

I was afterwards informed that the tall gentleman was a hymn writer of some distinction and regularly attended such showings as this. He claimed to be able to detect the Hand of the Lord in the most unlikely places.

After a while most of the people began to drift off and quite soon, apart from the three of us, there was only a small knot of some half a dozen or so gentlemen. Cousin Algernon suggested that we all withdraw to a smaller room that opened off one end of the gallery. He then came over to have a word with us, announcing that Babette herself was about to make an appearance.

'In the flesh?' I asked.

'Not immediately,' he answered, with a quick smile. 'But if you would like to stay on with your friends, I am sure you could be accommodated.'

'Some entertainment is afoot?' asked Gwendolen.

'In a matter of speaking,' he answered. 'Several of the gentlemen gathered here belong to a private club. They dabble in oils in a strictly amateur way. Since they are also collectors and valuable customers, I have arranged that they be given the opportunity to sketch Babette from Life.'

'What an enticing idea,' said Gwendolen. 'But will we not be something of an embarrassment?'

'I suggest that you all act as my assistants. You can help with the arrangement of certain properties, take Babette's robe from her when the moment comes to reveal all. That sort of thing.'

'This sounds great fun,' said Gwendolen. 'But I promise we will behave ourselves and do nothing to prejudice your commercial interests.'

We were ushered through to the smaller room. Various items of a domestic nature were heaped in one corner. They included scrubbing brushes, a mop, a portable washtub, a couple of flat irons and a neatly folded pile of linen. It was obvious that Babette would be able to display herself in any number of household chores.

'What's that?' asked George, indicating a stout wooden pole with a cross piece at one end and a round piece at the other with five short legs.

'A poss stick,' said Cousin Algernon. 'It is used to stir up the washing in a tub when it is soaking in the hot water.'

'I am afraid that George, like so many men, has never paid proper attention to the domestic duties that have to be performed in any household,' said Gwendolen.

'I used to venture into the servants area at home when I was much younger,' said George, 'But I was firmly excluded after my mother found me helping one of the maids to adjust her clothing. There was also the small matter that she was holding my youthful prick in her hands and licking the tip in a most attentive fashion.'

'I assume from that that you have led an active life,' said Cousin Algernon. 'A man after my own heart. But for the present, could you give me a hand in setting out a nice derangement of objects. Our amateur painters can then make the decision as to which pose they would wish Babette to adopt.'

At this moment Babette herself swept into the room. Truly a magnificent creature, she was wearing a regal purple robe which entirely swathed the bountiful promise of her body but yet which hinted at the well-fleshed splendours it concealed. We were quickly introduced and she embraced us all warmly but briefly.

'Cecily, I have heard all about you from Algernon,' she said. 'Do either of your friends have any knowledge of the world of the artist?'

'I have a distant cousin who is employed as a designer of pottery at Messrs Doulton's establishment,' said Gwendolen.

'But she does not have to appear in a state of undress?' asked Babette.

'Not at her place of work,' answered Gwendolen, 'Although on more private occasions she is frequently quite eager to reveal herself in a state of nature.'

'Perhaps I might be introduced to this cousin,' I interjected. 'She has the sound of a person of sympathetic disposition.'

'You will have much in common,' said Gwendolen. 'Fucking and being fucked is her chief delight. What a quartet we will make.'

'Quartet?' I queried.

'She has a sister of similar tastes. Their mother is also a woman with refreshingly unconventional ideas. They now also have staying with them Rosalind Murphy. You may remember her. She was a year behind us at school.'

'Rosie!' I exclaimed. 'Rosie with the rosy bottom. What fun it will be to meet her again.'

'Enough of this chatter,' said Cousin Algernon. 'Our would-be painters will be making their entry shortly.'

With this we fell to sorting out the pile of domestic articles. George and Cousin Algernon pulled the mangle into place and a woman appeared with pails of warm water with which the washtub was filled. In a trice the stage had been set for

Babette's performance.

Our amateur artists were led in. For a moment they fell silent in awe and anticipation at the sight of Babette. She, as yet fully clothed, moved among them, exchanging greetings as they were introduced. Ranging from the middle-aged to the elderly, one and all appeared to be respectable and sober representatives of the professional and upper commercial classes. Two, I vaguely recognised as men of some importance in Public Affairs. Two others were of military bearing and a third, of Gallic appearance, had the ribbon of the *Légion d'Honneur* in his lapel.

'Gentlemen, I am honoured to welcome you to our Private Master Class in painting from Life,' said Cousin Algernon. Let us now prepare ourselves.' Easels, paints, palettes and canvases were produced. There was a intent bustle of activity. Babette advanced on them with an armful of smocks.

'To avoid any splashes,' she said. 'Painting is an enjoyable but messy exercise.'

She passed among them, removing coats, slipping the smocks over them, buttoning them or tieing them briskly at the back. Many of the gentlemen were clearly quite excited at the touch of her hands. One who in turn attempted to place his hand on her splendid rump, had it firmly removed but all was done with a half-smile on her face and a twinkle in her eye so that not only was no offence caused, but a teasing air of promise caused the gentleman to become somewhat purple with pleasure anticipated.

'Gentlemen,' said Cousin Algernon, 'Madame Babette will now take up the first pose of the evening. However, the choice is yours. Would you have her at the tub, at the mangle, or possibly on all fours in her imposing imitation of a servant engaged in scrubbing?'

A veritable babble of competing voices was raised.

'The mangle,' cried one.

'No, no, for myself, I would prefer to see her leaning over the wash,' said another.

Two others were adamant that they could only do justice to their subject if she was crouched down. Yet one was all for her presenting her bottom to the class whilst the other, somewhat confused about domestic positions, I considered, wished to see her on her back.

'As though she has had a slight mishap on a slippery floor,' he explained somewhat unconvincingly.

Cousin Algernon let the argument rage for some minutes until it quickly became apparent that no one faction was in the ascendancy.

'Gentlemen,' he said, raising his voice to cut through the uproar. 'Since I can see that agreement is not be to easily reached, I have an alternative idea.' With that he clicked his fingers and a small but sturdy kitchen table was conjured up, along with a rolling pin and a large quantity of dough.

'May I present *Madame Babette Kneading Dough*!'

With the flourish of an experienced actress, Babette marched across to the table and in one flamboyant motion, shed her purple gown.

A gasp of admiration rose up from the assembled gentlemen artists, for underneath she was utterly and hugely naked. With an exquisite sense of timing, she leant over the table and seized the soft, pliant mound of dough. As she forced her hands into it, squeezing it back and forth, then shaping it and thumping it flat again, her breasts swung between her arms, her belly rubbed against the table and her tremendous buttocks jiggled up and down with the effort of her labours.

Her audience stared at her open mouthed, hardly moving, so transfixed were they by this vast vision of nakedness. From the back of the assembly there came a stifled groan.

Several were visibly shaking with suppressed artistic inspiration.

Then first one and then a second, pulling themselves together, took up their brushes and squeezed paint on to their palettes. Next there was a scraping of easels and stools as a number of them began to move into their preferred positions. I noticed that he who had been loudly in favour of the kneeling-seen-from-behind pose rapidly moved into the appropriate line-of-sight. I also noticed that he stationed himself within no more than an arms length of the twin subjects of his delight as they rose and fell in their majestic rhythm.

'Alas, I grow increasingly short-sighted,' he said hurriedly in order to justify his close proximity to Babette's bottom.

'A more convincing excuse if only he were wearing an eye

glass or spectacles,' whispered Gwendolen, nudging me gently. The three of us were now standing quietly against the wall as this amazing *tableau vivant* unfolded itself before our fascinated eyes.

Now the gentlemen fell to their painting with a quiet but splashy intensity. Brushes charged with full loads of paint were slapped and smeared on canvases. By the sweeping motions of their paint strokes I could understand that the great curves of Babette's body were being energetically, if none too skilfully, transferred to canvas. Cousin Algernon, in his role of teacher, moved from one to another, advising and encouraging. Here he deftly showed one how to mix a convincing flesh tone. There he demonstrated how to achieve the fullness of texture demanded by the subject.

Meanwhile Babette plunged and swung and thrust and kneaded. At one point the self-declared short-sighted gentleman crouched down on the floor peering intently up between her massive thighs.

'So difficult to catch the play of light and shade low down,' he muttered, with even less conviction this time.

'Ah, yes, a close scrutiny of his subject is a sign of a true artist,' replied Cousin Algernon. 'But you would not wish to impede the view of your fellow artists I believe.'

A little reluctantly, the myopic enthusiast withdrew, understanding that a polite reprimand had been given. Then Babette paused in her labours.

'Please, gentleman. A moment's rest for Madame Babette,' said Cousin Algernon.

A subdued ripple of disappointment ran round the room but this was instantly replaced by a collective sigh of pleasure as Babette stood upright and then slowly stretched herself. All eyes were on her as she displayed the full splendour of her body. Paint dribbled unattended from wavering brushes. Several of the gentlemen sat down with shudders of emotion, some almost bent double as if in pain. Trousers were hastily adjusted and first one and then another hurriedly left the room in order to answer an urgent call of nature.

Babette turned to our direction, her lush pussey hair standing out proudly against her flesh, and winked very slightly at us. I smiled back but swiftly resumed my most demure countenance. George stepped forward and handed her her robe which she put on with an easy but most provoking twitch of her shoulders.

'A short break for refreshment before we resume our artistic endeavours?' suggested Cousin Algernon as a decanter and glasses made their appearance.

After ten minutes or so, Cousin Algernon called upon his class to resume their places.

'Another three quarters of a hour will be enough,' he said to us quietly. 'I find that my more mature students can only stand a couple of hours. Such is the intensity of the artistic experience that for the most part they will be quite drained and more than ready to adjourn quietly to their clubs or their homes.'

So the second half of the art lesson passed. Babette, clearly a woman of considerable stamina, ploughed her swaying, quivering way through a second mountain of dough. As she sprinkled flour on hands and board to prevent the mixture sticking, smears of flour and dough transferred themselves to her face, her forearms and even to the Himalayan mounds of her bosom.

As first a lump of dough clung from one dark plum-like nipple and then as a sifting of flour settled on her luxuriant bush, so the brush work of the amateur artists became more and more wild and erratic. As though in sympathetic response, flecks and gobbets of pigment landed on smocks and faces. Whilst some were working themselves up to a positive frenzy of strokes and dabs, so others began to grow slack and exhausted. Eyes began to glaze over and brushes wilted in trembling hands. Soon several members were standing open-mouthed, sucking air into their labouring lungs like athletes at the end of a long foot race.

Babette herself began to move slower and slower, though still driving and pummeling the dough. Beads of perspiration stood out on her forehead and trickled down her heaving flanks. As she breathed ever more deeply her chest expanded and contracted and her enormous breasts undulated, rising and falling in a surging tide of flesh. Her well-planted legs flexed and trembled while her short-sighted posterior attendant, knees buckling, lowered himself on to his stool and sat there gasping for air like a landed trout.

'Time, gentlemen, please,' said Cousin Algernon. 'I feel we have accomplished enough for one evening.'

There was a half-hearted groan of disappointment but fatigue had indeed caught up with the best part of them.

'I hope though that you will all come again,' he continued. 'I suggest we reconvene in two weeks time at the same hour. I propose to join you in attempting to do justice to *Babette Kneading Dough*. If I am satisfied with my own work, I might, when it is completed, put it up for auction, restricting the bidding to those here present.'

This scheme was enthusiastically welcomed. The class began to filter out to the cloakroom in order to wash and generally make themselves presentable enough to face the outside world. Babette clutched her robe round her once more. She favoured the assembly with a sympathetic but slightly roguish smile as she stalked out to her dressing room. A few last lingering glances were directed at the generous hemispheres of her buttocks as they disappeared, like a double eclipse, behind the enveloping draperies of the curtain. Then the *amateurs de la peinture* bid their goodbyes and ambled out into the early evening air.

'You must all stay while everything is tidied away,' said Cousin Algernon. 'Babette will be rejoining us in a few minutes, as soon as she is refreshed and clothed once more. I have a couple of bottles of claret and some whisky also. We must all take a little wine in order to celebrate what I believe to have been a highly successful event.'

We fell to drinking and light conversation. Presently Babette reappeared. A glass or two restored her to full vigour and animation. We plied her with questions about the rigours of life as an artist's model.

'It can indeed be tiring at times,' she said. 'But that is generally the way with work, is it not? Yet I find that there is great satisfaction to be gained from it so long of course as one does not mind appearing unclothed before members of the opposite sex. For my part, I must confess that I have always had a certain yearning to appear upon the stage, in the theatrical limelight.'

'Do not artist's models usually pose motionless,' I asked. 'I know that, clothed or unclothed, I should find it impossible to keep still in one position for more than a moment or two. Would one not suffer terribly from aches and cramps?'

'Holding a pose for any length of time is indeed a demanding discipline,' she agreed. 'It is one that can be learned quite easily, but I confess that I do infinitely prefer your Cousin's moving presentations. If I am an actress *manqué*, then Algernon is an actor-manager *manqué* and an accomplished Master of Ceremonies as well.'

'I see that there are attractions to the job,' I answered thoughtfully. Babette looked at me with an appraising gleam in her eye.

'Do not take this amiss, Cecily, but I think that you may well have the makings of a model. I suspect that under that modest but quite charming dress there is concealed a fine display sufficient to hold the attention of the most discerning audience. Might I be allowed to . . .?'

'Oh, no!' I said, as natural modesty vied with a little tingle of excitement, 'No, I don't think I possibly could . . .'

'Madame Babette,' interrupted Gwendolen. 'Although it is two years since I saw Cecily, my memories of her are such that I can indeed confirm you in your beliefs. Cecily unclothed is a sight for the connoisseur's eye. Cecily, we are all friends here. I do implore you to allow us the pleasure of seeing your lovely titties. If Madame Babette will give you some instruction in the art of posing . . .?'

'Why, yes indeed,' she answered. 'I would be delighted to be confirmed in my belief that you have a most fetching figure.'

'Mouth-watering,' said Gwendolen. 'Oh Cecily, how excited I am. Two long years since I last feasted my eyes on your titties. You do not know how often I have dreamed of them and longed to nestle against them once more.'

'Dear, sweet Gwendolen,' I said. 'What a wonderful speech. How can I possibly refuse you.'

'I should perhaps withdraw from the room,' said George. 'I would not like to intrude upon such an intimate scene.'

'I also,' said Cousin Algernon, although with a marked hesitation.

'No,' said Gwendolen. 'Cecily, it would be too cruel to deny them a first sight of your bountiful charms.' She turned to them. 'All Cecily's body is a sight for sore eyes. She has the nicest, best-shaped bottom that I have ever clapped hands on. Her waist is adorable and I swear her pussey is the warmest, most welcoming pussey in the whole wide world.'

'Gwendolen,' I said, 'You go too far.'

'Oh! don't be cross,' she answered. 'I am so looking forward to an unveiling.'

'Well, I said, a little shocked and confused with the daring of such a plan but beginning to tremble with the excitement of it all. 'You will have to help me.'

Gwendolen eagerly hugged me. She buried her face in the nape of my neck and then before I had time to protest any further, I felt her fingers dextrously begin their work at the buttons of my dress. There came the sudden breath of cool air upon my now exposed back. I crossed my arms protectively over my bosom with a quick pang of shyness. Light hands played for an instant along my bare flesh and then my dress was pushed forward over my shoulders.

As I stood there, huddled and uncertain, Babette strode across to me, lifted my chin and looked me straight in the face.

'Not like that, Cecily,' she said. 'Keep your head up. You should be proud, not shamefaced. You are about to present your audience with a show for which they should be privileged and grateful.'

Emboldened, I did as she said. I straightened my back and stretched out my arms. George and Cousin Algernon unbuttoned my cuffs and Gwendolen pushed my dress and chemise off my shoulders so that it descended and gathered in a rustle of silk at my waist. I turned and presented my bared breasts to Gwendolen for her approval. Then, hands on hips, I deliberately twisted slowly round to the rest of my audience.

'Cecily,' said Gwendolen. 'How lovely they are. Surely they are even larger and more delectable than I had remembered. You have grown a little since I last saw you.'

'Such succulent fruit,' said Couson Algernon with an expansive gesture. 'Oh that a man might suck sweet nectar from those ripe nipples.'

I recalled that Cousin Algernon had always tended to the florid in his manner of speech. George meanwhile was quite tongue tied. Babette, her hands on mine, held me at arm's length and gazed with professional approval at me.

'You are a delight, my dear,' she said.

'Such beauties belong to the world,' Cousin Algernon went on. 'You are Aphrodite and Bathsheba and Lakshmi, all rolled into one.'

'Lakshmi,' said Gwendolen, 'is surely the Indian goddess with *eight* breasts. I think you are getting a little carried away.'

'Now turn round again. Slowly, slowly,' said Babette. 'Remember you are on stage.'

Quite overcome by the attention, all shyness was forgotten as I felt my nipples begin to stiffen and my breasts to swell with excitement. Arching my back, my hands clasped behind my neck, I held myself out to my enthralled audience. Then a sudden thought came into my mind. What if Miss Bradshaw were to see me now. Would she not fall in a swoon to the ground? I burst out laughing and, cupping my breasts in my hands, advanced on Gwendolen.

'If I am still pleasing to you, pray show me with your soft mouth that you are as loving and eager for me as I am for you.'

I smiled, the picture of a shocked Miss Bradshaw beside herself at such unladylike behaviour looming large in my mind's eye. Gwendolen, as though she could read my thoughts, smiled back.

'Schooldays,' I said.

'Schooldays,' she replied.

Forgetting my other admirers, I enfolded her in a warm embrace. As she responded, I kissed her. Gwendolen kissed me in return. Our tongues touched and probed. A familiar glow of expectation warmed me and my titties seemed to throb with anticipation. Each nipple rose, engorged and hungry for love. A little mew of pleasure escaped my lips. Breathing more heavily, I pressed her to my half-naked body and whispered to her.

'Gwendolen, I am becoming very damp in another place.'

Then as her hands slyly cupped my breasts, I bit her ear, trying to stifle the gasp of sheer pleasure that welled up inside me.

Gwendolen, with her well-remembered skills with tongue and hands was rapidly bringing me to a first climax of ecstasy. I know that my whole body was flushed and my breasts aching with the need for relief. Gwendolen was now becoming quite rough in her fondling and massaging. My hands on hers, I pressed them hard against me, spreading out her fingers so that they encompassed the twin orbs of my breasts. She squeezed and stroked and then suddenly pinched each erect peak. She steadily increased the pressure until I cried out. Pain and pleasure mingled. My heart was beating as though it would burst.

All at once I was aware of a sudden wetness between my legs and I closed my eyes, lost and drowning in the flood of sensual delight that swept over me. As I clung to her, she disengaged herself and moved her hands down to my waist. She eased me round to face and display myself to my audience.

'Cecily,' she said, 'Truly you are God's gift to all those lucky enough to behold you.'

The others were enraptured. Cousin Algernon and George were both standing, open mouthed. Great bulges betrayed their manhoods, each thrustingly erect and eager to be released from its bondage. Babette was smiling her approval.

'This is such pleasure,' said Cousin Algernon, 'What can we possibly do to repay you for this lovely display?'

'I think I'd like . . .,' I replied faintly, 'I want . . . I want very much to be fucked. Now! Fuck me now, please.'

My legs felt suddenly weak and I half leaned against Gwendolen. She held me tenderly and led me over to a table. Realising what was to come, I eased myself up and on to it, lying back and raising my knees so that my cunney was opened out before my audience. Gwendolen came round to my front and eased her hands under the cheeks of my bum as I raised it towards her sweet face.

She buried herself in my bush before sliding out her tongue and finding my clit. Licking and sucking delicately at it, she brought me in an instant to the very verge of coming. Then she withdrew her lips and tongue and ran one finger down the length of my cunt lips.

'See, the parting of the ways,' she said.

As I groaned, she looked round the room. 'George, Algernon, which one will be the first to volunteer to fill this aching need?'

Fumbling and overcome by the urgency of the summons, they responded. First Cousin Agernon's and then George's prick sprang out into full view. Each was rigid with the desire to thrust its way forward into the dark depths of my cavern. Yet courtesy was not forgotten.

'George, it is for you to make the first entrance,' said Cousin Algernon.

'No, I am an outsider here,' replied George gallantly. 'Surely you would wish to keep it within the family.'

'I insist,' answered Cousin Algernon. 'Besides, I know that dear Babette will take me in hand if needs be.'

Without waiting for further urging, George stepped forward.

'Cecily,' he said, 'I am at your service.'

'Fuck me!' I panted in reply. 'Fuck me! No more talking.'

Then, as I watched, he placed the tip of his immense prick at the gateway of my desire. At the first pressure of that swollen, empurpled head, I opened wide and reached forward to cradle his balls in my hands. I held them for an instant, feeling their heavy weight and sensing the spunk that was already beginning to force its way up his prick. Impatiently I pulled him straight into me so that the entire length of him slid its way up and up to the very hilt. I gripped him fast and then released him.

Needing no further urging, he commenced to thrust backwards and forwards, up and down the gaping depths of my cunt. A fever of excitement ran through my body and I became senseless with the joy of fucking. Vaguely I was aware that I was crying out, quite abandoned to my longed-for fate. Steadily the tempo of our coupling increased. We thrust against each other, all our strengths concentrated in the intensity of our fucking. Hunger fed upon hunger in mounting need.

Suddenly I felt the first long drawn-out shudder of my coming sweep over me. At the same moment he cried out and the first surge of his spunk shot out of his prick, jetting into the innermost recesses of my cunt. His cream flooded into me, mingling with the love juice that flowed in me, soaking the already moist forest of my fanny.

Gripping him with my thighs, I forced him still deeper into me.

'More! More!' I heard myself cry out, desperate to prolong the moment of our fulfillment. Gamely he drove on. I swear that never had such copious quantities of cum deluged me, overflowing and running down into the crevice of my bum so that I began to slip and slide in a veritable pool of our juices.

All good things must come to an end, as my governess had often said to me, and George's Thing had indeed come to my end – and his. One last spasm wracked our bodies and I was borne down by the full weight of his body, as he fell exhausted on me. I felt his distended prick relax inside me and we clung together, panting with our exertions. We lay still for a little while and then I pushed him from me in order to bend forward and lick the last milky drops of his cum from the tip of his now-softening prick. I ran my hands over his balls and rubbed them in the stickiness of his manly forest. I held him lightly by the wrists and drew his hands down to my wet cunney. He rubbed and fondled me until I raised his fingers to my lips. Sucking and swallowing, I licked him clean. Taking his cue, he similarly first kissed and then sucked my fingers.

Then, as I smiled up at him, he was pushed to one side and Gwendolen was crouching between my opened thighs, nuzzling and lapping at my wetness.

'Darling Gwendolen,' I murmured weakly, 'What a wonderful *bonne bouche* after such a feast of fucking.'

Contentment and a delicious fatigue suffused my body.

'Like a cat that has stolen the cream,' I heard Cousin Algernon say.

'Not stolen, but offered,' said Babette, with a little laugh.

'Oh dear!' I said, remembering where I was. 'You must all think me very forward.'

'Backward *and* forward!' said Cousin Algernon. 'Backward and forward. A most energetic and enthralling display. What a subject to be immortalised on canvas.'

'Certainly not,' I said, sitting up in alarm and pulling my dress down over my knees. 'If you dare . . .'

'Only my little joke,' said Cousin Algernon. 'I have long reached the years of discretion.'

'The very idea!'

Smoothing my skirt I stood up, glaring haughtily at him and then realising that my stance was less than impressive, since I was still naked to the waist. Angrily I reached down to drag my dress up over my bosom.

Gwendolen came forward, hugged me and calmed me. Next she deftly covered my embarrassment, slipping my arms back into my sleeves and buttoning me up at the back. For a quick instant she reached inside my dress to fondle and caress my titties before they were finally hidden from view. We kissed gently and she pushed a stray lock of my hair back into place.

'There, there,' she said. 'Cousin Algernon was only teasing. You must remember that he has just had a very teasing time himself.'

As Babette solicitously linked her arm in Cousin Algernon's and whispered something in his ear, Gwendolen released me and went across to poor George who was standing there looking somewhat crestfallen, unmindful of the fact that his trousers were still lying in a crumpled heap on the floor.

'George,' she said, 'You have played your part manfully. Now we must all get dressed and ready to go home but I do hope that you will in turn entertain me with that same part in the very near future.'

As she helped him into his trousers, tucking his now pliable prick back inside and making all secure, she kissed him also with friendly affection. He brightened up, glad that the little spat had passed.

'Thank you, Miss Cecily,' he said gravely. 'That was the most magnificent fuck that I have enjoyed in a very long time.'

'Next time, I hope that we can enjoy it for an even longer time,' I said with a quick smile so that he could see that I was no longer annoyed. 'I was quite beside myself with the need to fuck.'

'So endeth the art lesson,' Cousin Algernon. 'We must finish the decanter.'

So saying he poured out the last of the claret. 'A toast,' he said as we raised our glasses, 'To the Muse of Painting.'

'And of Fucking,' said Gwendolen.

'I don't believe there is one,' said Cousin Algernon.'

'Gwendolen's grasp of the Classics is not so secure as her grasp of anatomy,' I replied.

'Never mind. Let us drink to the missing Muse,' said George.

'To practical matters,' I said. 'I am in need of a bath and a change of clothes. George, would you escort me home in a cab. I had not intended my exposure to the world of the artist to be so prolonged or so complete. I have to dine with my Great Aunt Tabitha tonight where we will doubtless talk of her scheme to establish a Home for Aged Horses.'

Hurriedly I made arrangements to call on Gwendolen the following afternoon. Babette bade us Goodbye.

'I had not intended your first lesson in posing to be so active,' she said, 'but you are cordially welcome to return, possibly to Algernon's studio, in the near future, when we might continue your course of instruction. Gwendolen, I hope that you will accompany your friend, and George also.'

'I believe that I am developing a taste for such things,' I responded.

We kissed all round and George and I went out into the evening.

THE END

Introduction to Part Three

Since the first publication of extracts from the *Oyster*, there has been a certain amount of interest as to the real identity of 'Sir Andrew Scott', for unlike Doctor Parsifal, 'Scott' hides behind a pseudonym. In her Introduction to *The Oyster 1* (New English Library, 1985), Antoinette Hillman-Strauss speculated that the writer of these memoirs was one of the writers eking out a living on one of the burgeoning group of popular magazines that catered for the newly literate mass-market. Further research by Farquhar Platting and Huish Hampton brought in the names of Gerald Burdett and Oswald Holland, authors of the spectacularly rude Victorian underground novel, *The Adventures of a Ram*, as being possibly responsible for this witty, light-hearted romp.

But it now seems that 'Sir Andrew Scott' was none other than our old friend Sir Lionel Trapes (1826-1908) who appears both in *Oyster* and in other similar magazines. Trapes was a high-ranking Treasury official and a wealthy man in his own right, having inherited close on a quarter of a million pounds from his father, the third baronet in the line.

Sir Lionel was a member of the fashionable South Hampstead set amongst whose members were H Spencer Ashbee ('Pisanus Fraxi') and the notorious Doctor Jonathan Arkley whose own extraordinary story will hopefully one day be written. Both these gentlemen were indefatigable collectors of erotica and Doctor Arkley, a fashionable medical man in Harley Street just over one hundred years ago, was known to have organised orgies for the very highest in the land. So limited – and exclusive – was the circulation of the *Oyster* that the use of real names became something of an indulgence, a curious private joke.

It is interesting to compare Sir Lionel's deft writing with his staid little book on the Kentish water colourist Lawrence Judd-Hughes which he published privately in 1896. Judd-Hughes name of course, is mentioned briefly in the present volume – an illustration of the playfulness of an author writing not for the general public but for a close, private world of which he was so enthusiastic a member. Further research is in progress which will, it is hoped, shed light on the identities of some of the other characters in these writings: it seems highly likely that many are based on intimates of the author(s).

Jack Axelrod
Newcastle-Under-Lyme
November, 1988

A Further Episode in the Sentimental and Erotic Education of Mr Andrew Scott

For new readers, the story so far:

The young Mr Andrew Scott, his schooldays at Nottsgrove Academy now behind him, has moved to London and is in lodgings in Bayswater. The house is owned by a widow, Mrs P---, a longtime friend both of Andrew's Godfather and also, as it transpires, of his old Headmaster, Dr White.

Mrs P--- is a woman of refreshingly progressive views in matters sexual, believing such activities to be both natural and healthy and to be indulged in without shame with but the one *caveat*: that both parties should be equally willing. Her views have been long matured through her experiences in India where her acquaintance has included Mr Richard Burton, later to find notoriety as the translater of such Eastern classics as *The Perfumed Garden* and the *Kama Sutra*.

Also resident in the house are Mrs P---s two daughters, Becky and Hannah; the first follows the vocation of nursing, the latter is a skilled artist and designer employed at Messrs Doulton's Lambeth manufactory. The household is completed by two maids, Mary and Emily.

The detailed description of Andrew's ups and downs, his ins and outs in this most liberal of establishments has been set down in previous issues of the *Oyster*. It remains only to add that, as our story continues, Andrew has returned that very afternoon from a trip to the West Country, whence he has escorted Mrs P---'s Ward, Rosie who has been peremptorily expelled from her school for offences against the school rules involving her friendship with the Art Master and her growing interest in the skills of photography.

Now read on:

Dinner that evening displayed Mrs P---s household apparently in more conventional guise. Mrs P--- presided at the head of the table. Both Hannah and Becky were present and correct. Rosie, who had been installed in one of the two guest bedrooms, had been formally introduced to the household and now took her place with a display of maidenly decorum that would have been entirely convincing to any outsider who had not before been exposed to her wayward nature.

I was at once eagerly pressed on all sides to describe everything that had taken place on my trip to Bristol. For my part I was of course careful *not* to describe all that had gone on. I was only too aware that while Rosie had been placed in my care by Mrs P---, I had at certain points discharged my duties in a way that might have seen lax or even improper by conventional standards. Thus I glossed over a great deal of what had transpired on the railway journey, in particular omitting the fact that Rosie and I had enjoyed a First Class Great Western fuck all the way from Chippenham to Swindon [see *The Oyster vol. 2*] and mentioning only, with approval, the efficiency and punctuality of the Railway Company.

Rosie for her part was reticent to the point of near silence concerning the events that had led to her summary expulsion from her Academy for Young Ladies in Somerset. Nonetheless the soup course passed pleasantly enough, although without any great incident. When this had been cleared away, a fine roast joint was brought in and placed before me to carve. (Mrs P--- was quite firm in her view that, as the only man present, I should undertake this traditional male chore).

As I rose, carving knife and fork in hand, and made the first incision in the mouthwatering piece of beef in front of me, I was suddenly grabbed from under the table round the ankle by what I judged to be a small but determined hand. Startled, I looked down but could see nothing since the table's edge and the overhanging table-cloth concealed all.

Saying nothing, but glancing rapidly round the table to confirm that all the family were indeed in their places and that both the maids Emily and Mary were visibly going about their duties, I manfully carried on carving while the unseen hand began to stroke and explore first my ankle and then the lower part of my calf.

With what I felt was a praiseworthy determination to abide by the standards of polite society, I managed to carry on with my task while at the same time continuing a light conversation as though nothing untoward was going on. Meanwhile of course my mind was racing. Was this some typically high-spirited lark by either or both of the daughters? Discreetly I looked about me. Both Hannah and Becky were already beginning to eat with their usual gusto. I could detect nothing evasive or furtive about their expressions, no sideways glances in my direction or suppressed giggles. Mrs P––– and Rosie were engrossed in an animated conversation on the merits, or lack of them, of life in the country. All was innocence and order except for the wandering hand under the table.

Then as I sat down, took up knife and fork and savoured a first delicious mouthful, the hand all at once moved lightly but speedily up my leg, along my thigh and reached into my lap. There it rested for a moment but before I had had time to do more than register and then hide my renewed surprise, it moved again.

Burrowing beneath my table napkin, it felt for, found and squeezed the till-then dormant length of my virile member. Mr Pego at once responded, quite against my wishes at that moment, and began to extend into life.

'Tell me, Andrew,' said Mrs P–––, recalling my now wildly distracted attention with a jolt to the above-table world of propriety and social graces, 'Did Colonel and Mrs Moore have the opportunity to show you the sights of Bristol?'

Determined not to allow the increasingly strange turn of events get out of hand, so to speak, I swallowed and managed manfully to carry on a polite yet, I hoped, animated conversation. Mentioning my expedition to Clifton in the company of Rosie (but drawing a discreet veil over what had happened in the darkness of the *camera obscura* on the Downs [see *The Oyster vol. 2*] I expounded on the architectural and topographical merits of the city, gave my impression of the lively hustle and bustle in the streets that betokened its commercial vitality and embarked on what I pride myself was a not-uninteresting and well-informed dissertation on the Bristol origins of the phrase 'paying on the nail'.

Mrs P—— showed every sign of interest as I continued to inform her of the present state and past history of our premier south-western seaport. As she plied me with questions I was thankful that the good Dr White, my Headmaster at Nottsgrove Academy, had insisted that a working knowledge of Geography and the Commercial World should be instilled into his boys.

But behind my mask of calm, I was becoming more and more agitated. The hidden hand had now unbuttoned me, had reached in and exposed Mr Pego. A shrinking embarrassment at my predicament struggled with a swelling excitement as my prick was teased and stroked into life. Soon it was standing erect and throbbing. I leaned forward, seized by the disconcerting thought that the by now fat and dampening tip of my member might actually come poking up into sight above the table.

Desperately I carried on, trying to do justice to the meal before me and to keep my conversational end up. I was uncomfortably aware that the strain of appearing normal was causing me to clench my teeth at each new caress and I could feel beads of perspiration forming on my brow.

Deliberately drawing a deep breath and making a great effort to relax, I had just impaled and forked a large Brussels sprout, raising it towards my mouth, when the unseen hand struck or rather stroked again. Firm fingers wrapped themselves round the now near rigid shaft of my prick, forcing it down. There was a bumping and a boring between my thighs and the unseen hand was joined by an unseen mouth. Deliciously soft lips first kissed lightly and then opened to admit my pulsating cock. Inch by inch, I was sucked in while a probing tongue began to lick its way down the underside of my shaft and towards the very root of my straining manhood.

Convulsively I bit into the still steaming hot sprout, just as my invisible attachment nipped sharply at the open-eyed head of my engorged organ. I gasped as my teeth jarred painfully on the prongs of my fork and the soft inside of my mouth was scalded by boiling hot sprout. Again I gulped and tried to swallow my mouthful as at that very moment I became aware of the first rising spasm of my cum beginning to force its way up and along my distended shaft.

At once a slippery wet tongue was damped firmly down on the already weeping eye of my prick, bottling up the hot tidal gush of spunk that was now moving upwards.

For an instant I could feel a bursting pressure as my love juice was damned up. Just as a gardener will place his thumb over a watering hose in order to produce a more powerful jet, so my hidden succubus was engineering a veritable gusher of cum. Ecstasy and agony were mixed and I choked on my barely-chewed and burning Brussels sprout.

'Oh, dear', said Hannah. 'Something must have gone down the wrong way.'

With that she got to her feet and came round behind me to pat me on the back. As I coughed, my eyes watering and my throat on fire, I was unstoppered down below and a great geyser of cum shot uncontrollably, but safely, Thank God, into a now greedily welcoming mouth.

Hannah was now banging me heartily on the back as I doubled up, spluttering and drawing in great gulps of air while I was hungrily sucked and swallowed to an unforgettable climax. Shudders ran through my whole body. Mrs P—— looked at me with evident concern. Rosie and both maids all had the same idea and poured out glasses of water, pushing them or carrying them over to me. Wracked with pain and illicit pleasure, I waved my hands as though to say 'Just leave me alone. I'll be all right in a minute.' The last spasms of both my coming and my choking were coursing their way through my whole body. There was a momentary pause and I shuddered again as I felt at one and the same time the first blissful relief of being able once more to breathe freely along with the slow relaxing wave of sheer satisfaction at my relief down below.

As I mopped my brow, Hannah ran her fingers round the inside of my collar, helping me to breathe but also allowing herself the opportunity unobtrusively to rub her splendid titties against my back. My composure was rapidly being restored and I could feel myself being licked and tidied into quiescence. The last few drops of sticky cum were expertly sucked from the now withdrawing head of my prick. Fresh air helped to reduce my member back to more managable proportions and a more pliable condition. Hannah, with a last little squeeze to the nape of my neck, went back to her place. I was conscious of the very lightest of kisses to the very tip of Mr Pego before he was tucked away and I was made as decent down below as I was now composed above.

General conversation resumed although I now played a lesser part in the dinner table chit chat. I was tired, suddenly ravenous and had the best part of my roast beef, Yorkshire pudding and three vegetables still in front of me. As I ate I half-listened to Rosie who had now embarked on a description of the rigours of boarding-school life and a general denounciation of the educational system as it had affected her. I was left wondering Who? Who? I had looked down as unobtrusively as possible and had seen, nestling between my thighs, the top of a golden curled head as it lifted away from my still gaping flies but no recognition had dawned. Although the mystery presence had withdrawn, I knew that she was still there, hidden but close. I half-expected to feel her touch once more at any minute.

Tentatively I stretched out first one leg and then the other, feeling cautiously around me as best I could, hoping that I would be able to locate the golden-haired stranger. But nothing. Although all my other appetites were either well satisfied or well on the way, my curiosity was not just aroused but aflame.

Stretching a little too far under the table, I accidently half-nudged, half-kicked Becky who was sitting at my right. She at once responded in kind and then half-turned towards me, running her tongue lingeringly over her upper lip in an unmistakable gesture of promise. Just for a moment she fingered the upper button of her bodice and looked me straight in the eye before turning back to take her part in the great debate on education that Rosie seemed to have provoked.

The main course was succeeded by a tasty pudding. The maids went deftly about their business. Mrs P—— reminisced about Colonel Moore and the interesting times they had spent together in the Orient. The question as to who exactly was hidden under the dining table was of course unanswered. Coffee was served. Then Mrs P--- rose and excused herself.

'I have some reading to do,' she said. 'I will have to leave you young people to entertain one another.'

As the door closed behind her, I could contain my curiosity no more. Speedily I bent down to look under the table. But quick as I was, my anonymous explorer had been quicker still. As I peered underneath I saw the swish and flutter of the cloth at the far end of the table as an escape was made. Hastily I withdrew my head. Too quickly, as it turned out. I caught the top of my head a nasty crack on the polished mahogany, let out a sharp cry of pain and then set there in my chair, nursing my injured head in my hands while my eyes filled with tears once more.

Becky and Hannah were at my side in an instant.

'Oh, poor Andrew,' said Becky. 'What on earth is the matter with you this evening? First you choke on a vegetable and now you have banged your head.'

She pressed my damaged head to her delightful bosom. Then, running her fingers through my hair, she announced that a nasty little lump was raising itself on my forehead. Under the delicious pressure of her ministrations, I was aware that a rather larger lump was pushing against the tight cloth of my trousers.

'Becky', I said, my face still buried in her embrace, 'Something very odd happened earlier in the meal. I was about to carve the joint when I was approached from under the table...'

'How strange,' said Becky, 'But do go on.'

As I recounted the odd events, Hannah and Rosie gathered round me, concern growing on their faces.

'An hallucination,' said Hannah firmly. 'If it is possible to eat and talk and dream at the same time, then you have just managed it.'

'No!' I said. 'It really did happen. See, I was sitting forward, like so...' I recreated the scene, looking round the assembled company earnestly.

'When I felt a small hand, a feminine hand, reach out and grasp me by the ankle...'

At that moment a small, feminine hand really did reach out and grasp me by the ankle. I leaped to my feet in surprise. Three alarmed faces looked into mine.

'Not another hallucination?' said Hannah.

'I . . . I don't know,' I spluttered wildly. The unseen hand was now tugging peremptorily at my trousers. I sat down again with a bump. Hannah and Becky reached forward and seized me by the hands.

'Calm down Andrew,' said Becky, gripping me hard round the wrist. 'Rosie, pour him out a glass of water.'

Held as in twin vices as I was, I could not free myself. The unseen hand then reinserted itself into the seat of my passions, unbuttoned me all over again, released Mr Pego who sprang out once more. A soft, unseen mouth was clamped hungrily over the straining head of my prick and I felt a first greedy sucking.

'It's happening all over again,' I cried out, pulling at their hands to get free.

'What?' said Becky as she and Hannah resolutely resisted my struggles.

'There's someone under the table,' I said.

'Nonsense! You're imagining things. Now hold still and Rosie will massage the back of your neck,' said Becky.

'I am not,' I said while I strained to see downwards. 'I am being sucked off under the table by a complete stranger!'

'Such language!' said Becky. 'That is not a polite expression to use before three young ladies.'

'But it is true!' I yelled out despairingly.

The warm, loving mouth was now softly moving further and further up the distended length of my prick. Once again an eager tongue was licking delicately at the very tip of my member.

'Close your eyes,' said Becky. 'Take a deep breath. Rosie, sponge his forehead. Andrew is clearly suffering the most terrible pangs.'

Now I felt a gentle tickling as an unseen hand began to play lightly over my aching balls. I squeezed my eyes shut and wondered if I was going mad.

I must have groaned out loud for suddenly Hannah burst out laughing.

'We have teased him too much,' she said. All three released me and I rocked back on my chair, desperate to uncover what was going on.

There, nestling between my thighs was the same golden head that I had glimpsed earlier in the meal. Then, with one quick little nip, the mouth was withdrawn and the sweetest, most adorable little face was turned up to look me full in the eyes.

Starting backwards, I over-balanced on my chair. Flailing my arms I fell over. Rosie and Hannah jumped forward and just caught me before I measured my full length on the carpet. Pushing the chair upright, they allowed me to leap to my feet. Crouched before me a complete stranger. I barely had the time to register that this was a quite delectable creature, when she rose to her feet, smoothing down her dress and holding out her hand.

'Andrew,' said Becky, 'This is Gwendolen Bunbury. A cousin.'

'The Honourable Gwendolen Bunbury, to be precise,' said Hannah. 'Had you been looking out of the window at the right time on your journey from Bristol, you would have seen on the horizon the distant outline of her family seat in Berkshire.'

'Miss Bunbury,' I said, struggling to regain my composure but uncomfortably aware that the decorum of the occasion was marred by the fact that Mr Pego was sticking out of my trousers and was drawn up rigidly to attention and in full view.

'Mr Scott,' she replied, 'It is a great pleasure...'

With that, she dropped a greatly exaggerated curtsy and once more took the tip of my member in her mouth.'

'Do you come from these parts?' she said, looking up at me.

By now Hannah, Becky and Rosie were all in uncontrollable fits of laughter. Tears were flowing down their cheeks and they were holding on to each other, almost helpless in their mirth.

'This is your Welcome Home present,' said Hannah. 'Gwendolen is in Town after a long sojorn in the country and Becky and I thought that the two of you should meet. You in turn are Gwendolen's Welcome to London present.'

'But presents,' said Rosie, 'That I hope we can all share in.'

'It was Hannah's idea in fact,' said Becky. 'She thought that it would relieve the possible tedium of the dinner-table conversation. You are inclined, Andrew, to hold forth somewhat and we guessed that we might be subjected to a dissertation on the history and economy of Bristol. Poor Mama did very well in plying you with the right questions. You should have seen your face when Gwendolen started her ministrations on you. You went all flushed and for a moment I thought you were quite going to lose the thread of your argument.'

'This has all been very unfair,' I said.

'Do you not like having your cock licked into action by a young lady?' she said.

'Especially one as pretty as Gwendolen here.'

'Of course I do,' I expostulated. 'But not while I'm eating roast beef and three vegetables. And trying to carry on a normal conversation.'

'Think of poor Gwendolen,' answered Becky. 'At least you got something to eat. She must be positively starved.'

'I did in fact have a little to eat,' said Gwendolen. She licked her lips. 'And very satisfying it was.' She grasped my prick firmly in her hand. 'But I confess I am still a little hungry.'

'Very nicely said,' replied Becky. 'But we have saved some food for you. Andrew is not the only one who must keep his strength up!

She rang and Emily the maid came in.

'Emily, can you fetch something for my cousin to eat,' she said.

Emily bobbed a curtsy but then clapped her hand to her mouth. She went very pink and I realised that my member was still exposed.

'I'm sorry,' I said. 'I had quite forgotten...'

'Which, I suspect, is more than Emily has,' said Becky. 'We all here have the clearest, fondest memories of him. But for the moment, I suggest you put him away or you might catch a cold.'

'Here, let me,' said Hannah, as I began to fumble with my fly. 'You're all fingers and thumbs.'

'I am a little flustered, I must confess,' I said with relief as she busied herself. Soon all was proper again and as Gwendolen ate, the others explained in greater detail all the connections between them. Rosie could remember her very well at school although Gwendolen had been as she explained, 'One of the big girls.'

'How I envied you,' she said. 'You and Cecily . . . Cecily . . .'
'Cardew,' said Gwendolen. 'My dearest friend in the whole school.'
'All the younger girls had such a crush on the two of you. We used to loiter, quite against school rules, in the corridors, hoping that you would notice us.'
'You *were* noticed, Rosie,' said Gwendolen. 'And I am very, very happy to see you again. But I understand that you have recently left Miss Bradshaw's under something of a cloud. and rumour has it that there was an incident involving the Art Master.'

So the whole story of Rosie's sudden departure came out. When she got to the point where she was revealing her new interest in photography, I saw Becky and Hannah exchange meaningful glances. By now I knew them well enough to realise that an idea had crossed both their minds and that they would soon be hatching another of their plots.
'A group photograph,' said Becky after a moment's thought. 'Since you have a whole trunk full of photographic equipment up in your room, we must get everything cleared away just as soon as Gwendolen has finished eating.'
'What about the exposure,' I chipped in, rather cleverly I considered.
'Your jokes get worse and worse,' said Hannah. 'But you do have a point. Rosie have you the technical knowledge to do justice to your subject? We want two group studies. One with and one without.'
'One with and one without what?' I asked.
'With clothes and without clothes.' she answered. 'One that can be openly displayed and sent round to all our relatives. And one that will be kept private, restricted only to those of us here. And maybe sent privately to one or two carefully picked friends.'
'I have a better idea,' said Becky. 'It will take some time for Rosie to set up her equipment. I shall send an urgent message by cab to Catherine, asking her to come round immediately if she can. She might even be able to find the Scottish contingent.'
'Ian and Donald,' I said. 'It would be splendid if they could join in the fun. And I had the most warm, loving note from

Kate on my return this afternoon.' [See *The Oyster vol.2*]

So it was decided. A note was written and despatched. Rosie summoned me to help her unpack. Gwendolen volunteered to come with us. She squeezed my arm affectionately as we went upstairs.

'I hope you are not angry with me,' she said. 'I hope that when the photography is finished we can get down to the serious business of fucking. I have seen enough of you to know that I should like that very much.'

How could I refuse such an enticing offer? I hugged her to me.

'I'd like that very much as well,' I answered.

Rosie, who was a step or two ahead of us, turned.

'What about me?' she said sweetly. 'Can I join in?'

'Of course, Rosie dear,' said Gwendolen. 'This will be quite an old school reunion.'

That first photographic adventure was unlike anything that I had previously experienced. I had before been into a studio on two or three occasions. Formal portraits of my family had been taken. I had featured, two or three rows back, in a school photograph. I was accustomed to the slow deliberate proceedings as the photographer ordered his subjects, arranged his backgrounds, then buried his head under a black cloth. I knew how to pose motionless, staring at the camera. But to sit or stand, leaning on a classically styled pillar was one thing. To hold oneself immobile with one's virile member poking unmoving at the tender entrance to a generously spread cunney is a different matter.

Rosie was a paragon of brisk efficiency. As we helped her place the camera on its tripod, as she squinted though the viewing window, ordering us to close up or rearrange our groupings, she gave us a short explanation of the technicalities and the history of the craft.

We started with one or two more ordinary exposures, fully clothed. Catherine and the Fergusons brothers had not yet arrived although we had received a message that all three would present later on. Meanwhile Rosie was getting a little bored with the unrelieved decency of the proceedings.

'Andrew,' she said all of a sudden, 'I would like you to sit between Hannah and Becky. Gwendolen, would you sit on the carpet at their feet.' She looked carefully at us. 'Not very interesting. I have an idea. Andrew, would you take off all your clothes!'

'Just me?' I said.

'Just you for the moment,' she replied.

'This seems somewhat unfair,' I said.

'Hannah, Becky!' she called. 'Andrew is beng stuffy about this. I think you should help him out of his things.'

Before I could protest any further, hands were reaching out. Gwendolen had untied my shoelaces and slipped my shoes and then socks off my feet while jacket, waistcoat, shirt and vest were peeled and pulled off me. Rosie stepped forward and appropriated to herself the job of removing my trousers. As Mr Pego was all at once exposed to public view, I was suddenly somewhat bashful. I crossed my hands in front of him.

Gwendolen reached up from the floor and gently placed her hands on mine.

'Don't deny us the finest sight of the evening,' she said as she slowly pulled my wrists apart. Just as she did so, I felt a finger from behind. Whether it was Becky or Hannah I could not tell. As the cheeks of my bottom were parted, the finger was slipped gently but firmly into my back passage. With a jump, Mr Pego shot upright. Gwendolen and Rosie both gave a little cheer.

'Quick, sit down!' ordered Rosie. The rest of you, get into position.'

Hannah sat to my right. Becky to my left. Gwendolen arranged herself cross-legged at my feet.

'Gwendolen! He's beginning to flag,' said Rosie.

Gwendolen turned and stuck out her tongue, letting it play on the tip of my cock. It responded immediately. Then she traced out the line of the blue vein along the top until her hand came to rest at its root. She gave a short squeeze.

'That's it,' said Rosie. 'Cup your hand under his balls. Now, keep very still everyone.'

There was a flash of burning powder. The light seemed to fill the room. I heard the shutter click. Everyone held their breath while Gwendolen held my throbbing prick.

'Wonderful,' said Rosie. 'Now I want everything reversed.

Andrew, back into your clothes. Girls, off with yours'!'

Grumbling, I struggled back into my clothes. Mr Pego was by now most unwilling to lie down again and as I tried to force him back inside my trousers, the other three began to undress. At this Mr Pego became even more unwilling to bend to my will. Meanwhile before my enthralled eyes first Hannah's and then Becky's luscious titties were bared. Next their lovely rounded bottoms were revealed. Lastly I saw with rising excitement their dark and densely furred pussies. By now I was getting quite distressed with my unrelieved need to slip my prick into one of those welcoming quims.

'Andrew,' said Becky, 'I have a slight tickle. Here,' she said, taking my hand and placing it on her bush.

I felt its warmth and then the sudden yielding of her cunt lips as that first slick of wetness lubricated my finger.

'Just a little rub,' she said. 'And a little more.' She sighed.

'Not yet' said Rosie like some school ma'am. 'That comes later!'

Gwendolen, who had once again closed her hand gently over the engorged length of my cock, paused.

'What about you, Rosie dear?' she said. 'I am certain it would put us all more at ease if you were to appear in the same state of Nature.'

Hannah at once went across to help her before she could demur. Gwendolen had in the meantime handed me over to Hannah while she also began to divest herself of all her clothing.

Quivering, my hand still engaged with Becky's quim, I saw the full golden beauty of Gwendolen brought to light. What a mouth-watering contrast was there. The dark swelling mounds of Becky's and Hannah's pussies were contrasted with the fair silky down of Gwendolen's. Rosie's girlish, brown-haired beauty that I had examined so memorably on the train to Paddington was bared in turn. I was surrounded by the most welcoming but varied array of cunneys that any man could imagine even in his wildest dreams.

But Rosie was a hard taskmaster. I was forced back into my clothes and made to sit upright between the now naked Hannah and Becky. Looking down at Gwendolen I could see past the golden curls of her hair to her quite outstanding titties and then down again to the half-hidden promise of her pubic treasure.

Rosie, naked also, retired behind her camera. 'Smile', she said. We all smiled except I suspect my smile was more like a grimace as I held myself desperately in check, aware of the warmth rising from the eager bodies that surrounded me.

Then, just as Rosie bent to her camera, there was a soft knock at the door and Emily slipped in. She paused at the unusual display that met her startled eyes, then pulling herself together said 'Miss Catherine Ferguson and her Cousins have called.'

At once there was a bustle of activity. Hannah and Becky rose to meet their guests. Rosie, a little uncertain of herself now that strangers were arriving, contrived to hide most of herself behind her photographic equipment. Gwendolen stayed exactly where she was, cross-legged on the floor.

Catherine, elegant as ever, swept into the room, closely followed by Ian and Donald. With a social poise that I could only admire, she did not hesitate in her stride but embraced first the naked Hannah and then Becky warmly. Without blinking an eyelid, she then turned and gravely offered me her hand.

'I am happy to see you again so soon, Andrew,' she said. 'I hope you got my note.'

'Indeed yes,' I replied. 'It was waiting for me on my return from the West Country.'

Ian and Donald has been less successful at concealing their amazement at being so ushered into a room full of the most delicious bevy of undressed feminine beauty. They stopped dead in their tracks. They gulped in unison. Their eyes quite started from their heads. Then as Becky and Hannah went across to embrace them also, broad grins broke out on their faces. As each was hugged to a naked bosom, I saw both Becky and Hannah, as if each could read the other's thoughts, reach out a discreet hand and reach under their kilts. Both were drawn forward.

'Gwendolen, Rosie. May I introduce you to three very dear friends. Miss Catherine Ferguson and Mr Ian and Mr Donald Ferguson.'

Rosie, shyly came forward. Gwendolen rose with a lithe

grace from her seated position. Ian and Donald gasped at this sudden vision of golden haired loveliness.

'I am delighted to . . . to . . .' stammered Donald.

'To be at my service?' asked Gwendolen with a tantalising smile.

'Yes . . . Yes . . . To be . . .' stuttered Donald.

'I hope you can both recover your composure sufficiently to join in the fucking that is about to take place,' said Becky. 'But first, Rosie here is going to take all our photographs. Oh,' she went on, 'How rude of me. Rosie, there is no need to hide yourself away like that. I hope that you are going to take a full part in the events of the evening.'

Rosie allowed herself to be led forward and introduced.

'I hope that before long all our parts will be full,' said Hannah. 'I can see already that your Highland Things are showing a considerable interest in what is spread before them.'

I realised that mine was not the only cock that was bursting with life and a straining desire to find its way into one or more of the inviting treasure caves that surrounded us.

Ian and Donald rapidly tore off their kilts, sporrans and bonnets. As their erect pricks sprang into general view, Becky took one in each hand.

'The staff of life,' she said. 'Two staffs to be accurate.'

Rosie laughed, quite put at her ease by Becky's merry conceit. Catherine clung to me and whispered in my ear.'

'Let us be different,' she said. 'For a few moments let us remain fully dressed. At least until the photography is over. Then, Andrew, I want you to undress me. Slowly. I want to savour for a moment or two longer the thought that your prick will soon be sliding deep into me.'

Now it was my turn to gulp and try to keep myself under control. I tried manfully to think of anything other than the welcoming hunger of the cunt that I knew awaited me under that cool exterior.

'A slow fuck. A little time taken. That is what I need. But a very thorough fuck. A whole evening of fucking. Under all this clothing, she went on, I am already quite moist with expectation.'

I looked round the room. Gwendolen, very sweetly, was stroking Rosie and reassuring her.

'You're trembling a little,' she said.

'Oh, Gwendolen,' Rosie replied. 'I am indeed. This is very forward of me. When one is fresh from the schoolroom, it is so exciting to see not one but three such lovely big Things displayed before one.'

Gwendolen took Rosie's hand and placed it on her own blonde haired pussey. Then she drew a delicate finger along the cleft of Rosie's brown haired cunney.

'See,' she said, 'We are both the same. Both wet with the thought of what is to come.'

Rosie kissed her gratefully.

'How nice you are,' she said. 'I know that I am going to enjoy this.'

Suddenly there was an abrupt shriek of delight. I looked round. Two of our party had not been able to wait until the photography was over. Becky was bent forward while behind her Ian had sunk his shaft right up to the hilt in her generously displayed cunt.

'That's it,' she cried out. 'I want it right in. I want to feel all of it right up inside me. I need to be fucked fast. Now.'

Ian needed no urging. Spreading her legs even wider open with his thumbs, he plunged again, and again into her. She staggered under the impact of his mighty thrusting but still cried out for more. Ian rose manfully to the occasion, driving her on and on until she was beside herself with ecstacy. Surely Becky and her sister must be unrivalled in their sheer prick-hunger!

Hannah meanwhile was standing before Donald, squeezing and offering her magnificent breasts to him. Naked but for his argyle socks and sturdy brogues, he gasped in amazement.

As he bent to suck hungrily at her dark, swollen nipples, she clutched him by the cheeks of his bum and commenced to rub herself against him. Rosie, for her part, was now staring unashamedly at the activity. As she stood there, Gwendolen had crouched down before her and I saw her tongue bury itself deep in Rosie's young quim. Rosie began to tremble quite uncontrollably, instinctively opening herself up to Gwendolen's mouth.

Becky's first coming was upon her. She was kneeling down on all fours, her bum raised, perspiration covering the flush that was spreading over her whole body. God knows what

Gaelic oaths were being forced from Ian as she cried out and great shudders of desire shook her. Then her cries reached a crescendo of pleasure and the first fuck of the evening reached its climax.

But now Catherine regained my attention. With an insistent hand on my prick, she led me over to a corner of the room.

Enough of this watching,' she said. 'The time has come for us to begin that slow fuck that I need.'

Another memorable evening in Mrs P—' establishment was well under way.

[To be continued]

A Letter to the Editor of The Oyster from Lady Louise Kitely-Brown

15th June, 1891

Sir,

I am sure your esteemed readers will be fascinated to know of a most interesting and enjoyable experiment in which I took part last week with my good friends Doctor Jonathan Arkley and the Honourable Noreen Ravenswhite.

Both Noreen and I are twenty one years of age and though not entirely unschooled in *l'art de faire l'amour* we are neither of us as sophisticated in such matters as the good doctor who is of course somewhat older and who is known to you and many members of Society as one of the great fuckers of our times.

We had dined at Jonathan's house and fired by the warmth of the glorious summer evening and the fine champagne we had quaffed in abundance, it was perhaps not entirely surprising that we found ourselves in Jonathan's large bed. We were all quite naked and enjoying a delicious threeway kiss; pressing our lips together and wriggling our tongues around in each other's mouths.

Jonathan then turned to me and said: 'Louise, my dear, I have the strongest fancy to see you kiss Noreen's pussey. Would you humour me and go down upon her. Noreen will have no objection, will you my sweet?'

'Far from it,' laughed the pretty girl, 'I do so enjoy having my cunt sucked off that I don't care who does it. Indeed, in my experience, girls know how to tickle my clitty far more effectively than boys!'

I was more than willing to oblige especially after Noreen's agreement. It felt a little strange at first as although I had been in bed with other girls before, we had never made love together in the presence of a man. But I did enjoy the thought of making love to this cheeky young girl who lay in her proud naked glory at my side. She was certainly a beauty with large snowy bosoms, well separated, each looking a little away from the other, each perfectly proportioned and tapering in perfect curves until they came to two rosebud points. Her belly, smooth, broad and dimpled in the centre with a sweet little button, was like a perfect plain of whiteness which appeared the more dazzling from the thick growth of dark black hair which curled in rich locks in the triangle between her legs.

Jonathan quickly pressed my head down onto Noreen's gloriously large breasts and the lovely girl sighed with delight as I moved my tongue from one bubbie to the other, twirling my tongue around her erect little red nipples.

At first she lay passively but then with a cry she put her arms round me, holding her soft body to me as I continued my nibbling and sucking of her titties which were by now like little red stalks as I teased and suckled them up to new heights. Now I let my tongue travel the length of her velvety body, lingering briefly at her belly button before sliding down to her thighs. Her skin was so soft and smelled so clean that this was a real pleasure and I felt my own motte beginning to dampen.

The gorgeous girl whimpered as I pulled her long white legs apart and nuzzled my full lips around her curly dark bush. My own hands clamped around her firm bum cheeks as my tongue flashed unerringly around the damp pubic hair and her pussey seemed to open wide as she lifted her bottom which enabled me to slip my tongue through the pink lips, licking between the groves of her clitty in long thrusting strokes. With a groan of ecstacy, I lost myself in her delicious cunt, licking and lapping the sweet juices of her honey pot.

'Ah, that is heavenly!' she gasped. 'More! More! Oh, Louise my darling, you are making me spend!' My tongue was now revelling in her sopping muff, out of which her clitty was now protruding between the pouting lips. I took her clitty in my mouth, rolling my tongue all round it as Noreen quivered all over and began jerking her body all over the bed. It was hard for me to keep my tongue on her clitty as her legs tightened around my head. Then she arched her back and with a second all over shudder she screamed: 'Oh! Oh! Oh! There, there, suck my juices, Louise, oh, that's just divine!' I worked my tongue until my jaw ached sucking up her love juice as the lovely girl again heaved violently and managed to achieve a tremendous orgasm.

Noreen sank back exhausted but my blood was up and I was delighted to see that our little tribadistic encounter had excited Jonathan whose sinewy, stiff cock was now rock-hard. He frigged himself up to a gigantic erection but I had no intention of letting him waste his spunk by himself. I moved his hands away and took this monster cock in my own hands, peeling back the foreskin and running my tongue in the sensitive groove under the red, mushroom knob.

Jonathan groaned with pleasure as I leaned forward and took the dome shaped helmet between my lips, jamming down his foreskin and lashing my tongue around the rigid shaft. Then I sucked hard, taking at least half his shaft into my mouth until I could take no more. I sucked firmly, sliding my lips up and down the rock-hard shaft, gulping noisily as the head of his grand prick slid along the roof of my mouth to the back of my throat.

His cock was now throbbing furiously and I knew that soon he would be spending. I continued to gobble the pulsating tool as the rogue cupped my breasts in his hands, deftly flicking my titties with his fingernails. I began to give him sharp little licks on his swollen rod followed by a series of quick kisses up and down the stem, encompassing his hairy balls, thrusting his cock in and out of my mouth with a quickening rhythm, deep into my throat and then out again with my pink little tongue licking at the tip at the end of each stroke, lapping up the drops of creamy white fluid that were beginning to ooze out of the tiny eye at the top of his knob.

As soon as I felt he was on the verge of spending, I made ready to swallow his love juice. Jonathan thrust upwards and his cock shuddered violently between my lips and then in one long spasm he emptied his balls, first a few early shoots and then woosh! My mouth was filled with juicy, foam as his cock gushed almost uncontrollably as I held it lightly between my teeth. I let the sweet juices run down my throat as I washed his now spongy knob with my tongue and then, very gradually, I allowed the wet shaft to slide free.

Now it was Jonathan's turn to sink back gracefully next to

Noreen – but still here was I, instigator of their bliss still unsatisfied myself! This was quite unfair and I had no hestitation in telling them so!

'We are well rebuked,' cried Noreen, 'and you certainly deserve a beautiful fuck, Louise. Now, how shall it be, by cock or by tongue? The choice is yours.'

'Perhaps by both,' I replied gaily, 'although I would not want either of my dear friends to think me greedy.'

My two dear friends insisted that I deserved the fullest attention. Jonathan disengaged himself and stood by the side of the bed, allowing me to admire his magnificent nakedness, his wide chest, his flat belly and his enormous cock that stood up so excitingly from its thickest of pubic hair. Yet how could I neglect the sweet Noreen who lay stretched out besides me, her hands jiggling her firm, uptilted breasts in such an exciting fashion?

I lay down beside her and leaning over, kissed her upright little nipples, flicking them up to a fine state of erection as I lay on top of her. Gently, the dear girl caressed my buttocks and pushed me onto my back as she now took over as mistress of the revels.

I spread my legs as Noreen bent down in front of me and began kissing my pussey. Instinctively, I opened my legs to make my wet, swollen cunney lips more accessible and Noreen paused for a moment to savour the musky aroma before quickly kissing my pink pussey lips which were aching to be opened by her questing tongue. Lovingly, she began to eat me, forcing her tongue deep into my juicy love-channel, sliding up and down my crack until I screamed with pleasure as she found my engorged clitty. I tried hard to keep still so that Noreen could suck my clitty but she had a difficulty staying with me as I rubbed myself off to a delicious spend against her mouth.

Now it was my turn to take a more positive role so we changed positions. Now it was Noreen flat on her back with her head still clamped between my legs, eagerly lapping up my cunt-juice as I returned the compliment, placing my knees either side of her beautiful breasts and leaning forward to nuzzle my own head between her legs. This left me sitting on Noreen's face which enabled her to continue pushing her pretty face deep into my crotch, kissing and sucking until I could feel the moisture fairly dripping down the inside of my thighs. Naughty, but nice!

Doctor Jonathan was so taken by this action that he positioned himself behind me and after anointing his huge tool with pomade positioned his cock between my bum cheeks. I raised my backside in the air, opening my legs slightly so that he could guide the tip of his cock into my bum-hole. At first I felt some discomfort as his cock penetrated my bum-hole but then it felt quite delicious as he started pumping into me with swinging thrusts and my arse arched up and down to receive his delicious rod. We rolled about happily, the three of us, we two girls sucking each other's cunts and Jonathan fucking my bottom so stylishly. I could feel his build-up coming as his big balls slapped against the back of my legs. As his climax juddered to boiling-point, I felt the throb of liquid fire rage inside me with every throb of that divine cock as his creamy froth spurted inside me just as my saturated clitty sent jets of spend into Noreen's wet mouth.

We continued our threesome for some time aftcrwards. Noreen and I sucked off our mutual man. We both nibbled and licked at his stiff, pulsating cock but I could not contain myself with an hors d'oevres so I brought his mushroomed knob to my salivating lips and tongued the dome, tasting his salty juices. I then grabbed his shaft with both hands and hungrily stuffed it into my mouth as far as I could. He pumped further and further down my throat until I felt that he was again ready to spend and whilst I have no objection whatsover to swallowing spunk, I had a fancy for Jonathan to fuck my cunney.

I pulled his prick from out of my mouth but it was now too late. The juices were oozing from out of the tip which I lapped up instantly and then the first creamy jet of sperm came hurtling out of his prick. The first jet hit me on the right cheek but I hastily sucked on the jerking shaft, enabling me to gobble up as best I could the jets of frothy white spunk. As his spurting knob rested on my tongue, I swallowed quickly to keep pace with him. Then, as his spend passed its peak, I took his whole cock back into my mouth and sucked for all I was worth to extract the very last drops of love-juice from his twitching prick.

We lay silent for a spell and I declare that we would have

been happy to stay together all night but Noreen and I could not afford the chance of being discovered with the good doctor in the morning so reluctantly, we decided to take our farewells at about half past midnight.

Before we left, however, Johnny made us all some coffee and Noreen brought up a most interesting matter into the conversation which I feel is well worth relating here.

'My good friend Caroline Seale has a problem, Jonathan,' said Noreen, 'I think you have met her at one of Sir Andrew Stuck's parties. She is a very pretty girl and not averse to a little nookie.'

'You are being too kind,' I murmured somewhat unkindly, 'It is well known around Chelsea that she fucks like the proverbial rattlesnake as our American cousins are wont to say.'

'A curious analogy,' mused Jonathan, 'for as far as I know, the rattlesnake has a somewhat quiet sexual life.'

'Never mind all that,' said Noreen with some impatience, 'The simple fact of the matter is that she is conducting a discreet little affair with Sir Andrew whilst his other *amorata*, Mrs John Paterson-Thyme, is out of town.

'Her problem is that Sir Andrew enjoys oral sexual activity and Caroline is unschooled in the art. Furthermore, despite his urgent pressing of the matter, she has confided in me that she relaly does not want to learn the art of *fellatio*. Surprising though it may sound to either of you, she recoils at the idea of taking a cock in her mouth. Yet she longs to please him and make him happy but the thought of pleasing him in this way is to her, well, horrid. So we have an impasse, Jonathan. What do you suggest? Or indeed, Louise, perhaps you have an answer to this dreadful situation.'

'A lot of her problem is probably based on ignorance,' said Jonathan, stroking his chin.

'You would be surprised how many girls are kept unaware of the pleasures of sucking a thick prick or having their pussies licked out – or if such ideas are even obliquely mentioned, they wuld be banished by friends in whom they have confided. Why, one girl who came to me with a not dissimilar problem even thought such activity was illegal!

'My own opinion is, as you know, that when two people love

each other, almost nothing they do in private should be considered wrong or harmful. As my old friend Mrs Patrick Campbell has said: "All I ask is that they do not do it in the street and frighten the horses.'

'But any activity that for whatever reason is repugnant to one partner could become physically or psychologically harmful and no-one should be pressured to perform bedroom antics that make them feel uneasy.

'Yes, I do remember Caroline who seemed like a very nice girl to me. I am sure that she longs to give Andrew sexual bliss but if she just cannot bring herself to suck his prick then alas, both must simply find more compatible sexual partners. There's no magic cure, I'm afraid, Noreen, though you might like to tell Caroline that she should at least try her hand, or rather her tongue I should say, for I believe you should try everything once!'

'She will take your advice, I think,' said Noreen, 'for I know how much she values your opinion. Meanwhile, let me pay you a medical fee in kind!'

She kneeled down in front of Jonathan and opened his robe, taking his shaft in her hands. His hands pressed down upon her head as if he wanted to force her head into his crotch but he didn't need to do so as she was more than willing. She licked the pubic hair that encompassed his stiffening cock and heavy balls and then she began to move her face slowly, enjoying to the full the sensation of feeling his cock hard and erect against her soft cheek. Now Noreen made strands of her hair and made a web round the shaft, stroking it slowly, feeling it throb and grow even harder as she touched him.

Noreen moved her head across the red helmet of the handsome young doctor's knob and kissed the top which was already oozing drops of moisture. Then her tongue encircled his knob, savouring the juices as she drew him in between her rich, generous lips, sucking lustily as Jonathan instinctively began to push forwards and backwards as her warm hands played with his hairy, hanging balls.

She sucked happily away at her lollipop and Jonathan bucked wildly as his huge cock slurped in and out of her hungry mouth. He gasped: 'I'm spending, I'm spending, I cannot hold it!' and Noreen began to swallow in anticipation. She was proved to be right as Jonathan sent spurts of white frothy cum crashing into her throat. She sucked and nibbled greedily, milking his trembling cock of every last drop of love-juice.

'Ah, Jonathan, I do enjoy sucking a nice thick cock like yours,' Noreen said with a smile. 'Caroline may not enjoy it but I could happily suck your cock for hours. It never lasts that long of course and like all you men you squirt off in just a few minutes.'

'I've heard it said that General Aspis, the Belgian Chargé d'Affaires can keep going for half an hour,' I interrupted.

'That's probably just a rumour,' said Noreen. 'Anyhow, I just adore sucking and swallowing for nothing tastes so clean and fine. And there is the additional benefit of knowing that I can enjoy myself without getting in the family way!'

'So very true,' added Doctor Jonathan, 'but I hope you and Louise realise that whatever tricks you get up to in bed, the essential core of enjoyment lies in choosing an understanding and tender partner.'

With these wise words ringing in ours ears, we went home. Although Noreen was staying the rest of the night with me, we were back well after the time we had promised my Uncle Stanley. Fortunately, he had gone to sleep and Baigue the butler was not averse at telling the occasional white lie to my Uncle for the not unreasonable price of half a sovereign so Noreen and I went unpunished for our escapade. Hastening to our beds, completely worn out by our interesting little sexual experiments, we fell into a delicious sleep from which it was almost eleven o'clock before we awoke.

A final thought, Sir, before I end this letter; all animals copulate but only the human species is capable of extending a physical need into an act of love. This ability to combine sex with passion sets us aside from other animals though it is surely an unfortunate fact that far too few people recognise and develop this unique talent with which we are all blessed.

I am, Sir,

Your obedient servant,

Louise Kitely-Brown
Allum House
26 Piccadilly
London, W.

Preface

This final extract from The Oyster dates from July 1894 – not long after the Prince of Wales was involved in a somewhat sordid affair at a country house weekend where one of the guests was accused of cheating at cards. The Prince's involvement (and his threatened exposure as an adulterer in a separate juicy piece of scandal) did little to enhance his reputation.

We now know that in all probability the novelette (serialised in the magazine throughout 1894) was written by Phillipa Lintern, the wife of a wealthy London printer whose factory churned out the popular 'French postcards' during the 1880s and 1890s.

The narrator of the yarn is 'Estelle Bicklah', a young music hall artiste whose current amour is an aristocratic Army Officer, Captain Woode who takes her to a weekend shoot on the Scottish Moors. Most of the action is confined to the mansion and to her delight, Estelle learns that one of the guests at the party is the Prince of Wales.

Taylor Cuthbertson
Falkirk
December, 1988

I well recall the evening that I was first fucked by the Prince of Wales. I was chatting with my old friend Captain Marcus Woode about the events of the previous night when Lord Montmorency bustled up.

'Come on, you two,' he cried, looking anxiously at his watch. 'I've been looking everywhere for you! The Prince will be here very shortly, and we must be ready to welcome him. Everyone else is assembled in the Great Hall.'

Relieved that I was beginning to feel a little more like myself again, I did as I was bade. Shortly afterwards, almost exactly on the stroke of twelve, I found myself in the exalted presence of Royalty for the first time in my life.

To say that I was honoured would be an understatement. I, whose own life not so very long ago had been such a very quiet one, was almost overwhelmed by the occasion! As I curtseyed before His Royal Highness – Lady Montmorency had given us instruction on the correct mode of behaviour in the Prince's company – I felt faint with nervous trembling. But Lizzie – who as the daughter of a Lord is much more familiar with the high and mighty than I am – said afterwards that I was splendid, and acted impeccably, and that at the luncheon which almost immediately followed the presentation the Prince had asked his hostess to tell him more about me, as he was particularly struck even on so short an acquaintance by my beauty, and courtesy, and pleasant disposition, so much so that I blushed quite hotly and told her that she must be making it all up, for who would be so bold as to say such things about a little orphan-girl such as myself. But it was all true, she insisted most forcefully.

We decided among ourselves that for the duration of the Prince's stay there must be no repetition of the wild debauchery which had so far been the way of things at Montmorency Castle. At all times we were in danger of discovery – a fact which nonetheless added a certain spice to proceedings – but were word to be let out that such goings-on had taken place in the presence of Royalty, then our disgrace would be swift and final. Marcus would be certain to be stripped of his command, and reduced to the ranks. Thirkettle would lose the title he confidently expected would be his in the next Honours list; the Count and Countess of Courtstrete would very probably be forced to quit Society forever, and go and live abroad; while Lizzie and her parents – though they themselves were entirely innocent of any blame – would never live down the opprobrium that would be heaped on their heads, and the ruin of the name of one of the greatest families in the land. That afternoon the gentlemen accompanied the Prince to the butts which had been specially prepared for the Royal party, while we busied ourselves in innocent pleasures at the castle. Marcus told me at table that evening that the Prince was a capital fellow; an excellent shot, to be sure, and the owner of as fine a pair of guns as any he had ever set eyes on either in military or civilian life, but also a most companionable fellow – very ready to hand round his hip-flask, incidentally, and a fund of good stories. Now that the ice had been broken I was able to talk to him with a little less stiffness and nervousness than before, and found as we spoke for a few minutes by the fire in the Great Hall that evening that he had a ready wit and good ear for what other people had to say to him – an attribute which, I am sorry to say, is not always to be found among those whom fortune has chosen to elevate to life's higher stations. Though of scarcely more than middle height, he was quite a handsome man in my book, with lively eyes and an easy smile.

'And you are looking forward to the ball tomorrow evening, Miss Bicklah?' he asked me.

'Oh, yes indeed, your Highness. It is the social highlight of the week, and I am sure everyone is greatly honoured by your presence here.'

'You are too kind, dear girl. I do enjoy dancing a great deal, I must confess. Perhaps you would do me the honour of allowing me to mark your dance-card when it is available? They say I am the devil at the *mazurka*.'

My heart almost stopped beating.

'Why, I would be honoured, your Highness,' I managed to stammer at length.

'Good! Then it is fixed then – we will dance the *mazurka* together. Montmorency has engaged the services of the finest musicians in all of Scotland for the evening. I suggested he do so, because after a fortnight at Balmoral one might possibly have heard the "Gay Gordons" once too often. Strictly between you and I, the sound of pipes is guaranteed to set my teeth on edge. Had Montmorency had nothing but pipers and fiddlers on hand I think I might well have made my excuses and left for London as soon as my train could be made available.'

Even on so trivial a matter, I was sincerely flattered to be taken into the Prince's confidence. I was even more delighted that I should have taken the liberty, once I knew that there would a grand ball at the end of my stay in Scotland, of having a spectacular ruffled gown in black *crêpe de chine* run up for me by Lizzie's superb dressmaker, Madamoiselle Thérèse, and to have the not inconsiderable fees for her work charged to Lizzie's own account. Worn with my very finest jewellery, I was sure that this was precisely the right outfit in which to make an impression on the Prince. What a pity that he would not be able to see the divine set of undergarments which Madamoiselle Thérèse had made up specially to go with the dress. Though white has for so long been popular, these were exclusively in black, a fantasia of silk and lace that, when I first tried the garments on and saw my reflection in the glass, seemed the very epitome of womanly loveliness. Ah well, I reflected, if the Prince would not see them I was sure Tom or Marcus or whoever would be delighted to help me out of them when the time came.

On my best behaviour, though not without a certain longing, I retired to bed a tad before eleven that evening. Truth to tell, my head still rang a little from the night before, and I was glad of an uninterrupted night's sleep. My pussey, too, had felt a little sore and inflamed – especially as a result of the double stretching I had received when spitted on the Count's prick and enculed in rear by Tom. A night's abstinence would enable my body to make a full recovery, ready for the adventure of the morrow.

By all accounts, the shooting went extremely well in the morning. The Prince was sure there were more birds than he had ever seen before on the Montmorency estate, and certainly none plumper. Lord Montmorency's careful husbandry had obviously had the desired effect.

Before the sun was too high in the sky – Tom Feather told me that the deep shadows cast by the noonday sun were to be abhorred by every photographer, since out of doors they quite obscured the features when a hat was worn – a splendid series of photographs was taken, first of the Prince in the company of his Lordship and some of the more distinguished guests in the party, then of all the guns grouped together, with the morning's 'bag' before them, and finally of the entire party, ladies included, lined up on the great terrace outside the library.

After that, it being such a fine day, with nary a cloud in the sky, a wonderful luncheon was enjoyed at tables set out on the lawns of Montmorency Castle. I spent the afternoon with Lizzie and Miriam – we were all on first-name terms now – and we discussed the latest fashions, and the season's taste in hats, and the best new plays in London, and all the little tittle-tattle which makes intercourse between ladies so delightful.

With so many birds there for the asking, the Prince was keen to be out with guns and dogs again in the afternoon, a wish with which the gentlemen readily concurred. A high-tea in the traditional Scottish style was taken at five by those who wished to avail themselves of it – a buffet supper was to be served at the ball – and what a delightful repast it turned out to be. The species of kippered fish known, I believe, as an 'Arbroath smokie' was perfection in itself, as were the quail's eggs and the almost limitless range of cakes and other delicacies with which we were tempted. As for myself, I am afraid, I succumbed all too readily, and it was only the fear that I might so fill my stomach that I would be unable to squeeze into my new black ball gown that stopped me making an utter pig of myself.

By seven I was in my bath and by eight, freshly talcumed and scented, with my hair already dressed, I was stepping into my new black undergarments for the first time.

'My goodness me, Estelle, you look a picture,' exclaimed Lizzie, who was sitting on the edge of the bed in her underthings. 'I think, if I were a man, I would ask you to keep them on while I made love to you. I'm sure I never saw a lady attired in such a provocative way.'

'You can thank your Madamoiselle Thérèse for that,' I replied, flattered by her kind words. 'And perhaps I will keep them on, at least for a little while.'

'It does seem to delight the gentlemen so, does it not? Harry insists that I keep my stockings and garters on when we are in bed together, and I am always happy to oblige.'

At half-past eight we all stood in line as the Prince, with Lady Montmorency on his arm, led the way into the ballroom. The band struck up the anthem, and then Lord Montmorency made a brief speech. Then, at last, the great event was under way.

My first partner, for the waltz, was Marcus, who looked most dashing in his full dress uniform. Then, for the polka, it was the turn of Tom Feather. Next came General Yardley of the clacking teeth and after that Lord Montmorency himself twirled me around the floor for a turn or two, during which I was quite convinced that his hand was deliberately placed a good deal lower on my back than is normal for a dancing partner, especially as he contrived to squeeze my bum a few times as we glided along. But he is a dear old boy nevertheless, and as generous a host as one could ever hope to be entertained by.

A vigorous fox-trot followed, in which I was partnered by the Count. So energetically did he dance, that I was quite glad to regain my seat afterwards, and to refresh myself with a water-ice from the buffet. The Count sat beside me, and applauded the musicians loudly as they played a selection of popular overtures.

'Montmorency must certainly have some influence in musical circles,' he whispered in my ear, 'for some of the Empire's finest musicians are in this ballroom tonight. See, there is Goulthorpe, the oboe player, and Cripps, playing the fiddle, and is that not the great Mr Webb himself performing on the piccolo? How strange it is, that man with so huge a physique should be able to coax such marvellous sounds from so tiny an instrument. I am sure that at times he must almost lose it in that great beard of his, and yet they say that he has no peer in Europe.'

I drank some more champagne, and listened to the band, and began to feel most delightfully happy. The convivial atmosphere evidently communicated itself to everyone in the room, for even when Marcus – who is not, I am sorry to say, the most graceful of dancers – had the misfortune to propel me directly into the path of the Prince and the Countess of Courtstrete, the Prince was most insistent that it was himself who was at fault, and that he had two left feet to be sure – even though I knew him to be as elegant on the dance-floor as is a swallow in flight – and that he hoped Marcus and I would forgive him for his appalling clumsiness.

'It is the *mazurka* soon, is it not, Miss Bicklah?' he said as we waited for the beat. 'I have not forgotten your promise.'

Round and round we went, and then there was champagne, and more dancing, and I am sure I never knew so delightful an evening. By the by I stepped out on to the terrace – it had become quite warm inside the ballroom, and I was glad to feel the cooling air on my face. I stood there breathing in great draughts of God's sweet wine when the Count came up to me once more.

'How absolutely ravishing you look tonight, my dear. I am sure I never saw you looking quite so beautiful.'

'You flatter me, Count. I was only going to say how gorgeous the Countess looks herself. She and the Prince made a fine picture as they danced the polka together.'

'They are old friends, Estelle, and have known each other many years. Once, in fact, before we were married, they were closer friends still, if you see my meaning. But what I wish to say to you now is this' – and he dropped his voice a little.

'Although we have already agreed that there should be an embargo on our amatory exploits for the duration of the Prince's visit, his Highness has discreetly suggested that, were a select group of us to desire to carry on after the ball is over in a little private entertainment of our own, he might even be favourably disposed towards joining us. Would you care to be among our private party?'

A voluptuous thrill of excitement coursed through me like burning brandy.

'Of course I would,' I breathed. 'It would be an honour indeed.'

'Good. Then I will no doubt speak to you later.'

Just then the waltz came to an end, and I realised it was time for me to dance the *mazurka* with the Prince. I dashed back inside, and found him waiting for me by the dais.

'Miss Bicklah!' he cried, his arms extended wide in greeting. 'Or may I call you Estelle now?' he murmured as we took the floor (I had not the nerve to address him by *his* Christian name!)

The band immediately struck up the tune in triple time, and we were away! Oh! how we danced! The Prince was everything I had dreamed of as a partner, leading me this way and that, holding me with a light but firm grip, until I felt myself to be mere butter in his hands. On and on the tune went, and my happiness knew no bounds. The other guests stood back to admire us as we swept by, and I even heard a smattering of applause as we executed a particularly intricate turn with perfect grace.

'You dance divinely,' I found myself murmuring in his ear, and then momentarily rebuked myself for what might seem excessive familiarity.

But he seemed entirely nonplussed, and held me closer, and whispered compliments so delightfully unexpected that my whole heart melted. As I abandoned myself to his arms I could clearly feel his prick pressed firmly against me, in a manner that suggested the gesture was hardly accidental. As we rejoined our friends when the music was finally over, I had already accepted his invitation to join his private party later.

The rest of the ball passed in a flurry of delightful anticipation. What kind of entertainment could be in store? I was almost beside myself with expectation, but when the Prince partnered me again for the *schottische* he gave no further hint.

A little after midnight a select group assembled in the Prince's private chambers: the Prince, the Count and Countess, the Thirkettles, Miranda Welsh, Lizzie, Marcus, Tom Feather and myself. I had not previously visited these rooms before; they were, so Lizzie told me, reserved for the exclusive use of Lord Montmorency's most exalted guests. In luxury and elegance they far outstripped any accommodations I had ever seen before: beneath twinkling chandeliers of pure crystal the walls were hung with the finest paintings, and the floors were draped with exotic rugs of Oriental manufacture.

Champagne quickly loosened our tongues and made us forget any inhibitions we may have had concerning our situation. Nevertheless, I was more than a little taken aback when I saw the Prince and the Countess disappear into the royal bedchamber together.

'I see your wife and the Prince seem to enjoy each other's company,' I observed to the Count.

'Of course they do! He's fucked her with my blessing countless times. At the very least, it puts me in good favour with the Palace.'

'Don't you mind, Count? Are you not taking your loyalty to the Crown a little too far.'

The Count laughed.

'Not a bit of it!' he exclaimed. 'Why should I mind? A woman like Miriam needs a spot of excitement to keep her in trim. Besides, the Prince knows a thing or two about satisfying a woman. He's probably got his prick in her already – he's not one to mess around – and a fine one it is too, as Miriam never ceases to tell me. Perhaps he will consent to let me watch them fuck one day.'

'Why do you think we're all here?' I asked in all innocence.

'Because the Prince likes his pick of the pretty ladies, my dear. Goodness me! That was quick! Here's Miriam now.'

Visibly purring like a contented cat, the Countess emerged from the royal bedchamber and rejoined her husband. The Prince emerged shortly afterwards.

'Ladies and gentlemen!' he called, clapping his hands together. 'As my old friends will know, a visit to Montmorency Castle is never complete without our rounding off the evening with a small, intimate gathering such as this. This year I am delighted to say that we have a novel entertainment. Mr Tom Feather, whose acquaintance I am delighted to have made during the course of my brief stay at the castle, has some splendid lantern-slides to show us which I am sure we will all enjoy enormously. If you would make yourselves comfortable, Mr Feather will let us see some choice examples of his art.'

The room was dimmed, and the beam of a lantern speared the darkness. An evening of lantern-slides? How unusual, I thought. However, my curiosity soon turned to amazement when the first slide was projected on to the wall. There was the glen by the castle, and there was I, as naked as the day I was born, with my bosom and cunney shamelessly exposed to the camera. The darkness hid my blushes, but I need not have feared for my modesty for it was followed by an image of Lizzie and Miriam licking the Count's cock.

'Capital! Capital!' cried the Prince, who was evidently delighted with what he saw. Miriam, I noticed, was sitting on his lap, with her hand inside his shirt.

Next, Tom showed a sequence of pictures showing Marcus and Effie fucking, of which I had seen prints earlier in the day.

'Is that your girl, Woode?' called the Prince. 'She's a fine one, isn't she? She's a goer, all right, I'll wager! Does she enjoy a cock in her pussey?'

'She certainly does, Your Majesty,' replied Marcus, sounding slightly embarrassed.

'Don't bother with that "Your Majesty" business here, old boy! That's just for public consumption. We're all chums here, aren't we, what? My goodness, look at the size of those titties.'

I now knew what kind of an evening we were in for. The Count took my hand and placed it on his cock, and I played with it through his trousers as we watched the sequence of slides. When the lights came up at the end, the Prince and the Countess were to be seen kissing passionately, without any inhibition.

This seemed to act as encouragement to the rest of us. Soon the air was filled with soft sighs. Angelica Thirkettle quickly undressed both Marcus and herself and in a trice they were fucking with gusto on the floor in front of us. Lizzie and Angelica's husband were similarly engaged elsewhere, while Miranda Welsh showed her gratitude to Tom by kneeling down in front of him and lustily sucking his sinewy cock in tribute to his talents.

Not wanting to be left out, I arose up and divested myself of my ball-gown. Immediately all eyes were drawn to me as I stood there in my black underthings, which had been so lovingly crafted by Madame Thérèse that they seemed to accentuate rather than hide my womanly attributes. In a trice the Count and Tom, both naked, were at my side, and I could feel their stiff pricks pressed against me through the black silk and lace of my chemise.

The Prince, too, paused in what he was doing – licking Miriam's cunt, by the look of things – to admire me in a way that I found particularly gratifying. Fixing him with a soft and wanton stare, I slowly divested myself of my finery until I stood there naked but for my black stockings and a wasp-waisted corset of similar hue.

'Here, Estelle!' called Marcus. 'Come and sit on my prick.'

He was laid down on the floor, quite naked, with his member standing up proudly as though in salute to our guest of honour. I squatted over him and made him lick my cunt while I took his prick in my mouth. Then, changing positions, I was just on the verge of impaling myself on his cock when a lewd idea struck me.

'Put it up my bum, Marcus,' I whispered. It was not easy, with Marcus lying flat, but eventually the insertion was achieved. Marcus's great prick filled my rear passage most delightfully but I was still not satisfied.

Tom and Miranda were next to us and I took hold of Tom's prick while Miranda leaned over me and licked my titties, her delightful pink-tipped nipples brushing against me as she did so. I found that by stretching slightly I could also frig Mr Thirkettle at the same time – three pricks at once, but still my apetite for *recherché* eroticisms was not satisfied!

While Lizzie, Miriam and Angelica amused themselves with the former's splendid ivory-shafted dildo I bade the Count straddle over me and I licked his balls and his prick stem until he was driven almost insane with desire. I could see that the Prince was watching me intently as I took the Count's cock deep into my mouth and sucked hard on its purple tip.

'My God!' cried the Prince, unable to contain his lust any longer. Tearing at his clothes and throwing them heedlessly down about him, I was at last rewarded by the sight of a member of the highest family in the land – nay, even in the world! – as naked as the day he was born. Miriam was certainly right about the royal cock: it was among the biggest I had ever seen, so long and thick that I wondered if I could take it up me even if I did not already have Marcus's splendid prick in my arse!

I parted my stocking-clad legs as wide as I could before the Prince. In a flash he was upon me, and that great royal tool was at last within me. With the light of pure lust in my eyes I frigged two cocks and sucked on a third, but my senses were all attuned to what was in my cunt. How the Prince pumped into me, and how the walls of my pussey seemed to part to allow him entry! In a delirium of lust I sucked even harder on the Count's prick, and pressed my bum wantonly against Marcus as he fucked me from beneath.

The air was filled with bawdy oaths and cries of lust and longing, and I sensed that my spending was upon me. And even as I came, again and again, in a great tidal wave of pleasure I could feel the Prince's spunk shoot into me, and Marcus come boiling forth into my bum, and two more jets of spunk shoot out on to my tits even as the Count's prick seemed to shudder and convulse and deluge my mouth with spendings, which I greedily sucked down until I felt I would choke with happiness.

And afterwards, when the others had retired to their separate bedchambers, the Prince and I spent the whole night together, and enjoyed every conceivable kind of eroticism, many of them so novel to me that when I awoke in the morning it seemed they were but a dream were it not for the photograph which was placed by the bedside.

It had been taken by Lizzie – to whom Tom had entrusted the alchemical secrets of his the photographer's art – and the two of them had evidently been up half the night with their bottles of solution to have it ready for the Prince when he departed in the morning. In full and graphic detail, it showed the remarkable climax to our evening's enjoyment – all the more noteworthy, since Lizzie seemed to have captured the exact moment when all six of us – the Prince, the Count, Tom, Marcus, Thirkettle and myself – spent simultaneously in a crescendo of passion. I placed the print in its gilded frame back on the table by my bedside in the royal chamber. And as I lay back on pillows of the purest goose-feather my hand stole down under the bedclothes towards the still-sleeping royal phallus, which would shortly receive as delightfully rude an awakening as any it had hitherto enjoyed...

MORE EROTIC CLASSICS FROM CARROLL & GRAF

- ☐ Anonymous/ALTAR OF VENUS $3.95
- ☐ Anonymous/AUTOBIOGRAPHY OF A FLEA $3.95
- ☐ Anonymous/THE CELEBRATED MISTRESS $3.95
- ☐ Anonymous/CONFESSIONS OF AN ENGLISH MAID $3.95
- ☐ Anonymous/CONFESSIONS OF EVELINE $3.95
- ☐ Anonymous/COURT OF VENUS $3.95
- ☐ Anonymous/DANGEROUS AFFAIRS $3.95
- ☐ Anonymous/THE DIARY OF MATA HARI $3.95
- ☐ Anonymous/DOLLY MORTON $3.95
- ☐ Anonymous/THE EDUCATION OF A MAIDEN $3.95
- ☐ Anonymous/THE EROTIC READER $3.95
- ☐ Anonymous/THE EROTIC READER II $3.95
- ☐ Anonymous/THE EROTIC READER III $4.50
- ☐ Anonymous/FANNY HILL'S DAUGHTER $3.95
- ☐ Anonymous/FLORENTINE AND JULIA $3.95
- ☐ Anonymous/A LADY OF QUALITY $3.95
- ☐ Anonymous/LENA'S STORY $3.95
- ☐ Anonymous/THE LIBERTINES $4.50
- ☐ Anonymous/LOVE PAGODA $3.95
- ☐ Anonymous/THE LUSTFUL TURK $3.95
- ☐ Anonymous/MADELEINE $3.95
- ☐ Anonymous/A MAID'S JOURNEY $3.95
- ☐ Anonymous/MAID'S NIGHT IN $3.95
- ☐ Anonymous/THE OYSTER $3.95
- ☐ Anonymous/THE OYSTER II $3.95
- ☐ Anonymous/THE OYSTER III $4.50
- ☐ Anonymous/PARISIAN NIGHTS $4.50
- ☐ Anonymous/PLEASURES AND FOLLIES $3.95
- ☐ Anonymous/PLEASURE'S MISTRESS $3.95
- ☐ Anonymous/PRIMA DONNA $3.95
- ☐ Anonymous/ROSA FIELDING: VICTIM OF LUST $3.95
- ☐ Anonymous/SATANIC VENUS $4.50
- ☐ Anonymous/SECRET LIVES $3.95
- ☐ Anonymous/THREE TIMES A WOMAN $3.95

☐ Anonymous/VENUS DISPOSES $3.95
☐ Anonymous/VENUS IN PARIS $3.95
☐ Anonymous/VENUS UNBOUND $3.95
☐ Anonymous/VENUS UNMASKED $3.95
☐ Anonymous/VICTORIAN FANCIES $3.95
☐ Anonymous/THE WANTONS $3.95
☐ Anonymous/A WOMAN OF PLEASURE $3.95
☐ Anonymous/WHITE THIGHS $4.50
☐ Perez, Faustino/LA LOLITA $3.95
☐ van Heller, Marcus/ADAM & EVE $3.95
☐ van Heller, Marcus/THE FRENCH WAY $3.95
☐ van Heller, Marcus/THE HOUSE OF BORGIA $3.95
☐ van Heller, Marcus/THE LOINS OF AMON $3.95
☐ van Heller, Marcus/ROMAN ORGY $3.95
☐ van Heller, Marcus/VENUS IN LACE $3.95
☐ Villefranche, Anne-Marie/FOLIES D'AMOUR $3.95
Cloth $14.95
☐ Villefranche, Anne-Marie/JOIE D'AMOUR $3.95
Cloth $13.95
☐ Villefranche, Anne-Marie/ MYSTERE D'AMOUR $3.95
☐ Villefranche, Anne-Marie/PLAISIR D'AMOUR $3.95
Cloth $12.95
☐ Von Falkensee, Margarete/BLUE ANGEL NIGHTS $3.95
☐ Von Falkensee, Margarete/BLUE ANGEL SECRETS $4.50

Available from fine bookstores everywhere or use this coupon for ordering.

Carroll & Graf Publishers, Inc., 260 Fifth Avenue, N.Y., N.Y. 10001

Please send me the books I have checked above. I am enclosing $________ (please add $1.00 per title to cover postage and handling.) Send check or money order—no cash or C.O.D.'s please. N.Y. residents please add 8¼% sales tax.

Mr/Mrs/Ms ________________________________
Address ________________________________
City ____________________ State/Zip ____________
Please allow four to six weeks for delivery.